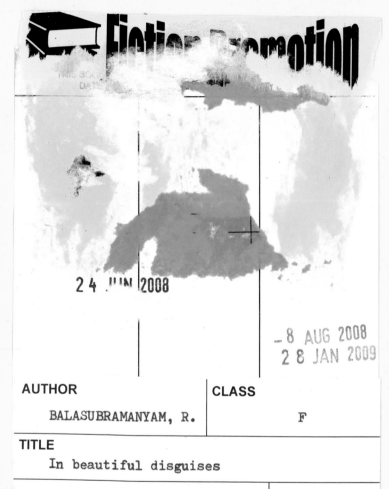

Fiction Promotion

24 JUN 2008

-8 AUG 2008
2 8 JAN 2009

AUTHOR	CLASS
BALASUBRAMANYAM, R.	F

TITLE

In beautiful disguises

IN BEAUTIFUL DISGUISES

IN BEAUTIFUL DISGUISES

RAJEEV BALASUBRAMANYAM

BLOOMSBURY

First published in Great Britain 2000
This paperback edition published 2001

Copyright © 2000 by Rajeev Balasubramanyam

The moral right of the author has been asserted

Bloomsbury Publishing Plc, 38 Soho Square, London W1D 3HB

A CIP catalogue record is available from the British Library

ISBN 0 7475 5341 6

10 9 8 7 6 5 4 3 2 1

Typeset by Palimpsest Book Production Limited,
Polmont, Stirlingshire

Printed in Great Britain by Clays Ltd, St Ives plc

For Maya and Ayesha

Part One

Have done with all dualities, stand ever firm on Truth;
Think not of gain or keeping the thing gained, but be thyself

The Bhagavad Gita

1

I was born a girl and remained so until I became a woman.

My birth was fast, efficient and businesslike, without mysterious portents, flaming meteorites or phantasmic deluges of blood descending from the sky. Everything was over as quickly as it had begun. I probably let my parents down.

I was the third child. Before me came my elder sister and my very elder brother. My father was an office clerk. My brother, Ravi, was an office clerk, and my sister was a sister, daughter and niece.

It is a little more difficult to classify my mother. The best description is probably *domestic philosopher*. She thought a lot. She cooked, and served, and cleaned, and thought. Nobody asked her what she was thinking about. When she spoke, if she spoke at all, it would be gossip and banalities, but she definitely had her own private world. Whether this world was profound or otherwise is largely irrelevant. She married my father when she was young, very young. I have no idea if he was aware of her private world. Probably he wasn't. This is not to say that he didn't understand her. He understood her fairly well, but she also had a purely personal dialogue, as do all people. It is my theory that the less flesh a woman exposes in public, the more expansive is her imagination, and my mother always kept her ankles covered. Whilst I would not dare to speculate on the content of her inner monologues, I would guess she was largely unaware that she was doing it at the time. I would contend that my mother was aware

3

of only two worlds, domestic and social. However, she definitely had three; domestic, social, and, let us say, internal. She passed this trait on to me and I pushed it to its logical extremity.

By the time I was fifteen I had developed problems distinguishing between fantasy and reality, or rather, I could make the distinction, but somehow I would invert the significance. I had a habit of trapping myself in that place that lies between dreams and consciousness, and I would stay there until someone pulled me back. Usually it would be my brother as he returned for lunch with his customary eloquence.

– You lazy bloody girl! What are you doing sleeping in the middle of the day?

– I was dreaming, Ravi.

This one had been an especially nice dream. They were all nice in fact, but this one was nicer than most.

– And I was working, working so you can dream. I want to eat.

Ravi wasn't as bad as he sounded. He was bad-tempered and prone to giving orders, but in his defence, he *needed* to give orders. He would wave his arms around and scream about incompetence. *Where are My Shoes? Such Incompetence! Where is My Food? Sheer Incompetence!* etc. etc. Incompetent was an odd word to use, especially about his sister, but Ravi was only off-loading his own failings. I'm sure they called him *Incompetent* at the office, several times a day, and so he had this backlog of incompetents which he tried to shift by heaping them on to me. But even if he had done nothing but shift incompetents day and night, he would never have been able to clear it. I was glad that, being the next down in the great chain of being, I was able to be of some assistance. I never felt the need to clear any incompetents from my own head because, as I believe I mentioned, I didn't take reality particularly seriously.

– Those bastards!

Ravi only used foul language in my presence. It was our secret. When he swore at me it was like a conspiratorial oath, a way of saying that he trusted me.

– Those *bastards!* Bloody corrupt incompetent *bastards!* They think they can treat me how they like! They think I am a dog! I am not. They cannot. Tomorrow I'm going there with a big smile and I'm going to piss all over their arrogance.

This was another show of affection. It was his way of saying, *I'm Weak and Powerless and I Know it and Can't Do Anything About It.* I silently acknowledged the confession.

I brought his food to the table and watched him eat, my hands folded under my chin.

– Why do you have to stare at me? Go play! Go see your friends!

He knew that I didn't have any friends, but again, this was part of our understanding. It was so bound up with private complexities and riddles that anyone looking in would think he was bullying me mercilessly. It pleased Ravi to bask in this illusion, but we both knew he was a failure, and an unhappy one. All failures reach a point where they decide to be happy or unhappy. Ravi had decided to be an unhappy failure, and this was his most admirable quality. We both knew that I could easily hurt him, but still he pretended to be in control.

– All right, I'm going.

This was my release. He would behave as though he were making me go, and I would act as though what I most ardently desired was to sit and watch him belch and slurp his way through his meal like a lawn mower. It was as though Ravi believed that someone was watching and making careful notes on his performance. Perhaps my father had paid someone to hide at the window? He would have to maintain this complicated and personalised etiquette at all times.

I smiled. He smiled back, and then hunched his shoulders over his food, knowing he had let his guard down. Maybe the spy at the window had seen the smile. Maybe, at this moment, the spy was busily constructing an artist's impression of that careless smile, and tomorrow it would be all over the newspapers. Ravi tried to pretend it was a grimace, hoping this would fool the spy. As I was leaving he shouted, by way of an additional defence, *There's Too much Salt in the –*

It didn't really matter what there was too much salt in, because I was already out of earshot, but the spy at the window would be interested so Ravi finished the sentence.

– Too much salt in the *rasam!*

There wasn't any rasam on the table! Ravi was panicking. Perhaps the window-spy wouldn't notice.

Poor Ravi, sometimes I could almost hear him thinking, screaming, *Why are You so Happy! You're not Supposed to be Happy!* Life had cheated him. He was thirty-one, unmarried, trapped in a menial job where he was treated with perpetual disdain, and he hated the way I would smile and gaze into space with such serenity. Sometimes he dismissed it as stupidity, he would call me *The Smiling Fool*, but most of the time he just wondered, puzzled.

I left the house and walked, relieved to be outside. The day was hot, but not unpleasant, and I liked the stickiness of the late afternoon. I liked looking at the sun. He seemed so tired after burning his merciless fury all day long. Five o'clock was the only time when the sun was amiable and fairly civilised, yet still full of life. Any later and he became depressed with the futility of his spent fury and retreated into himself. The next day he would seem to have forgotten, and would rise again, as violent and angry as ever.

Dust settled between my toes as I walked. I liked the way it felt. Unpredictable cyclists veered around me like insects. Some boys were waiting at the bus stop and they shouted as I passed, but I didn't catch what they said. It didn't matter. People interested me from a distance. Up close, when you could smell their sweat, they lost all attraction. There were people all around me in fact, boys playing cricket by the side of the road, girls walking back from school with satchels, the ironing man ironing on the street. I watched them for a while, but my mind was elsewhere.

I was going to *Majick Movie House*, the only place I ever went. It wasn't bad as movie houses went, very cheap, and I had my own seat in the front stalls which everyone else avoided without having to be told. Why life had chosen that dirty seat to deposit its innermost truths I had no idea, but there it was. It was my secret, and I didn't like having to say it. It was there that I felt my lover's caress. It was there that moist lips bewitched my neck. It was there that men carved themselves into pieces with long knives in a delirium for my love. I would sit in my seat, the lights would dim, voices would fade, and it would be me and the screen, and then, those lights and colours and sounds would somehow surround me until there was no screen, only lights and colours and sounds, with me in the centre. One day – I was certain – I would be a movie star, and in my mind, for those two or three hours every day, I already was.

I reached the movie house and paid the man at the window. He smiled. He saw me almost every day. I gave him a shy, distant smile, the only sort of smile I ever gave. He knew I wasn't afraid of him, as most young girls were, and I suppose he also wondered why I was so happy with my ridiculous life.

The movie wasn't a good one. I had seen it twice already and every time it had been just as bad. I didn't like this sort of thing, all guns and blood transfusions, but still it swept me, as all movies did, into another world, *my* world. The quality of the movie didn't matter so much. I knew I could carry it with me into my bed, and in my dreams it would be filtered and softened into something nicer. The only problem was that Ravi would wake me up. He had taken to coming home drunk, and he could be a real nuisance when he was drunk. Generally I tolerated Ravi, but sometimes he could make me angry, especially when he woke me up from some nice dream. He knew it, and at times he was afraid of me, because whatever he was doing had to be really wrong if it made me angry. He would assume that I merely disapproved of his drinking. It didn't occur to him that I could have certain pleasures of my own. But, as he judged all his actions by my reaction, and as I ordinarily gave no sign of having any tangible emotions, my anger gave him a sort of otherworldy fear. I was, against my will, Ravi's moral thermometer.

As I walked home I tried to imagine the scene I would confront when I reached the house. My father would have returned, drunk. Ravi would be just about to return, hopefully sober. My mother would be cooking, in her usual meditative way, thinking her own, private thoughts. And my sister would be there, talking some nonsense. I rarely listened to her, she reeked with the banality of the real world, which reminded me that the worst possible outcome in life could also happen to me. One day, the real world might catch me and enfold me in its terrors.

I was fifteen. Not old. But not as young as I would have liked.

I entered the house quietly, hoping to escape notice. The house had four rooms. There was my parents' bedroom. I never went in there. I suppose my parents' bed hinted that mine might not have been a virgin birth, and this was hardly something I wanted to be reminded of. At times I overheard my parents talking, or rather, I heard my father shouting. My mother rarely responded.

Upstairs there was a small room where Ravi, my sister and I slept. I was rarely able to disappear upstairs without someone screaming my name, but I found I could actually get more privacy by sitting in the kitchen, surrounded by people. The radio was usually on, and if I concentrated hard enough on the music then the room around me would disappear until it was just me, alone in a strange, though not unfriendly, world. I could often get away with this for ten or fifteen minutes, until someone would disturb me.

As soon as I entered I could tell something was different. The scent of whisky and cigarettes was fainter than usual, and I could hear the sound of my father's laughter. From this I drew two fairly alarming conclusions. He was laughing, obviously, and he wasn't drunk. The sound of my mother's laughter ambled across the room like a slow scream in a dream. At this time of the day she was usually enduring somebody's drunkenness with tightly sealed lips, like a cat who closes his eyes hoping it will make him, or at least everybody else, invisible. But this evening she was laughing. This really looked serious.

I took a deep breath and walked into the kitchen. They were all smiling. They looked ridiculous, like children with stolen sweets behind their backs. Everyone was silent, but there was a deafening buzz. It took me a few moments to realise that the room was humming with suppressed excitement. My mother broke the silence.

– Your sister is going to be married.

I said nothing. There was nothing to say.

My sister was staring at me, looking very frighténed.

– Isn't that good? Aren't you happy?

I struggled. Try to smile! Make some positive sign. Give official endorsement. *Smile!* Couldn't smile. Couldn't speak. God knew what my eyes were giving away. Must say *something!* But what a waste of time! I was forever trapped in situations where I didn't know what I was supposed to do, and wouldn't want to do it if I knew. That was why I didn't have any friends – I didn't like their games.

They were still watching me. My mother wasn't laughing any more. Her eyes were trained on the point where my nose met my forehead, as though to extract her own frightened genes from my heretical brain.

In the end, I did the only honourable thing left in such situations and burst into tears. Luckily, this was the appropriate response, and was mistaken for uncontrollable joy.

Vijay Kumar, twenty-six.
Single, obviously.
Five feet ten inches.
Brahmin, obviously.
Good-looking, less obviously.
Rich, allegedly.
Very real, very terrifying.

Tears had formed on my pillow that morning and had crystallised where they fell. Like tiny mirrors they captured my fear and thrust it at me saying, *Here, Embrace Me, This is You.* I swept them up in my hair where they floated amidst falling curls, laughing and shining with mischief. I bathed twice, but they wouldn't go away, and so I had to carry them with me to visit Vijay Kumar, his mother, his father, and his inevitably senile grandfather.

– Did you wash your hair this morning?

My mother had an eye for mischievous crystallised tears.

– Yes, twice.

– Is this the house?

– Yes.

My father had insisted that we visit them in *their* home, under the pretext that the grandfather would find the strain of walking to our house difficult. The real reason, of course, was that he wanted to know if their alleged wealth really existed, and because he didn't want them to see our very real lack of it.

We entered, and there was Vijay Kumar, exuding confidence, delighted to meet the family that would be enraptured by his wit and dazzled by his looks. My sister was shining like a polished raisin. My mother looked like a mother, only more so than usual. Even my father looked reasonably dignified. I looked towards Ravi for support, but he was also grinning like an idiot. His reflection in their very expensively marbled floor made his head look doubly oily and his nose doubly bananaesque.

Vijay Kumar touched my father's feet and sat like a smiling patriarch, one leg neatly balanced over the other. He was an engineer for a German company and had spent three years in America, which accounted for his ability to release perfectly audible words through his nose whilst moving his lips like a ventriloquist's dummy. As we drank coffee and ate sweets, I began to wonder whether American universities forbade their students from speaking through their mouths in traditional fashion.

I hoped no one would talk to me, but luckily, though unsurprisingly, Vijay Kumar dominated the conversation, talking mainly about himself. I, and his evidently senile grandfather, seemed to be the only ones in the room who did not consider him part man and part deity. I concealed this behind my usual impenetrable silence, which people usually mistook for stupidity.

His *hopelessly* senile grandfather made no attempt to disguise his belief that the entire meeting had been arranged for his personal amusement. I liked him. And I rarely liked anyone.

– When I was in America I used to eat the best chow mein in Boston for only two dollars a box. All the other students went to Mr Chen's, where you ate the same food for five dollars and the service was incredibly slow. But *behind* Mr Chen's, a van was parked between one o'clock and three o'clock. There the service was fast, and you could eat the best chow mein in Boston for only *two* dollars. And the hilarious thing was that the owners of Mr Chen's were *Chinese*, and the owners of the van where I bought *my* lunch were *Indians!*

Everyone, except for myself and the grandfather, agreed that this was indeed a hilarious thing, and praised Vijay Kumar for his hunting and gathering skills, and praised those entrepreneurial Indians for their ingenuity. Ravi was particularly interested.

– Yes, I have also heard that those Chinese are an incompetent lot.

– And they eat cockroaches. Cockroaches and *dogs!*

That was the grandfather. Astonishingly, even though he spoke at twice the volume that the eardrum usually splits at, nobody seemed to hear a word he said. Ravi would probably have heard, had he chosen to, but he was busy trying to stamp his authority on the gathering. He had decided that Vijay Kumar was his equal, and he was bent on demonstrating this.

– I have to deal with all sorts of incompetent fellows at the office. It is enough to make a man lose all his patience. Those Germans, they are an efficient bunch, aren't they?

– Oh yes, very.

– I admire their nationalism. They will never go down on their knees to anyone.

Ravi's politics had always been a little suspect. The grandfather, it turned out, also had a keen eye for political debate.

– Not like that bugger Nehru, licking the buttocks of the British, fornicating like an elephant.

I think everyone heard that one, except of course for Vijay

Kumar who had plenty of other things to say. He seemed to view these interjections as something like the applause after each act of a play.

– America is also a very efficient country. Not at all like India. In India, people are poor and it is their tragedy. A fate that, at least in this life, is enduring and undeserved.

He paused. All sentences dripping with poetic tragedy must be followed by a respectful silence.

– But in America, money is *there*. If you want it, you work for it, and you take it –

– And you buy cockroaches and dogs from the Chinese buggers!

I laughed this time, I couldn't help it. But then I caught my sister's eye, which was smouldering, and I tried to concentrate very hard on a drop of Ravi's hair oil that was soon to add to the brilliance of the very expensively marbled floor.

– Yes, America is not a bad place, but after some time I began to miss India. I missed the honest, hopeful faces of the children. I missed the cows on the street. I missed –

My mother yawned. It was a tiny yawn, especially by my father's standards, but it caused him to step rather hard on her two smallest toes. She smiled a tight, controlled smile.

As his grandson continued to display his verbal agility, the old man fell asleep and began to snore like a buffalo in heat. Eventually, he woke up and smiled brightly at seven people determined not to acknowledge his presence. Slighted by this cold-blooded negation of his existence, he invited me to join him upstairs. We skulked away, seeking hard to avoid eyes which, in any case, were preoccupied with more important matters.

I was beginning to like this old man more and more.

– Do you know what marriage is?

– Yes.

– Let me make my meaning more precise. Do you know what is the *purpose* of marriage?

I conveyed my unwillingness to answer with a shrug.

– When a woman marries a man, she makes an agreement to

fulfil certain obligations. If she does not fulfil these obligations, then she is divorced. I hope we understand each other.

Again, I shrugged.

– On the night of marriage, the bed sheets must not be unsoiled. Some time afterwards, there will be children. Understand?

– Not really.

– Do you know what is meant by sexual behaviour?

That was an interesting question. I regularly saw dogs writhing in the street, so I had a reasonable idea of what he was talking about, but I wasn't about to admit it.

– You see, your sister is about to make a commitment to shed blood from her womb in the name of God, and to allow no other man to taste her flesh, in the name of morality.

– And what does she get?

– She gets food, clothing and shelter.

– I see.

There was a knock and a short man with friendly eyes entered. He looked shy and his shoulders and moustache drooped. The grandfather smiled at him.

– How are you my friend?

The short man smiled and looked at me with embarrassment. The grandfather crossed the room and gave the man's cheek an affectionate squeeze.

– Don't worry about anything. It's all settled, all settled.

The short man smiled again.

– You have a destiny my friend. You needn't worry. Come again and see me tomorrow.

The man acquiesced and touched his forehead several times. The grandfather patted him on the back and returned to his chair, which he pulled forward with a snort. He leaned towards me.

– Do you know who Manu is?

– I think so.

– Manu made laws. The law says that, after marriage, a woman must never refuse her husband sexual activity. Manu said that *Woman is as Foul as Falsehood Itself. When Creating them, the Lord*

13

of Creatures Allotted to Women a Love of their Beds, of their Seat, and Ornaments, as well as Impure Thoughts, Wrath and Dishonesty, Malice and Bad Conduct. From the Cradle to the Grave a Woman is Dependent on a Male; in Childhood on her Father, in Youth on her Husband, in Old Age on her Son.

I didn't say anything. I was feeling sick. I had never realised that being a woman was this bad. But I wasn't a woman yet, so everything was OK for the time being. But I did have a love of my bed, so perhaps I was already on my way.

The grandfather was staring at me.

– I am telling you this because I can see you have a fertile young mind. You do not take things lying down, so to speak, and this is a good trait, a noble trait.

He pinched my cheek, and I could smell his breath which reeked of onions.

– I don't think I shall ever marry.

– A wise policy. You must, of course, learn the arts of producing milk, cotton and bricks with your soul. It has been done before, by many great ascetics.

– I don't want to shed blood for anybody.

– Very sensible. When I was a boy we used to box with pieces of wood for gloves. This was all part of becoming a man. Were I a boy again, I would refuse to become a man. A very costly habit, in terms of blood.

– Are you telling me that to become a woman I have to shed blood?

– It is usually seen that way.

– And after shedding blood I will –

– You will receive food, clothing and shelter, and will no longer be a burden to your father.

– So becoming a woman is a good thing, in a way?

He paused, and the veins in his forehead bulged.

– In a way.

– Am I really a burden to my father?

– Certainly you are.

– Then I must become a woman and shed blood.

– Unless you can produce milk, cotton and bricks with your soul.

– I see.

An important question occurred to me.

– Does my sister know all this?

– I don't know. You could ask her.

– Yes, I suppose I could.

– But I wouldn't advise it.

– Why not?

– Some people are sensitive about these matters.

– I see. Is that good or bad?

– That depends.

– On what?

– On what you are seeking.

– I see.

– What *are* you seeking?

– I don't know.

– Good. Better to remain that way. When you tell me you know what you are seeking I will worry for you. If you tell me you've found it, well, it will be time for me to die.

He laughed and then coughed for some time and then laughed again, and he brought his face close to mine and grinned so I could see the cataracts in his eyes.

There was another knock and my father entered, glaring at the old man as though smelling subversion. I tried to look as innocent as possible, which made my father doubly suspicious.

– We are leaving.

– All right, Appa.

I turned to say goodbye to the grandfather, but he was already on his feet, grinning mischievously.

– Your daughter and I have been discussing the merits of Chinese food.

He looked at the floor, as did my father in spite of himself, and there was a large cockroach, running frantically to escape our stares. The grandfather rubbed his stomach and burped.

Delicious, he said, and winked at me. Without another word, my father grabbed my arm and pulled me down the stairs.

We walked home. My sister looked frightened and Ravi was in high spirits. My mother hid her face in a shawl. I tried to listen to her thoughts, but remembered that that was impossible. My father, unusually, did not say a single word, but that night I had my first bad dream.

I was dancing with my father who was spinning me around like a tyre and I was shrieking with delight and the ground whirled under my feet and the blood began rushing to my head and I didn't like it any more and I yelled at him to stop but he just kept on dancing until my ears started to swell and drops of blood pushed against the hair inside my nostrils and my lungs hurt and I thought I would faint. I screamed again and he shouted, *Don't you Like Playing with your Father?* and I shook my head until little rhythmic pearls of red shot across the sky like a premature sunset and he suddenly stopped and threw up his arms and let me drop and I fell into bed shouting, *Am I a Burden to You?* and he sighed and put his head between his knees and rubbed his cheeks with palms callused like coconuts and I cried for him to stop but he couldn't hear me and he rose and spat, drenching me with fury, and ran in torment like a young man until I couldn't see him any more but could only hear him say, *Enough Play, Time for Work.* And I walked to the mirror and examined my face and I could see small wrinkles forming under my eyes and white hairs curling against my cheek and my skin looked yellow and my neck reminded me of a gnarled old tree baking in the shade and I pulled a razor down from the shelf and held it to my skin, watching as the light from my eyes cast shadows over the blade. I lifted the hem of my night-dress and humming to myself I fixed my reflection with a stare of denial and plunged the blade between my legs until the looking glass dripped with shame and I caught my father's eye looking back at me behind a veil of blood saying, *Thank God, Better Late than Never*, and he laughed paternally at my discomfort and at the mess between my legs and I smiled as brightly as I could, hoping that would make him go away.

When I awoke the sheets were wet and I ached all over. I could see Ravi's back, turned towards me, glistening like a pig's. I looked at the lizards staring wide-eyed, upside down on the ceiling.

I was seventeen and my sister was pregnant. The marriage had been a success. Ravi was still unsuccessful and nobly unhappy, and my mother talked even less and my father drank even more. The grandfather and I had become friends. He took me to movies, sometimes two in one day. My father disapproved, but most of the time he didn't know. My sister's initiation had begun. She was turning into my mother, except that her private world was smaller so she had fewer defences. I worried for her, and I worried for myself.

I knew that if I didn't become a movie star soon then I would be in real trouble, but my acting career didn't seem to be going anywhere. Vijay's grandfather told me not to worry, *At Least you are Watching Plenty of Movies*, he would say, *The First Thing an Actress needs is a Passion for Cinema*. I wasn't convinced. I had started dreaming while I was awake now.

There was a robbery at Ravi's office. He was badly beaten. They threatened to cut off his penis and Ravi didn't speak for five days. When he finally did speak, his first words were, *Cut the Fucking Thing Off!* But it was too late, they had only nicked it, just for the pleasure of hearing him scream. Ravi didn't work any more. The company had been generous to him, after all, he had undergone severe trauma in the act of defending company property. He used the compensation they gave him to install cable TV, and he stayed at home staring at the television. He had also taken to giving long, philosophical speeches in doomsday style. My father worked harder and harder. His liability column now consisted of my mother, Ravi and me.

In a way I was glad of Ravi's downfall. I liked having him around, sometimes, and I especially liked his new contribution to the house. I watched whatever he watched. Until now, I had seen Hindi films at *Majick Movie House*, and had occasionally watched black-and-white Kannada or Tamil films on the old television. My father liked these, but I found them boring; too many women crying and they all looked like my mother . . . though I think this was why my father liked them. But now I watched everything, including English films and comedies. Ravi liked them for the naked women, which were plentiful. It seemed that Americans took their clothes off for no reason at all, and at the most extraordinary times of the day. Anyway, Ravi loved this, and I was happy because it proved my theory. But it was through Audrey Hepburn, who never took her clothes off, that I learned what film stardom was really about.

I saw *Breakfast at Tiffany's* four times, and by the third time I had almost become Holly Golightly. Whenever Ravi leaned over the banister to hurl some abuse at me, I would stare hard at his face until he became Mr Yumioshi, *Miss Golightly, I protest! This Time I Call the Police*. And whenever I saw Vijay Kumar I would say to myself, *Quel Rat!*

My other favourite was *The Sound of Music*, but I thought that the life of an actress was infinitely preferably to that of a nun turned governess, so Audrey Hepburn remained at the centre of my world. Ravi, of course, was completely opposed to her. *That Bloody Incompetent Woman*, he would say, *Look at Her! She Looks Like a Sparrow! All those Jewels and She doesn't even Eat!* I would just smile and say to myself, *What a Thumping Bore!*, although, in fact, Audrey Hepburn wasn't much thinner than I was, so I was secretly delighted every time Ravi opened his mouth. Since I was a child I had had Aunties and Uncles pointing their fingers at my ribs, telling me how sickly I looked, so Audrey Hepburn was my secret salvation after years of torment.

It was then that I learned that I was also to be married. I suppose my father was trying to clear his liabilities as fast as possible, and Ravi was one that refused to go. Had my father been honest with himself, he would have hired a pair of goons to split Ravi's head in two like a lemon, but like Ravi, my father lacked imagination. He wouldn't let his world oscillate too far towards the poles of good and evil. He preferred to occupy the neutral territory in between, where fewer bombs fell. My father had learned that nobody criticises the man who stays in the middle.

My impending marriage caused a strange thing to happen. For two whole weeks I didn't have a single dream and hardly saw any movies. I consulted a number of people about this most critical situation.

Ravi

Why are you complaining? Don't think they'd find you some incompetent bugger. They'll find you a good man I tell you. Look at me. Now I have time to think and believe me, death can take you away at any time and there are certain things to be done first. I never married because women have trouble understanding me, for which I do not blame them. But I understand married life better than most men and I know it is not something to run away from. People respect my judgement on such matters. Don't you know that when I was a child it was prophesied that I would either be a ruler of men, or that I would renounce material things for a life of contemplation. So why do you think I now sit here every day instead of leading those hopeless fools? I chose to be a quiet man of truth and wisdom. It is quite proper that you came to me for advice. I have known you all your life. Marriage raises a woman from the level of lazy ungrateful idler, the level at which you find yourself now, to the level of creator, friend, mother, sister and wife, a level at which you will find gold right under your feet. All women find this sooner or later. Ask your mother, she knows that . . .

My mother

. . . you mustn't listen to Ravi . . . ask your sister about marriage . . .

My sister

. . .

My father

. . . ha . . . nervous? . . . so was your mother . . . look at her today . . .

My mother
. . . she will tell you that . . .

Ravi
. . . you shouldn't think so much . . .

My sister
. . . when you grow older . . .

My father
. . . respected and contented . . .

Vijay Kumar's grandfather
. . . living without seeing . . . everything is broken up in time . . .

My sister
. . . and more confused . . .

My mother
. . . I should not tell you anything . . . I cannot . . .

Vijay Kumar's grandfather
. . . but if you can live without thinking . . .

My sister
. . . feeling as though you can't . . .

Ravi
. . . talk is for girls . . . you mustn't . . .

Vijay Kumar's grandfather
. . . learn that life is pain . . .

Ravi
. . . think! . . . dream . . . cry . . . it gets you nowhere . . . it only hurts . . .

Vijay Kumar's grandfather
. . . in the end . . .

My mother
. . . you reach a time in life . . . when you . . .

My sister
. . . behave like a child and like a . . .

Ravi
. . . bloody incompetent . . .

My father
. . . old senile fool! . . . stay away from that old man or . . .

Vijay Kumar's grandfather
. . . we'll die after all . . . and . . .

My father
. . . I'll put a stop to all this nonsense . . .

My mother
. . . learn that the purpose of marriage . . . is to . . .

Ravi
. . . fuck! . . . fuck those incompetent bastards . . .

Vijay Kumar's grandfather
. . . when all is said and done . . . time doesn't always heal . . . truth is never warm like the rain or cool like the breeze . . . never easy . . .

My sister
. . . like a part of something else . . . a spoke on a wheel . . . I know that I . . .

My mother
. . . give without expecting reward . . . and . . .

Ravi
. . . they think they can treat me how they like . . . fuck them . . . I am . . .

Vijay Kumar's grandfather
. . . always hurting . . . but you must suffer . . . so long as you are a heart . . . you must suffer . . .

My mother
. . . never think of yourself . . . I know I will never be . . .

Ravi
. . . a strong man . . . a big man . . . my own man!!!

My sister
. . . I don't want to be alone.

My mother
. . . his equal.

My father
. . . some things have to be done!

Vijay Kumar's grandfather
. . . only suffering can purify.

In the end I didn't have a choice. Six months later I accompanied my parents, together with Ravi, to meet my future husband.

2

We walked. Ravi kept up an incessant stream of moral philosophy at which my mother smiled sympathetically. My father did not say anything. After a time he reached around my mother's shoulder and slapped Ravi hard on his shiny bald head. After that we walked in silence, until Ravi cursed the heat, cursed the sun, and then saw my father and fell silent again.

It upset me to hear Ravi curse the sun like that, especially in the late afternoon, my favourite part of the day. It was October and it wasn't every day that the sun shone with such abandon. Sometimes it would rain, ferociously, and I loved it, but sometimes it would be dry and overcast, which I hated. I was glad that today it was sunny. It seemed a good omen. I tried to walk faster than my shadow but gave up because that's hardly the sort of thing a girl should be doing while on the way to meet her husband.

I remembered the story of Sanjna, the girl who fell in love with the sun. She used to spend all day gazing skyward, dancing and playing while her friends wilted in the heat and ran indoors. Her parents eventually approached Surya with an offer of marriage (as any considerate parents would). Somewhat surprisingly, he accepted, but despite her love of daylight Sanjna could not withstand her husband's heat and was unable to look him in the eye. Surya became furious and, being terribly sensitive, Sanjna ran away and turned herself into a horse to escape discovery. She asked her shadow to take her place at Surya's side.

After some years Surya realised that the shadow, although very beautiful, was not the girl he had married. What tipped him off was that his surrogate wife would only beat Sanjna's children, whilst pampering her own. One of those children happened to be Yama, god of death, but this is treated as an irrelevant detail. Anyway, after hearing reports of a talking mare, Surya deduced that this *must* be his wife. Using all the charm at his disposal he succeeded in enticing Sanjna to come back to him, and the problem of his fiery enthusiasm was solved by Sanjna's father who, as luck would have it, was the celestial architect and chiselled away one eighth of Surya's brilliance. They lived happily ever after.

I hoped my marriage would be something like that, except for the Yama part.

When we reached the house and had been seated and served with coffee and compliments, and after I had been examined from head to foot (I call this *visual autopsy*), I decided to make up my mind about this man who sat opposite me and was to be my benefactor-provider-soulmate in this life and the next. He was dark, spindly and thin, and although none of this interested me, it would certainly irritate everyone else. What bothered me was that I had not yet seen his eyes. He hadn't looked at me once, not even a furtive glance when he thought I was looking the other way. *Nothing!*

I gave him the opportunity occasionally, by turning this way and that, rubbing my eyes and looking at the ground . . . but still nothing. I changed tactics and stared at him wide-eyed, eyelashes touching eyebrows. Still nothing. Maybe he was blind and my parents hadn't told me. Maybe my parents didn't know he was blind. Maybe *his* parents didn't know! Well, what other reason could there be? Vijay Kumar had talked incessantly about his own dynamism and had proudly displayed his magnificent pupils to the entire room. This one had not said a word. He just sat between his parents looking at his shoes. Maybe he was a poet! Maybe he was eulogising on the fate of poor downtrodden shoes . . .

So far the conversation had been dominated by his mother,

punctuated by staccato interjections from my father, and oiled by Ravi's tuneless burbling, much to everyone's discomfort.

– I received a magnificent farewell from my company after single-handedly defending them from robbers.

– You know, *our* home was broken into a few months ago, and last month a man put a snake in our kitchen and asked for two hundred rupees to take it away.

– You should have called me, I would have broken his nose.

– Next time I'll call you.

The mother seemed to like Ravi.

– Please do. It is my business to help those in distress, particularly women.

– For how many years have you lived here?

My father was desperately trying to steer the conversation in a direction that Ravi couldn't follow. Unfortunately, whilst there were many areas where Ravi was unqualified to participate, he was unaware of his limitations.

– My great-grandfather built this house.

– Really?

– Apart from the third floor, that was my husband.

– Really?

– Yes.

Silence. Then Ravi rescued the conversation from awkwardness with dashing flamboyance.

– I have built several houses.

This one even startled my mother into speech.

– *Really?*

– Of course.

Finally, *He* spoke. Well, actually he never quite managed it, because his six-year-old sister came running into the room, but he was definitely on the brink of opening his mouth, and it's the intention that counts.

– I want to see the girl! I want to see the girl!

I liked her, and as I said before, I rarely liked anyone.

– Sit down Savitri, be polite. Don't call Auntie *The Girl*.

This time *He* really did speak.

– Savitri, this is not a girl. This is my wife.

Now that was a bit excessive. Admittedly, everything was more or less settled, but I didn't like his tone one bit. The child tugged at my sleeve and told me that I looked like her elder sister who was dead now.

– Are you *really* going to marry my brother?

This was asked not only with childish innocence, which I approved of, but also with a hint of amazement, which worried me. I was faced with a double dilemma. First of all, how was I to deal with this question? I could use the technique I had stumbled on three years ago, of bursting into tears, but I was a bit too old for that one now. A more elegant approach, befitting an eighteen-year-old about to enter the adult world, was to pretend not to hear, which, given a little licence from the adults in the room (the girl had a piercingly loud voice), proved more or less acceptable. The second problem was more serious.

He was looking at me now. And his look went way beyond visual autopsy. His eyes scuttled over the folds of my clothes like a cockroach across a kitchen floor. At strategic locations he would pause, as though finding some sweet morsel buried in the dust, and then continue, furtively shifting his glance at intervals as though afraid a heavy boot might suddenly descend on his head.

I looked at his eyes. They couldn't conceal his intentions. I looked at his trousers and they proved equally inadequate. This didn't look good.

– What's that thing?

Savitri had calmly pointed out her brother's rather obvious erection. I wasn't sure whether the others realised or not, but *He* certainly understood and crossed his legs while unleashing his second sentence of the evening.

– Hush Savitri. Don't interrupt.

Ravi once again rescued the room from embarrassment with a wholly unconscious blend of tact and charm.

– In America one can eat very cheap and very delicious Chinese food, if one knows where to find it that is.

Ravi's words fell like gentle rain and I looked at his large hands and thought how glad I was that my big brother was there for support. This thought soon faded, and I tossed it on the heap where I keep other thoughts that stalk me in moments of desperation.

Savitri continued talking (while ignoring her brother's glares) to my delight, amusement, and anxiety.

– I have never eaten Chinese food, but I like ice cream.

I approved of this topic.

– I like ice cream too.

– What flavour?

– Pistachio.

– Yuck.

I smiled. For a second I had forgotten about *Him* and his uncontrollable organ.

– Shut up, Savitri. This conversation is for adults.

Despite his attempts to hide it, *His* adulthood was still in full view.

He was grinning with a face caked in jubilance. Our eyes locked and I fought it but I couldn't break that grin. I had seen it before in other faces, though never with my mother sitting next to me, drinking coffee. His gaze was uninhibited now, resilient under the pressure of my resistance, like pins, twisting my arm behind my back. I stood with a snap, like the cracking of a bone, and my coffee cup was in fragments on the floor and I hissed, *I don't want you!*, between clenched teeth. The grin flickered and was gone, replaced by feigned surprise, but the sinewy grip of his eyes was still there, lazier now, like a muscle relaxing after impact. I had not drawn breath for some time and it came rushing out in a moist sigh over which I heard my father's voice, predictable as a trip-hammer, straining against necessity.

My mother was trembling. Ravi looked perplexed. And like a crane my father's grip practically lifted me from the house. One or two stray apologies fell impotently, bereft of any weight, and we left, but not before Ravi had informed them that I was a nice girl, though quite mad, and that he would easily sort the situation out.

27

Outside, Ravi pronounced the visit a success and my father slapped him seven, maybe eight times, much harder than usual, and Ravi screamed, arms flailing like meat from hooks. It was almost dark. I looked back at the house and it veered towards me, groaning against bricks and mortar, like a dog whose teeth tear against the muzzle that binds it. I tried to run, but my father only held me tighter, his fingers cold like knives. I struggled but I could hear him slapping Ravi with his free hand, so I stopped struggling and walked. I didn't look at my mother, it wouldn't have been fair.

When we reached home my mother went into the kitchen to make coffee. My father pushed me into a chair, and Ravi hovered, afraid to stay, but not wanting to leave. I didn't cry, but looked straight in front of me, expressionless. My father stared at me, knowing that I could feel his stare, demanding a response. I looked hard at his shoes and he took off his belt which slithered in his hand, and then, without taking his eyes off me, he gave Ravi a couple of quick licks with it and Ravi squealed and ran upstairs. My father stared harder, as though his look would break glass, but I stayed silent and when my mother returned with the coffee he turned on his heel, snorted, and wrenched the coffee from her hand before pouring it on to the floor in a thin, noisy stream. He left without a glance at either of us.

I looked at my mother for a moment. She returned my look, but I couldn't see anything but worry behind her eyes. She mopped up the spilt coffee with a cloth before returning to the kitchen to cook.

I wished Ravi would come back, but I knew he was hiding, licking his wounds. I wouldn't have blamed him if he had asked himself why my father hadn't hit *me*, but this wouldn't have occurred to him. There were tiny flies bouncing from the light bulb which swung back at them, spitting. Its electric glare was so artificial that it would never run out of anger.

I hated those idiotic flies, spinning like fools. And I hated that bulb, so bright, so fierce, and it couldn't even shake off a few flies. And it would go on all night, and then the next day, and then the next, until all of a sudden that bulb burnt itself out. It was all such a waste of time. I got up and turned off the light, and within seconds my mother was in the room, asking why and turning it back on in one breath. I mumbled something and she half smiled, and then returned to her cooking.

I stayed in the chair all evening, and didn't eat, much to my mother's anguish. I had ruptured my father's world, and now I was starting on hers. Like a clockwork ritual she kept insisting, and I kept refusing. And it went on and on, until they all went to bed.

I stayed in my chair late into the night, watching the flies, and then I also went to bed and lay down beside Ravi, listening to him snore. Ravi snored so pitifully, like a little child. I knew I would have to leave him, and I knew he wouldn't understand why. He was afraid even when he was asleep, or perhaps everyone was, but Ravi lacked the hardness of character to disguise it. Though I knew him so well, his sleeping form was a mystery to me, a mystery because I couldn't hold it, couldn't take the pain away. I watched as his chest rose and fell, and he shivered a little, a childish shiver, his *own* shiver, that he couldn't have prevented were all the world standing over him, waving their fists. If I couldn't take that shiver away then I couldn't take his pain away, and I would have to leave him for him to understand.

In the hall the clock struck four. The room was cold and I rose to shut the window. The rain was slanting down. I looked at the tree outside and pushed my face into the night, feeling leaves brush my skin and rainwater trickle down my neck. I craned my neck to see the top of the tree, but I couldn't. The rain splashed breathlessly against the leaves in a complicity so timeless that my father seemed to shrink in my mind until he became more an object of pity than fear. I shut the window, shutting out the smell of the leaves and the rain. I wanted to say goodbye to them, but once such ceremonies had begun it would be impossible to leave.

I pulled a few things into a bag, not quite knowing what to take, and thinking that taking anything would be useless. But still, I had to take something, if only to convince myself that I was indeed leaving. Ravi rolled over and muttered something. I ran downstairs and into the night.

Running away was difficult. Every street was familiar, each echoing a familiar route that would lead me back home. This was *their* time – the anonymity of the night where every shadow was a part of their world – and I felt their adult warnings prick my insides. I walked faster and faster, turning down roads I only half-knew, until I was lost.

Watery lamps lit the street and I wandered like an erratic gust of sea-swept wind. A red glow bloomed on the horizon like a sleeping dragon opening a fiery eye, taunting me. I turned into streets with no name. I saw dogs with their stomachs torn open, the wind caressing their insides. I saw children with the faces of old men sleeping in beds of dust. The sky glowed a painful red, as though a giant needle had ruptured the night in a thousand places.

Rain splashed into the gutter where it moaned, lashed by the wind, and clung to my ankles like a curtain. The wind was closing in, forcing its way into my eyes. I thought about lying down and waiting for a better life, and then I thought of *Him* and the dark revelation he held cocked in his fingers. I thought of my father. He would have snorted like a bull and shouted *What are You Doing in the Rain? There are Things to be Done and You are Standing in the Rain!*

The sky seemed calmer and I could see light shining through with a surreptitious smile. My reflection stared up at me from the puddle around my ankles. My face looked pale. I thought of Holly Golightly, standing in the rain, her face crushed with tears. Didn't I look like her, just a little?

I lifted my feet and walked.

The road wound on, turned to earth, and then lights, and I reached the edge of the town. A wide road stretched ahead of me. A lorry rattled down it, frenziedly declaring its existence to whoever cared to listen. The rain had almost stopped and there were lights and voices up ahead. I craved human warmth so much that I almost ran . . .

It was a roadside coffee shop with a dozen or so people and the smell of food. I sat down, trying to look inconspicuous in my sodden clothes.

To my right was a group of lorry drivers. They talked quietly, often lapsing into a bored silence during which they would watch the six men in front of them. The men were dressed in virginal white cotton, arguing about a debt that a seventh man, sitting defiantly amidst them, had incurred. The remorseless debtor glowed with outrage at any accusation, including those that were so straightforwardly factual that it was ludicrous, and not even helpful, to deny. He seemed determined to seal his slighted pride with blood.

The lorry drivers left, with their weary, unflappable instinct for trouble, and the six men dragged the still protesting debtor from his chair. Two held his arms while a third punched him like a technician who knows the best results are achieved through patient repetition. The unfortunate victim's head bounced from side to side like an onion. He closed his eyes and smiled at the sky like Joan of Arc. I waited for him to break into a eulogy on the power of truth to heal all sin, but it was hard for him to talk with a mouth full of salty blood. His stoicism seemed to irritate his assailant, who discarded his methodical pummelling in favour of wildly swinging his fists. The actual purpose of the beating seemed long forgotten as Joan of Arc abandoned his poise and begged for mercy like a baby. The man stopped pounding to listen to what he had to say.

The debtor sobbed through his teeth about the plight of his family and how he had desperately wanted to repay the money but how his wife had persuaded him not to. Getting excited by this one, he wailed that women will always turn an honest man into a snake, how she had wracked his mind with threats and pleas, how his mother-in-law had taken a stick to thrash him for being such a useless husband and how his wife had laughed and told her friends and now the whole village knew and none of this was fair and didn't they understand how much pressure he was under and how he would prove that he was a man of his word and needed two more weeks and had deserved the beating to show him the way and how grateful he was for it and how in the morning everything would be different, and he would be different, and the world would be a better, fairer place.

The men appreciated this fine speech, although the one who had been administering the beating disappeared during one of the most eloquent moments. When he returned he was carrying a rifle. The debtor screamed. The goons lashed him to one of the wooden pillars that supported the roof. I studied his eyes. One of them had half-closed and folded upon itself like a baby's fist, but I could see the dull, grey light droning inside. The other eye looked lazy, and with a start I noticed that he was watching me with some interest. The man raised the rifle and took aim.

I looked at Joan of Arc once more, and then turned my head, leaving him to his fate. The gun roared. When I looked back the wall behind him sported a smouldering hole where the bullet had entered, and the man was weeping gently. The tall man lowered the gun, *You have Two Weeks, if the Money is not Paid, then See What Happens To You*. They turned to leave. The tall one pointed the gun at me for a second, and then slung it over his shoulder, winked, and was gone. I felt a flush of disappointment. The movie had ended . . .

Joan of Arc was still lashed to the stake. He whimpered, looking at me with a strange blend of curiosity, entreaty and fear. The old couple who owned the coffee shop, and had silently disappeared when the beating started, now returned and untied Joan of Arc, who collapsed to the floor. They helped him to lie down on a charpoy where he drank tea in silence. I didn't look at him, but walked over to the old couple and asked to use the telephone. I phoned Vijay Kumar's grandfather. It was early morning and he was awake. I asked the couple for our location, and he said he would come in twenty minutes. They brought me coffee and I waited, watching them talk.

They seemed untroubled by Joan of Arc now, who was still nursing his wounds on the charpoy. I couldn't hear them, but they seemed to be talking of idle things, like old friends. They even seemed happy. It was nice to watch them. The grandfather had sounded calm on the phone. I had told him that I was in trouble and he had sounded concerned, though unsurprised. I drank another cup of coffee, very carefully avoiding Joan of Arc's eyes. I knew he sensed my indifference to his plight, and I knew he was afraid of me, afraid of such indifference where there should have been only fragility.

The morning continued its shuffle towards us and the old proprietors stopped talking and returned to their work. Joan of Arc was snoring on the charpoy, but I still didn't look at him. My complicity in his pain was not to be questioned. I was as guilty as the tall goon who had spilt his blood. I couldn't look at the blood, staring brightly at me from the floor. Had Savitri been with me she would have asked, *What's that Red Stuff?* and pointed with childish amusement, and I would have used my newly acquired adulthood to turn away and stare in another direction, preoccupied with more serious things.

More serious things. What was more serious than blood? I closed my eyes to think but my mind had become opaque, congealed, resisting order, begging to soar, begging for release. Why should it interest me where men shed their blood? *Were I a Boy Again, I would Refuse to Become A Man. A Very Costly Habit, in Terms of Blood*. I pressed my hand to my wrist, searching for my pulse, finding the insistent thud. *My* blood, I thought, *my* blood. Not their blood. *My* blood. But who hadn't shed blood? Ravi certainly had, lots of it, from every part of him. *My sister?* I felt sick at the thought. Her veins gasping for air, her heart growling at this faraway violation, little capillaries trembling like children, turning their faces away in fear, and all the time Vijay Kumar would be there, claiming his right, feasting on blood, watching as it touched the sheets, as it screamed with cold, looking for the warmth it had left without warning, and then hardening, stiffening, silently dying, like a child.

I forced myself to look at Joan of Arc. He was still sleeping, but he looked calmer now and was smiling as smugly as a baby, a smile of greedy contentment, as though his satiation had left nothing in the world for him but sleep. I remembered his passionate, greedy defiance, a self-satisfied self-destruction – betraying his own creation – begging them to suck their fill of his bones, to splinter his face with sweet, succulent pain. And how, even when his mouth was full of blood, his cheeks bulging like bloated moons, he had longed for more, longed for more fear, longed for . . . a complete ordeal. He had denied everything, and admitted everything, he had protested wildly, and then eagerly writhed in his own baseness as though sucking milk. And now he felt safe, safe because his body was no longer his own. His mind had lost its centre and had spilt, like his blood, out and across the floor.

I felt no guilt any more. Only loathing and betrayal. And the way he had looked at me? The anger? The fear? The contempt? The childish entreaty? He wanted me to join him, lashed to a stake, hard fists pounding, blood freely flowing, and to lie down with him on that charpoy, sucking my thumb, with no body of my own, no mind, only a greedy surrender. And so this entry into adulthood was – what? – a retreat back to that womb that had hardly seemed to want me in the first place.

Joan of Arc awoke and looked at me with a quick, terrified glance. I looked back and he wiped an invisible blob of spittle from his face and then turned away, facing the wall, to sleep his greedy sleep. There was hatred in his turned back, in the leer of his buttocks. It was too horrible for me to look at.

– What happened?

The grandfather had arrived. I hadn't heard his footsteps, but he was looking at me with a calm which stopped me from shouting, but the fear was in my face and my voice. So hard was it to look away from Joan of Arc that I was shaking with the effort.

– I don't want to shed blood and I don't want to marry anyone.

– I have told you before, a wise choice, but –

But you must Learn the Art of Producing Milk, Cotton and Bricks with your Soul. He could tell I was in no mood to hear it.

– but I hope you know what this means.

I said nothing. I didn't want to consider it. Holly Golightly had never considered it, and she had lived alone in her apartment with her Cat.

– You should go home now, sleep, think it over.

– I don't want to go home.

– Your brother must be missing you.

He was manipulating me now. I hadn't expected him to do this. It seemed so unlike him, and so terribly unfair.

– My brother?

He smiled.

– I have told you before that truth is never easy. You must suffer.

– Must shed blood?

– In one way or another. It is very difficult not to.

I thought of Ravi's face when my father had whipped him with his belt. The moment before impact his face had stiffened, with a knowledge of what was to come, a resignation, though unlike that of Joan of Arc. And my sister? I thought of her face when three years ago I had wandered into the house to learn of her betrothal. I had seen her terror. Her fear of pain. And I hadn't managed to find one word, not even one.

– I know. But I will never marry that man.

– Did I say you must?

I shook my head but his eyes were twinkling and I found it impossible not to smile. He gave me his hand and we walked away to the car. He didn't speak as he manipulated the gear-stick, turning the wheel with a grimace. I wondered how he had suffered, but it didn't seem right to ask him about his life. I trusted him, and that was enough. I looked at the watch where his veined arm gripped the wheel in a tight, prisoner's clutch. It was almost seven o'clock.

– Will your mother be awake?

– Yes.

– And your father?

– Not yet.

– Good, good.

I had never really seen him as old, but the way he gripped

35

that wheel suggested that he was no more invincible than anyone else. He seemed almost afraid of the car that was so much more powerful than him, but he made no attempt to disguise his frailty, and I loved him for that.

– Will you tell your mother?

– I don't think so.

– I think you should.

I said nothing. Of course I wouldn't tell her, though it was my own fear that prevented me. I was more afraid of penetrating her private silence than I was of my father's belt. The unseen terrors inside her head were so much greater.

We reached the house very quickly, and I felt ashamed at how insubstantial my attempt to run away had been. I had felt as though I had crossed into another world, but it had been no further than a couple of miles. My mother probably walked that far every day in her endless circuits to and from the kitchen.

– There now, go inside, come and see me when you are ready. We shall talk it over.

He kissed me hard on the cheek so that I could feel his stubble, the dead skin scraping my face. I didn't meet his gaze but ran straight into the house.

The door was open, as it always was in the mornings, and I walked through and saw my mother sitting in one of the hard, wooden chairs in the living room. She was perched on the edge and her frame was very stiff. She looked up at me, her face reproachfully pale, with her familiar trembling stillness. I didn't know what to do, and I didn't want to say anything, so I acted as though nothing had happened and turned my back and went upstairs.

Ravi was sitting on the bed, looking at the bedclothes where I had slept. I came in and sat next to him, watching his big, foolish nose and his flabby, sack-like ears. He seemed to want very much to say something. This was unusual for Ravi. It was almost as though my disappearance had forced him into a spell of honest, unflinching thought.

– Where did you go?

– I went for a walk.

– Then why did you take a bag?

– I don't know. I thought, maybe, about running away.

He lurched backwards as though stung and then turned towards me, eyes wide with questions. I knew he hadn't the voice to say what was careering around his head, so, as always, I tried to give him a little gentle help.

– I don't want to marry that horrible man, Ravi.

– Why not? I know he was ugly, but so many men are ugly.

I had a feeling this comment wasn't entirely altruistic.

– It has nothing to do with him being ugly, Ravi.

There was a coaxing echo in my voice that I prayed would penetrate that thick forehead and lodge somewhere between his ears where he couldn't pull it out.

– Ravi, that man was *horrible*, completely *horrible*. I *hated* him.

– But *why*?

He seemed on the verge of tears, exasperated and afraid.

– Ravi, couldn't you see?

– See what? I know his trousers were –

He stopped. There were some subjects Ravi was incapable of talking about without revealing a thoroughly disturbing amount of information about himself.

– Not his trousers, Ravi, his *eyes*.

– You didn't like his eyes?

– No, I didn't like his eyes.

I wanted to leave it at that, leave him to think about it. But my hopes were crushed as the frightened look left his eyes and was replaced by his usual idiocy.

– Listen to me now. I know a lot about men and a lot about marriage. You may not like his eyes, you may not like his face, you may *think* you do not like him. But marriage is not something to run from. Marriage is something to face. It *grows*, like –

He paused, seeking poetic insight, and his eyes fell upon the window.

– like a tree.

Ha! I could feel his satisfaction rising. *Like a tree!* What wisdom! Poor Ravi.

– Ravi, please try to listen.

– It is not my place to listen. You are my sister and you are more important to me than life itself. I will protect you, if need be, as I have protected your sister. But I can tell you that that man is not a bad sort. I have promised I will settle this issue. I have promised them, and now I give my promise to you. I shall not rest until you are happy.

– Thank you, Ravi.

– Not at all.

He sat, arms folded like an emperor, and I sighed and pulled the bedclothes over my head. I badly needed to sleep.

– One more thing.

I pulled my head back out. The tears hadn't had time to form, but time was running out.

– Yes, Ravi?

– The next time you feel afraid, do not hesitate to come to me. No, you *must* come to me. It is best. I know things. You should take advantage of this. Your problem is you think too much. You think you know something of life. You should listen to me.

– All right, Ravi.

– Good girl.

He patted my head and trotted off to the mirror to shave. I pulled the bedclothes back over my head, and this time the tears did come, silent and fast.

Ravi left and I went on crying until I heard my father climbing the stairs. I made sure the blanket covered every inch of my face and I closed my eyes and breathed as heavily as I could. Such tricks were wasted on my father, who wouldn't have cared if I'd been in hospital in a coma. He pulled the covers from my head and yelled in my ear, *Wake Up Girl! Wake Up!*

I rubbed my eyes and frowned, trying to look like the baby girl who used to greet him in the mornings. I think this brought back bad memories for him, because he seemed even less sympathetic than usual.

– Your mother told me to give you this.

He thrust a cup of coffee in my face, spilling a little, scalding my hand which I sucked at, trying, again unsuccessfully, to arouse some sympathy. I knew what the coffee meant; it was his way of establishing his credentials as a warm, loving father before he put the boot in. It was nearly eight o'clock which meant he was late for work, and I knew that if I refused to wake up then he would have to leave without delivering his piece. Unfortunately, after burning myself with the coffee, I had no chance of feigning sleepiness.

– Six o'clock, we're going back. Be ready.

I nodded, and only a corpse could have failed to notice the tears swimming in my eyes. My father touched me on the cheek and smiled.

– You are a good girl, most of the time. And I want to be proud of you as I am proud of your sister. You are too clever for your own good. Behave yourself this time.

His smile faded with the additional effort of his words, and he left, ruffling my hair, which made me spill my coffee again.

I watched him leave, walking his quick military walk, clouded in stress like a thick, angry mist that obscured everything beyond his own nose. I needed to think fast, to make a plan. Vijay Kumar's grandfather had not, as I had hoped he might, waved his magic wand. He had been deadeningly practical. My father would never listen to reason, Ravi lacked the mental capacity to do so, and my mother might listen, but that was all she was capable of.

Six o'clock . . . time was running out. I didn't know if I could face him again. The grandfather had told me, in no uncertain terms, that everyone suffered. And it was true . . . *You must Suffer, Must Suffer. Must Suffer.* But hadn't he said that I didn't have to marry that horrible man? I didn't have to. Didn't have to . . .

– What time is it?

Ravi was standing above me, his face screwed up into a ball.

– Six o'clock. Appa is waiting.

– Six o'clock?

I had slept for ten hours.

– Where is Amma?

– She doesn't want to come. She has gone out.

Gone out! My mother never went out.

My father came storming into the room, looking terribly tired, and he grabbed my arm and pulled me upright.

– They are here.

– *Here?*

– Downstairs! Here!

– But I thought we were going –

– They said they wouldn't wait. You are to marry today.

– *Today!*

My father was moving faster than his body, his words were spilling out with a ferocity I had never seen before. Ravi was scurrying around the room, faster and faster, as though afraid to remain idle for even a second.

I didn't have a choice and so I pulled myself out of the bed with a wrench. I shivered. The air was bitterly cold and my father's grip was around my arm again, like a prison of bones. He dragged me downstairs, so fast that my feet spluttered and tripped over the steps. I could hear Ravi thumping down behind me.

– Here she is.

Ravi joined my father and beamed proudly. My father wore his widest plastic smile. His face looked about to crack under the strain. The horrible man and his father and mother were there. *He* was bare-chested, wearing a white dhoti, and there was a fire in the centre of the room, rising from the floorboards. My sister was standing by the door in front of a shadow which must have been Vijay, the trans-Atlantic demi-god. Her face was a mask of pain and tears. I looked to her for sympathy. *Why Don't You Want to Do it? Aren't you Happy?* She was crying as she said it, making no attempt to hide her tears.

He rose from his seat, his wraith-like frame shining with moisture. The room stank of sweat. I saw Savitri playing in the corner, skipping near the fire. The flames cast orange streaks across her face. She didn't seem to notice me. *He* crept closer.

Three drops of sweat poured from his forehead to the bridge of his nose. Gathering speed, they moved to the tip where they lingered before falling to the floor. I watched them. The obscene blackness of his eyes was reflected in their elliptical perfection, and I prayed that they would stay frozen in the air. I closed my eyes and felt him lifting up my clothes, baring my thighs. I looked at Ravi and my father, and they were smiling and nodding their heads. I looked at *His* parents and they were holding hands, watching proudly. He gripped my shoulders and I turned my face from his acrid breath and saw my sister, leaning against the wall, her hair swept back off her shoulders. She was smoking a cigarette in an enormous holder and was watching with faint amusement. *Quelle Bore!* she said, and tossed her head, shook her hips and sailed out of the room.

I awoke, blinking, and looked at the clock. Eleven o'clock. Ravi was sitting with his back to me, watching girls in bikinis on the television. I leaned back, feeling the softness of the pillow. I wanted to dream. I wanted to see my sister as she had been, with her hair swept back, smoking a cigarette with a languid smile. I wanted to keep that image, to hold it close to me. Predictably, Ravi turned around.

– So you have woken up?

– Yes, Ravi.

The tension in my voice was greater than usual, but Ravi didn't notice.

– Appa told me not to let you leave the house.

I rose and picked up the bag I had half-filled in the night.

– I just want to be outside for a while, Ravi. Don't worry.

Ravi looked frightened. I knew my father would beat him when he returned, but that was inevitable.

– Don't worry, Ravi. I'll be back.

– Where are you going?

– I don't know. For a walk somewhere.

– Be back soon uh? Don't go too far.

I looked at Ravi's bulbous face, his walrus belly bulging beneath

41

his belt. The girls in bikinis were still prancing behind him, but he wasn't watching any more. His fear of my father had been replaced by something much more unsettling. I stood facing him, meeting his gaze, using the osmosis technique that I had often tried (unsuccessfully) whereby understanding was supposed to seep into his head. I knew the longer I stood in front of him the more pathetic he would make himself appear, so I turned and walked downstairs, trying to shut his face out of my mind.

The living room was empty and the door was wide open. I could hear pots banging in the kitchen, a sound which had long been a surrogate for my mother's voice. I paused, listening, hoping her private truths could be siphoned through the din of the pots. I left the bag by the door and walked into the kitchen.

She didn't turn around but continued to scrub a blackened vessel, digging her nails into the charcoal embedded in the bottom. She had heard me enter, but still she cleaned on, only turning around when the task was complete. Two cockroaches appeared from wherever cockroaches appear from and ran across the floor in terrified, exhilarated defiance. My mother, her eyes narrow with concentration, took a spoon from the sink and crouched low before stunning one of the renegades with a precisely aimed stab to the head. He reeled, turning on to his back, kicking his spindly legs before flipping over and disappearing from sight.

She looked up at me and it took some time for her eyes to right themselves. They still looked like dark, narrow tunnels, with room only for infidel intruders in her kitchen and the relentless punishments that awaited them. For a moment I thought she might rap me with the spoon, but then her pupils dilated and were flooded with brighter shadows.

– Drink your coffee now.

I shook my head, but she moved to the stove and began to pour coffee into a tumbler. I felt impatient. There was so much to say, and so much that would be left unsaid, and she was pouring coffee.

– I don't want coffee, Amma.

She looked at me in surprise.

– And I don't want to marry that man.

Her face relaxed. Everything was all right now. The inexplicable had been explained.

– Appa is angry.

I knew that.

– Amma, I'm going now.

– Going where?

– I have some things to do.

– Have your coffee first.

– I don't want coffee, Amma. I just want to –

To say goodbye.

– to go now.

– All right. Go.

It was extraordinary. My father was angry because I didn't want to marry, and my mother was upset because I wouldn't drink my coffee.

– Amma, do you want me to marry that man?

The coffee was boiling over on the stove. She ran to it, abandoning my question for a more urgent cause. I sighed, loudly, but she didn't hear. Her body was moving to its kitchen rhythm, a clashing and a banging that drowned all other sounds, taking over the body and jerking its limbs in time to its never-ending needs.

She restored the coffee to health and turned with a face that said, *Marriage can Wait, There is Coffee on the Stove*.

– Amma, I don't –

– Go for your walk now. When you come back we will talk about it, after you have had your coffee.

She smiled, though, as always, it was a tired smile. I smiled back, and then turned to leave. By the time I reached the door the tears had returned, but this wasn't a time for tears. My mother was determined. She was silent and sorrowful, but determined. I would follow her example.

The walk to Vijay Kumar's grandfather's house was short, but eyes would be watching me every step of the way. As I turned left by *Majick Movie House*, I knew that Ravi would be watching from the window. I shuddered but kept walking, looking ahead.

I passed the court house on my right and I noticed a man from my father's office, leaning on his scooter in front of the building, chewing. Our eyes met and he smiled a knowing smile, and I looked ahead, certain he could read my mind. I turned the corner without looking back and crossed the street.

In the centre of the road was a statue of Shivaji on his horse, holding his sword aloft. He was looking at me, and I looked at him, as everyone did. And then I looked at the horse. The eyes were dead, probably because nobody looked at him. Shivaji's eyes were wild and alive. I tried to imagine what would happen if that horse suddenly bucked and galloped off. Shivaji would be left, lying in the centre of the road, probably still holding his sword above his head. And everyone would laugh as they passed him. If he hadn't been a statue he would have cut them down with a snarl. I could see him, standing defiantly in the street, waving his sword.

When Shivaji was young, the Sultan sent Afzul Khan to arrest Shivaji's father, as a warning. The Sultan then sent an army to attack him, but Shivaji defeated them twice, so the Sultan released his father. But then Afzul Khan sent him a message ordering him to surrender. Shivaji agreed to meet him, but the Khan ordered that he come with only two guards and no army. Shivaji was clever, he wore armour underneath his clothes and fastened tiger's claws to his fingernails. When they met, the Khan, with a great show of respect, made as if to embrace him, but Shivaji noticed him pull out a knife to stab him in the back. With lightning speed Shivaji seized the knife, dug his tiger claws into the Khan's chest, and killed him. So, if Shivaji's horse did make a run for it, perhaps nobody would laugh. Shivaji was not a man to be trifled with.

I looked at the horse again, condemned to stand for ever under the rain and the sun, carrying that fearsome warrior on his back. Shivaji's sword was curved, and tapered into a murderous-looking point. I wondered if he held it so high just to stop his horse from escaping; after all, there wasn't much else to do up there, waiting in the middle of the road. His enemies had long since died. The truth was that Shivaji was probably bored, but at least people looked at him. His horse just stood there, trembling, and nobody noticed. It occurred to me that if I did go to meet the horrible man then I could maul him to death when he came near me, but I was pretty sure that people would notice if I walked into the house with tiger claws growing from my fingers. No, when it came to it, I definitely wasn't a Shivaji. I was a Shivaji's horse. I wanted to see if Shivaji also had some growing excitement in his trousers, like the horrible man, but he was surely above such things.

It bothered me that not only could I never be Shivaji, but I would always, no matter how hard I tried, be afraid of him. I walked on, turning down the side road that led to the grand-father's house. I wondered if I should tell him about this. Most people would get very, very angry if I told them I was afraid of Shivaji, but I didn't think the grandfather would mind. I tried to imagine what Holly Golightly would say; *Quel Rat* would hardly be fair. Perhaps she would marry him, for his money, but that didn't seem very likely either.

I looked back but I couldn't see the statue any more. If Shivaji came to life now, and if he knew what I was thinking. I would be in serious, serious trouble.

I reached the house. Vijay's father would be at work. I hoped his mother wasn't there. Usually at this time she had gone out somewhere, but you could never tell. The door was open and I walked in and took off my sandals. I tried to hide them beneath the other shoes, but gave up. I couldn't see his mother, so I ran up the stairs as quietly as possible. The grandfather was in his chair, reading the newspaper.

– Ah, good morning, my dear, I was just thinking about you.
– Yes?
– Sit down, sit down. Now, how are you? Did you sleep?
The grandfather had a habit of making me wait.
– Yes.
– Good, good.
I hated this.
– I won't marry that horrible man.

– Good.

That was better.

– And I can't stay here. Not with my father.

– Of course you can't.

– So I have to leave.

– Yes, you do.

– But I don't know where to go.

I had met a girl from Bandipur once. I didn't have her address, but I supposed if I went there and asked around I could find her. She was very nice.

– Do you remember the first time we met?

– Yes.

– Do you remember a short man, with a moustache?

I just wished I could remember that girl's name.

– Well, anyway, it doesn't matter if you don't, but that man's name was Raju. I sent him north, a long way north, to The City.

– Why?

– Well, Raju is from a village, and things weren't so good for him there, and he needed work.

– Oh.

– And you need work, isn't that true?

– Yes, but –

– But you want to be an actress. Wait a minute. Now what is the first thing an actress needs?

He had told me this so many times already. I answered like a parrot.

– A passion for cinema.

– Right. Which you have, isn't it? Now what is the second thing an actress needs?

An apartment, diamonds, a friend in Sing Sing, a cat?

– I don't know.

– Some experience of life. That's right. Experience of life. Very important. *Profoundly* important.

What did he think I'd been doing with my time?

– I do have some experience of life, don't I, Uncle?

46

– Life. *Life*. Not dreams, not movies.

– I see.

I supposed he had a point, but this wasn't a very nice way of saying it.

– Now, I have arranged a position for you.

– To work?

– Of *course*. We all have to work, you know. All of us. I did, oh yes. But what did I tell you? Milk, cotton and bricks – food, clothing and shelter. Do you want to be a burden to your father?

– No.

– And do you want to marry the horrible man?

– *No!*

– Then you have to work. I have been busy this morning. Something in your face troubled me last night, so I decided to take matters into my own hands. I have arranged a position for you, as a –

Film star?

– maid.

– Oh.

He seized my hand in his.

– *Experience of life*, damn it! Don't look so downcast.

– Sorry, Uncle.

– That's all right. That's all right. At your age you want the egg without the rooster, and I understand that, but milk, cotton and bricks you know. And this will give you good experience of life.

– Where am I –

– Hold your horses. I'm coming to that part. You are to go north, right into the heartland, to The City.

– By myself?

– Of course by yourself. What did you think? You think I want to go with you at my age? No no, The City is for youngsters like you, full of passion –

He tugged at my cheek. I resisted, not because my distaste for cheek-pulling was greater than anyone else's, but because I was scared.

– full of *dynamism!*

Nobody had ever used that word about me before. I might have been pleased had he said this under less terrifying circumstances.

– My dear, you have a destiny. And, quite rightly, you have told me that your destiny is *not* to marry the horrible man, and *not* to remain here, with your father. This is not to say that your father isn't a good man, but he will never allow you . . . stardom, and, for the time being, unless I have misunderstood, that is what you are seeking, isn't it?

At that moment what I was most ardently seeking was a couple of hours in *Majick Movie House*.

– Yes, Uncle.

– There is a gentleman in The City called Mr Aziz, a Kashmiri. Mr Aziz currently employs Raju, as a cook. Now Mr Aziz is a very wealthy man, considerably so, . . . but he owes me a favour or two. We were together in the army, and the army does strange things to men. It brings them together in ways quite contrary to the laws of social behaviour.

He handed me a piece of paper.

– This is his address in The City. You will need a letter of introduction, which I have for you here.

– I have to go to see the man, at six o'clock.

– At six o'clock, my dear, you will be on a train.

– So *soon?*

– What did you expect?

– I don't know.

– Destiny is not an easy thing to manage. If we don't pluck it . . . it vanishes.

He clapped his hands.

– I see.

– And besides, there is no time. When you don't come home, where is the first place you think they will look for you?

My heart was beating so loud that I couldn't hear my reply, if I replied at all.

– Precisely. The crazy old fool's house.

I thought about Shivaji again. He had never had to do *this*.

– It is almost noon and the train is at four, which leaves us plenty of time. What do you have in your bag?

I wasn't sure, it seemed months since I had packed it.

– I don't know. Some clothes, my toothbrush.

The word *Toothbrush* aroused terror in my mind. I imagined myself in a cold, lonely room, pulling my toothbrush from the bag, putting it beside my bed.

– What about money?

I had precisely five rupees in my pocket. I shook my head.

– Well, I think it's a little foolish to forget money, don't you?

I nodded. He went over to his bed and took some notes from under the pillow and handed them to me. I stuffed them into my bag.

– Put some with your clothes and put some in your pocket. Keep it safe.

I did as instructed. I wasn't enjoying this at all.

– That's it. It isn't much money, but it should be enough for a week's milk, cotton and bricks. Rule number one is never, never give anyone your money. And don't keep it under your pillow. Keep it somewhere safe.

– Yes, Uncle.

– And don't look so sad. You're going to The City damn it. *Experience of life!* Lots of it. And movies, lots of them, lots and lots of them.

I had seen *My Fair Lady* a few days ago (for the second time). He sounded a little like Henry Higgins, *If you are Good, then you Will Have Lots of Chocolates and Take Rides in Taxis, but if You are Bad* . . . I couldn't remember that part, which was probably just as well. Thinking this lifted my spirits. A common flower girl, going to The City, with film studios growing from every pavement, with writers with their typewriters living just upstairs from me, with Cats and diamonds, and dark Brazilian men with large wallets.

– But what about Ravi?

– You can't expect *Ravi* to come with you!

49

– I know, but he . . . he doesn't like his life much.

He looked serious.

– And do you like *your* life?

– I did, until the horrible man.

– Well, yes. But hasn't it ever occurred to you that Ravi has his *own* destiny, and that, perhaps, his destiny may be best promoted by your leaving.

It had occurred to me, several times. But I couldn't even begin to imagine what Ravi's destiny could be.

– I suppose so.

– The City is far away, but not that far. I will write to you. I will keep you informed, and I will watch over Ravi and your sister.

And my mother? I supposed she was too old for anyone to watch over her. In any case I doubted she would have welcomed such attention.

– My dear, all you have to do is to follow your heart.

– I don't like leaving them.

– Of course you will leave a wound when you go, but you must suffer. And there are others who will understand. Keep moving, keep seeking. The City can be a treacherous place, and the minute you stop, those around you will encircle you and drag you down until you drown.

I looked at the floor.

– My dear, your dreams will never lie to you. You must turn your dreams into reality, that's the thing, turn them into reality.

He pinched my cheek again. I felt tired and didn't want to talk any more.

– Well, I think we should have some lunch, don't you? Lunchtime is always a good time for lunch.

He left me alone while he saw to the food. I thought about what he had said. I tried not to think about The City, or about my toothbrush, or about the money stuffed between my clothes in my bag. I thought instead about Ravi and his ambiguous destiny. The grandfather had made it all sound very simple, but I remained unconvinced.

I couldn't help Ravi to find his destiny, but the question was why? There was the glib, though very probable answer, that Ravi didn't have a destiny. But if I were to stay, then I could at least help to numb his pain a little. The grandfather hadn't considered this, or if he had, he hadn't told me. I couldn't help feeling that lurking in the midst of all of his philosophy was a hint of manipulation. And I couldn't help feeling that he *wanted* me to go, for himself, though I hadn't the slightest idea why. It didn't matter. I couldn't stay. I couldn't marry that man, not even if it meant saving the souls of all the unhappy failures in the world.

The grandfather called me and we brought the food upstairs and ate in silence. By the time we had finished and he had drunk his third cup of coffee, he pushed back his chair and looked at the clock. I didn't want him to say it, and thankfully, he didn't.

We left for the station. He carried my bag for me, and as we waited on the platform he didn't say much, but his movements were unusually soft. When he did speak it was only about practical things for the journey. The train arrived and he climbed on board with me and paid for my ticket, bribing the conductor to give me a bed on the uppermost tier, close to a family whom he seemed to know a little. I didn't want to talk to anyone, but he insisted I stay close to them. He sat with me for a while, saying nothing except that the view from the window would be very nice, and that the toilet seemed very clean. When it was time to go he did not say goodbye, but just squeezed my hand. I watched him from the window, until he was whisked away by vendors and bushes and iron railings.

The sky was dark and overcast. I hoped October wouldn't be so treacherous in The City. Here it would be like this for some time to come, and I had never known any other weather. It was strange to think that life would simply go on without me, and that no one in The City would ever know, or care.

When the clock struck seven my father would stamp out of the house, threatening violence for when I returned. He would have forgotten after his fifth whisky, but he would start all over again the next morning. My mother would wonder where I had

51

gone. She would ask Ravi, and Ravi would sulk. She would look outside, but only a little way outside. There would be too much to do. Rice had to be cooked, seven cups of coffee had to be boiled with milk and soaked in sugar. Then everyone would sleep, and she would worry.

Ravi would awake the next morning and be the first not to notice I had gone. By lunchtime he would curse me, because I always gave him his food. But secretly he would worry, for himself. He would be careful not to show it, there was the window-spy to think of. My mother would be distraught by then. Ravi wouldn't notice. By the evening my father would have returned, drunk. Ravi would also be there, hopefully drunk. My father would fly into a rage. He would shout at my mother and slap Ravi a few times around the head. After that I didn't know what would happen. It was better that way.

There was also my sister to think of. She would cry and be deeply hurt. She had married Vijay Kumar on the implicit condition that I, in turn, would marry whatever I was allocated. I had broken that condition and had made her look foolish, and for this I was sorry. I preferred to think of her as she had been in my dream, smoking a cigarette. I hoped Vijay would be nice to her.

Vijay's grandfather would be returning home now. He wouldn't say anything. No one believed a word he said anyway. I was glad that the one person who knew the truth had a reputation for insanity. The money he had given me was enough for six movies a day, and as yet, I couldn't think of a better use for it. I couldn't imagine what a maid's life would be like.

I didn't feel lonely. I was scared, but I was enjoying looking out of the window as the shadows fell and dusk approached. The movement of the train made me conscious of how slowly everything moved at home. The food was prepared slowly, my father drank slowly, my mother cooked slowly and talked slowly, if at all. Ravi thought slowly, if at all. Everything and everyone moved with an unquestioning, slothful obedience to unwritten laws.

The train was tearing along. From the window I could see

women carrying bundles with heavy, silent movements, and then the train roared forward and they were tossed into the past.

When I was six Ravi had been beaten up by his friends. His nose was very bloody and two of his teeth were cracked. His upper lip had ballooned to an astonishing size. He was very upset and told my mother and my sister what had happened, and then I came running downstairs (I had been sleeping), and he cried all over me. I was very interested to learn that it was his friends who had beaten him. He had come home bleeding before, but on all previous occasions he had been the innocent victim of Undesirable Urchins.

I asked him why his friends had done this. He said they had run away from him and whispered together, and when he ran after them they turned around with fists flying. We were all very sympathetic. We made him lie down and fussed over him until he was beginning to enjoy himself. And then my father came home. He took off his belt and said he would find those Undesirable Urchins and give them a thrashing they would never forget. Nobody would heap such ignominy on *his* family. Ravi stopped him and explained that it wasn't the Undesirable Urchins, but his own friends. My father found this totally unacceptable and gave Ravi a few good whacks with the belt. And that was that. From that day on, if Ravi came home with his face different from the way we left it, no one asked him how it had happened, and he never told us. My father would walk in, threaten to kill the Undesirable Urchins, storm out of the house with his belt, and go straight to his club. A law had been passed. Reality had been subtly, but forcefully, beaten into obedience.

I wondered what The City would be like. I had only scraps of heavily distorted information to work with. Ravi claimed he had been there once. Actually, Ravi *had* been there once, but anything Ravi said was to be treated as a claim. Ravi said that The City was a horrible, dirty place, full of uncultured ruffians. He said that people chased him wherever he went and that he had been punched by a rickshaw driver for the offence of requesting change. He also said that very few of the ruffians understood

English, which Ravi, in his usual way, considered to be a personal insult. He also said that it was impossible to get a decent cup of coffee anywhere, and that he had seen a man blow his nose into a chapati.

Ravi's comments weren't really enough to form a clear impression. His appraisal of both people and places tended to be somewhat idiosyncratic. Anyway, it didn't matter. My world didn't consist of odd slivers retained from Ravi's tirades any more. Nor was it to be circumscribed by my father's intricate set of rationality-defying laws. The grandfather had told me to turn my dreams into reality, but I thought of it a little differently. The City would be the land of my dreams, but would appear as reality, wild and untamed, not pummelled into banality. It would be the City of my Birth.

Part Two

Ah, my Beloved, fill the Cup that clears
TO-DAY of past regrets and future Fears:
To-morrow! – Why, To-morrow I may be
Myself with Yesterday's Sev'n thousand Years.

The Rubaiyat of Omar Khayam

3

The City of my Birth was a terrifying place, or at least the railway station of my birth was. It was as though a warlord had imprisoned us all in this dusty, high-ceilinged dungeon, awaiting his pleasure. And then, one by one, we were herded on to trains by whistle-blowing men, driven off to a fate in the next life.

Families slept on the floor, sharing faded blankets. Even the children refused to play. Everyone just waited, until their names were called by that hidden face behind the loudspeaker. I walked in a daze, hardly expecting ever to leave this place. Vendors were everywhere, selling, shouting. I saw some men in ties with shiny shoes and newspapers. They seemed exempt from judgement, administrators of this new order, carefully selected to shepherd the prisoners from one camp to the next.

There was light at one end of the vault. I headed towards it, expecting this was some trick, but as I drew nearer I saw faces and life outside. A blast of hot air lunged at my face. The noise was thick and choking. People were running and shouting. There were drivers everywhere, leaning on horns, whipping their engines into roars of obedience, accosting every face that emerged. I wandered through them, avoiding eyes, looking at no one in particular. No one noticed me. They looked over my shoulder, or else straight through me, seeking out business. When, to my surprise, I emerged from this mêlée into a road, I was too afraid to go back. I turned to my right and walked.

The sun was heating my head. I ruffled my hair to stop it

catching fire. Even though the air was so moist, there was none of the rain scent that hung in the breeze at home. The air had a sootiness to it; it smelt of petrol and hard, sun-dried excrement. Everything gleamed unnaturally, as though oppressed. Sanjna's story made so much more sense here. I could never quite understand how she could leave Surya – it had always seemed like the self-indulgence of a spoilt child – but here the sun was white, not orange, and split the air instead of warming it. His rays were metallic and discordant, like an invader's. People walked with tight, balled faces as though every foray outdoors was a torment. And the *cars*! They were rabid with heat, vultures with burning wings. Their pain was so great that they cared nothing for man or beast. I was shocked by the bravery of these people – or was it indifference to death? – who walked so matter-of-factly through this blizzard of stampeding metal. My own steps were so tentative that I wondered if I would ever leave this road. I felt like a castaway in hell, accidentally abandoned, at the mercy of these hardened street-warriors. Perhaps the sun that screamed down upon The City wasn't Surya at all. Perhaps this was different sky, ruled by different gods.

There was a billboard in front of me, a message from The City's police force. It said, *Wherever you go We Are Watching You*. I didn't like the sound of that at all. Underneath it someone had written, *Then Where Were You When I Wrote This?*

I wondered what was happening at home. Hopefully Ravi hadn't been beaten, but I couldn't see how else my father would vent his frustration. My sister would be in bewildered shock, and my mother, by now, would be very, very worried. I still couldn't believe that I was here, *me*, in The City. It was against the rules. And nobody knew I was here, and nobody here knew me. And I was going to be a maid! There was nothing that would shock my father more, or make him more angry. I tried to imagine what my mother would say, but that wasn't possible. Either I worked as a maid and my mother never knew, or I didn't work as a maid. Any other combination and my mother, together with the earth and The City and everyone in it, would explode.

There was a rickshaw on the other side of the road and I crossed and got inside. I fished Mr Aziz's address from my pocket and gave it to him, but it was written in Kannada and he turned it around a few times, making some amused noises, until I snatched it back and read it aloud. Without a murmur he revved the vehicle into motion and we set off in the direction I had come.

The driver drove with the same mania as the drivers at home, only amplified a thousand times. I felt distinctly sick, but I refused to close my eyes. I wanted to take a good look at The City from this position of (relative) safety.

The streets began to widen and I saw increasing amounts of greenery. We passed imposing buildings, with fountains and flags and hordes of policemen, and then we climbed a steep hill with trees at either side. At the top was another very wide road, but without any people, only cars. The heat had died down and the cars seemed less impassioned and more businesslike about their speed. The driver was singing loudly and shouted periodically at other drivers. His shouts were unsynchronised with the traffic, as though he were shouting just for the sake of it, declaring his presence to unseen gods.

The road was raised above The City and looking right I got a good view of this place that would be my home. All I could see were buildings in their thousands, which seemed to come in two different styles. Either they were dusty and brown, and squatted unfashionably like mushrooms, or they were black, shiny gods, tilting their heads imperiously to the sky. The sun glinted against the glass of the windows causing them to wink menacingly, as though warning me away from their presence. I wasn't sure who ruled this place. The sun obviously felt he had first claim, but he seemed far less important now. These buildings were like warlords, daring the masses to live beneath their steely gaze, commanding fear and obedience.

The road wound downwards like a snake and we entered a new district. The driver drove much more slowly, the engine making nothing more than a deferential chug. There was a sign in the centre of the road that read, *Drive Slow, Do Not Horn*, but I had a feeling that the driver couldn't read. Nonetheless, it was clear that, in this part of The City, cars were servants too.

The road was lined with tall trees, and between them I caught glimpses of palatial white houses, smiling out through iron gates at the distant order of the road. The driver leaned out of the rickshaw, craning his neck to see the numbers on the houses. He was so industrious about this labour that I realised he thought me a very important customer. It startled me to think that Mr Aziz owned one of these houses. I could see no traces of life behind the gates. The grind of The City didn't seem to penetrate through.

We were miles away from the stares of the buildings and the glare of the sun. Light fell in gentle showers, filtered by green leaves, which lent the houses an easy radiance. Sounds were distinct and individual. I fancied I could hear the rustle of each blade of grass and the murmur of each beetle as it crawled between them. The insistent pounding between my temples was the only discordant sound.

The driver found the house and I climbed out and paid him. He carefully counted out my change and I smiled, happy that Ravi's spell had been broken. I walked up to the gates while the driver chugged off, and standing behind them were three men, all dressed in jungle green and carrying lathis. One of them had a rifle. For a moment I thought I had the wrong address, this was clearly a military barracks, but then I saw the shiny plaque behind the gates which displayed only one word, *Aziz*. It was all becoming horribly clear. They had found me. My father had sent these men to bring me home. Well, I wouldn't go. They would have to shoot me.

None of them were looking at me, but I had a feeling that the fattest man with the biggest moustache was watching from the corner of his eye. They were trying to draw me closer, so they could grab me, but I wasn't going to be caught so easily. I wondered if they had my photograph, perhaps pinned to the inside of the gate; maybe that was what they were looking at.

I needed a plan, but I couldn't think of anything, unless . . . unless I could *bribe* them. I had almost four thousand rupees stuffed into my clothes, which would be a pretty effective bribe, certainly more than my father was paying them. I stooped and opened my bag, keeping one eye on the men, and rescued as much of the money as I could, folding the bills into my palm. The fat one was looking at me now. Probably he had seen the money, but that wasn't a bad thing. At least he wouldn't grab me straight away.

I walked towards him, keeping my gaze as still as possible, and when I drew near he moved closer and gave me an inquisitive smile. At least while we were on opposite sides of the gates he couldn't do anything (except shoot me of course, but I couldn't believe my father had instructed him to do that). When I reached him I held my head as high as possible.

– I am here to see Mr Aziz, sir. I am the maid.

Suddenly the word *Maid* had taken on an unprecedented status (as opposed to *Fugitive* or *Convict*). The man nodded. The other two still hadn't shown much interest. They were looking at the ground, but of course this was all strategy.

The fat man opened the gate and I jumped inside and thrust the money at him as discreetly as I could. He hesitated for a moment, and then looked towards the house. I hoped Mr Aziz wasn't in on this as well. I couldn't possibly expect to bribe Mr Aziz too – I didn't have much money left. The guard looked at me intently, then quickly, furtively, he pocketed the money and led me towards the house.

I was left waiting on the veranda while the man went inside. I could dimly see the other two guards, hugging their lathis close to them. The next moments would decide my fate.

The fat man returned. He was smiling, a fat smile, and he waved me inside the house.

Nothing had prepared me for this entry into – into what exactly? We passed through the veranda, through the door, and into a single corridor that went on into the distance, seemingly for ever. The corridor was wide enough for an elephant and his wife to stand quite comfortably side by side, and was lit by lamps perched on tall pillars in solemn procession. The floor was of polished marble in which I could see my reflection (which glared back at me), and there were paintings on the walls and statues in alcoves. On my right was an enormous painting of a white man dressed up as a soldier, sitting on a throne and putting a crown on his head. He was distinctly overweight, with stubby arms and a floury, podgy face that looked a bit like Ravi's, though the man's eyes were much beadier than Ravi's. Everyone around was watching him, fixated, and there was plenty of gold and finery. I wondered if this might be Jesus – hadn't he been a white man who wore some crown? – but then I remembered that Jesus had a beard. It was possible that the artist, through some act of incredible genius coupled with utter lunacy, had decided to capture one of Ravi's most private fantasies, but that obviously wasn't very likely. I bent to read the inscription, but the fat man hurried me along, tugging at my arm.

There was a wooden door to our right, about a quarter of the way down the corridor, and the fat man knocked, waited for a few moments, and then opened it, pushing me inside. The door clicked shut behind me. I was in a very large room with a piano, a bookcase, and plenty of big leather armchairs and sofas. Sitting to my right, quite a long way away, was a woman, the first white woman I had ever seen in real life. She was looking at me, but didn't say anything. I looked around but I couldn't see any sign of Mr Aziz.

I walked over to the woman and stood in front of her. She stared at my shoulder. I automatically moved my hand to the spot, hoping there wasn't a stain on my clothes. This seemed to annoy her and she sighed and shifted her look to my feet. My feet were not unattractive, they were slender and my toes were all neatly proportioned, but I had only got off the train that afternoon and had been running around The City, so I hoped she would find some more suitable part of my body to stare at. I shifted a little, placing one foot in front of the other, and this brought forth another, heavier sigh, and she switched her gaze to my left hip. I wasn't enjoying this game at all, but she didn't seem to want to do anything else, so I took the opportunity to have a good look at her.

It was hard to say how old she was. Her face was covered by a thick layer of cream beneath which all wrinkles would be well hidden. Her hands were thinly veined, and looked almost transparent, and the skin around her knuckles was raw. Her hair was tightly tied back and seemed damp, but not oily. She was wearing a purple silk shirt with the first button undone, revealing a string of pearls, and a very short black skirt that left her thin white legs and most of her thighs very arrestingly uncovered. Her eyes bulged at me behind spectacles with extraordinarily thick lenses, so thick that her eyeballs seemed to sprout from her face in a most unsettling way.

My hands had moved, this time more consciously, to my hips, which brought forth another sigh, and finally she turned her wobbling eyes to my face. I couldn't take this any more.

– I am looking for Mr Aziz. I am the maid.

Her face tightened.

– I know you are the maid.

She started speaking in a language I couldn't understand in a tone of extraordinary tenderness, quite distinct from the guttural rasp she had used at first. It was only then that I noticed the cat curled up next to her. She stroked its ears. The only words I could make out, which she used time and time again, were *Mon Shoe*.

I couldn't understand what she wanted me to do. Her stare, that had made me merely uneasy at first, now felt like a hot iron, pressing against different parts of my flesh. She sighed again.

– Follow me.

I followed.

– The house is very large, many rooms, all need cleaning, every day. There are two more maids, and four floors. You will clean downstairs. Do not go upstairs. Start here, in the sitting room.

I nodded and she opened the door. We turned into the corridor.

– Corridor. Wash the floor, then polish. Marble. Pay attention to your work, do not chip.

I almost smiled. The way she said *Corridor* sounded like the noises my father made in the morning. We walked to the end of the hall where there was a door. She flung it open.

– Toilet. Mop, scrub, inside and outside. Keep very clean.

This was an intriguing room. It was carpeted and the toilet was western, which I had seen before, and there was a shower, which I hadn't.

There was a door to our right, but she marched back to the beginning of the corridor. I almost had to run to keep up. I watched her legs, wondering about my theory. When we reached the beginning of the corridor she opened a door directly opposite the one I had first come through.

– Small bedroom. Nobody sleeping here. No need to change the sheets. Sweep the floor.

We started off down the corridor again and she showed me the kitchen which was on the left, and then the dining room which adjoined the kitchen. *Showed* is perhaps too strong a word; she hurled the door open and then slammed it shut again, saying, a little superfluously I thought, *Kitchen*. I wondered if she might be some sort of housekeeper, like Mrs Pearce in *My Fair Lady*. I was about to ask when a man emerged from the door at the end of the corridor. He was quite a long way from us, but I could tell he was definitely not white, definitely bald and definitely fat. He walked towards us with a peculiar, shuffling gait, his head seeming to hang from his left shoulder. His face was big, round and shiny, and I could see two dark patches of sweat beneath his armpits. He looked nervous, and when he saw me, without any attempt to disguise it, he ran his eyes up and down my frame as though checking for deformities.

– Ah, yes, hello. I am Mr Aziz. It seems you have met my wife.

I looked at her, unable to conceal my surprise. She smiled, and her smile was far more frightening than her stare.

– I am Mrs Marceau.

Mr Aziz looked like quite a nice man. I liked the way his paunch hung over his belt, it was a nice contrast to Mrs Marceau's razor-sharp legs.

– So, you have come all the way from the south. How are things over there? Good, good.

I hadn't said anything.

– Well, you must be hungry.

Mrs Marceau made a noise, somewhere between a cough and a shriek, and Mr Aziz shifted uncomfortably.

– Please excuse us for a moment.

They disappeared into the sitting room and I took the opportunity to read the inscription under the painting of the fat man. It said, *The Coronation of Emperor Napoleon*. The name was familiar, but I preferred to think of it as *The Coronation of Emperor Ravi*. I hoped his day would come. Mr Aziz would have liked Ravi; they seemed, superficially, to have a lot in common, and thinking this made me like Mr Aziz even more. But Mrs Marceau! *Quelle Beast!* I could hear them from the sitting room. They were arguing. Mrs Marceau was shrieking like a furious elephant and Mr Aziz was grumbling back at her. He sounded very apologetic and anxious. I heard her say, *But Why does that Concern Us? She is here to Work!*

When they returned Mrs Marceau glared at me icily, and then marched away down the corridor. Mr Aziz had the air of a man who had won, though at heavy cost.

– My wife has asked if you would join us for dinner.

What?

– Thank you, Uncle.

He became even more anxious.

– I would prefer it if you didn't call me that, not when my wife is present at least. She feels it is better for servants to call us sir and madam.

I nodded, but I knew I would never call him sir. The idea was ridiculous. It would be like calling Ravi *Your Highness*.

– Anyway, it doesn't matter much. You needn't call me anything if you don't want to. It's just my wife, you know, she can be very particular about such things. Anyway, come with me, come with me.

I was starting to feel as though I had some secret power over this man.

We went into the sitting room and Mr Aziz poured himself a whisky from the drinks cabinet. He asked if I would like some, and then retracted the question, telling himself how stupid he was.

We sat opposite each other and he gulped his whisky. He didn't seem to know what to say.

– So, I suppose my wife has explained your duties.

– Yes, Mr Aziz.

That was a good compromise.

– Good, good. My wife is French, you know.

– Oh.

French. I didn't know anything about French people, though Ravi had told me they ate donkeys.

– I am a Kashmiri.

He said it very proudly, puffing out his chest and holding his head up high. I was quite impressed by this.

– Oh, Kashmiri.

– Yes, yes.

He took another large gulp of whisky. I remembered the letter the grandfather had given me and I pulled it from my bag and gave it to him. It was quite crumpled now, but he opened it and read it with great concentration. When he had finished he put the paper in his pocket, took another gulp of whisky, and then crossed to the drinks cabinet. When he returned he looked very serious, and seemed on the point of saying something important, but instead he just looked at me with pursed lips.

– So, you are old enough to vote?

– Not quite.

I had seen this before. When men drank whisky and couldn't think of anything to say, they always talked about politics.

– And if you were old enough to vote, you would vote for . . . ?

– Congress.

66

I had known for years that we were Congress voters.

– Ah, good good. Glad to hear it. They won't last long you know.

It occurred to me that actually I *was* old enough to vote, but I decided to keep this to myself.

– No?

– No, they won't, they won't. The fools . . .

Mrs Marceau returned, drinking a beer. She sat on the sofa looking at us. Mr Aziz went to put more ice in his whisky.

– Well, it is time to eat now. Shall we go?

I nodded. Mrs Marceau drained her glass and fixed me with her eye.

– You eat meat?

I shook my head. She sighed and we proceeded through to the kitchen where two servants were frying meat. Mrs Marceau stopped and stared at the frying pan, the flames almost touching her eyelashes. Her cheekbones tensed in an alarming way. I had visions of bone ripping through skin. She turned to the servant nearest the frying pan, who was looking at me inquisitively.

– What is this?

– Ghee, madam.

Mrs Marceau picked up the frying pan, which was still sizzling furiously, and dumped it, with its contents, into the sink.

– This is disgusting!

She turned to look the servant in the eye, shoulders erect, not moving a muscle.

– Steak. Fry in butter. From fridge.

Before he had a chance to respond she marched into the dining room. The servant looked at me as the ghee spat furiously in the sink. I smiled. The other servant had buried his head in his hands and was sitting on the floor in the corner. Mr Aziz looked terribly ill at ease and seemed on the point of saying something, but then followed his wife. I trotted after him.

The dining room was very dark with wooden walls. The table was shiny, with legs carved to look like snakes, and was easily twelve feet long. Mr Aziz sat at one end and Mrs Marceau at the other. I wasn't too sure where I was supposed to sit, though I had a feeling Mrs Marceau would have preferred it if I sat on the floor. I must have spent quite a long time thinking because eventually Mr Aziz rose and pulled out the chair closest to him. Mrs Marceau suddenly shrieked.

– Raju!

Raju. I had forgotten.

– Raju!

Raju arrived, he was the one who had been frying steak in ghee.

– Have you fed Moustache and Carpet?

(Pronounced *Moostash* and *Cahrpett*)

– Madam?

– Poosy cats! Have you fed the poosy cats?

Raju shook his head and looked at his shoes. It was lucky for him that only I could see him grinning like a schoolboy.

– Then what are you doing?

Raju started to leave, but she screeched again as though someone had left a fork on her chair.

– Serve the meal first, for God's sake!

He left, but not before flashing another broad grin at me which I shyly returned. I looked at Mr Aziz, but he was staring into space as though pursuing some sort of transcendental state.

Raju returned with the food and announced, very proudly, *Avocado and Prawns*. I could see two forks, three spoons, two knives, and two glasses. My chances didn't look good. Of course I knew I shouldn't touch anything with my fingers, but that didn't help me much. I could see Raju watching, he seemed to find his job endlessly amusing. I hoped that cleaning would prove equally hilarious.

Mr Aziz wasn't eating. He said, with tremendous stoicism, that he didn't like it. This made my situation doubly difficult. Raju, very thoughtfully, hadn't put any of the little fishes inside my avocado, but I found this vegetable perplexing enough on its own. It looked like a guava, but it smelt of rain, which presumably meant it tasted like rain as well, though my chances of ever tasting it were slim. Mr Aziz hadn't noticed my dilemma. He was still staring into space, still soliciting divine intervention. Raju *had* noticed, but to him it was all part of the inherent comedy of domestic service.

Eventually I thought of a cunning way out, and with a feigned spasm of the right arm I sent a knife flying across the room. Pouncing like a tiger, before Raju could get to it, I jumped from my seat and picked up the knife.

Raju bounded from the room and returned brandishing a fresh knife. I just smiled in quiet satisfaction. Through this ingenious stunt I had learned that rain-smelling guavas, with or without fishes, are to be eaten with the small silver spoon that I had thought was for stirring tea. I smirked at Raju triumphantly. He grinned back, generously conceding my first-round victory.

The next course was steak, for Mr Aziz and Mrs Marceau. From Raju's quiet look, I wondered if this was the same steak Mrs Marceau had thrown into the sink, washed and refried in butter. I got an omelette. I wasn't supposed to eat eggs, but Ravi had once left an egg in the kitchen (Ravi ate chicken as well, which was his most closely guarded secret) and my mother had dealt with it with admirable self-control. Anyway, I didn't think Mrs Marceau would react well if I protested. She was watching me now, wincing as I picked up the nearest fork to me.

– Do you *ever* eat meat?

I shook my head.

– Why not? Because you think you are eating your ancestors?

– No.

– Then?

I watched her stuff a huge piece of quivering flesh into her mouth, her throat bulging.

– I don't know.

She snorted.

– I cannot live without meat. When I was in hospital after the birth of my son I ate raw horse flesh. I would have died otherwise.

My mother would have died a thousand times over.

– Raju!

Raju was filling their glasses with wine. He looked at me and I vigorously shook my head.

– Madam?

He flinched, as though expecting a slap.

– Poosy cats!

Raju left with the wine bottle, and only I saw him take a swig as he passed into the kitchen. Mr Aziz seemed to have abandoned his quest for the almighty. He leaned towards me.

– Our son has just finished university, you know. Oxford.

He said it pompously, but I found this undeniably impressive. My father had taken me out of school after I finished Standard Nine – even Ravi had protested at that one.

– Yes, yes. Very brainy, very brainy. You might see him tomorrow.

Mrs Marceau put down her fork and stood up.

– I am going to bed.

And she went, leaving Mr Aziz and me looking at each other.

– Please allow me to give you my condolences.

What?

– Thank you.

I wondered if these *Condolences*; were some sort of chocolate. I hoped so, I liked chocolates, though I didn't get to eat them much. Perhaps they were *French* chocolates.

– The loss of one's parents is a difficult thing to get over.

I said nothing. I was too stunned. This must have been the grandfather's work. Mr Aziz looked even more sympathetic, mistaking my confusion for sadness. His eyes actually looked moist.

– Well, I think I should join my wife. It is late.

It was nine o'clock.

– Yes, I have a lot to do tomorrow, a lot to do. Raju will show you to your quarters. If you need anything, ask Raju. Well, goodnight.

– Goodnight, *Uncle*.

I said it a little flirtatiously, unable to resist, and he smiled and then pursed his lips in discomfort. I had come to a conclusion about Mr Aziz's baffling display of hospitality. There was more to it than mere *Condolences*; he had recognised my star quality. It had mesmerised him. Things were going well.

After he left, Raju came in to clear the things away. I followed him into the kitchen. Raju didn't say anything for a while, and then –

– Stupid fucking woman.

I nodded my agreement.

– Stupid fucking cats.

I nodded again and Raju's mood seemed to lighten. He was quite a handsome man, dark, with a carefully groomed moustache and neatly parted hair plastered against his scalp. His eyes were deep-set and very obscure beneath the dense foliage of his eyebrows.

– So, the old man sent you.

– Yes.

– His health is good?

– Very good.

– Good.

– Is Mr Aziz a nice man?

He gave the question some consideration.

– Weak man, but good. The woman is trouble.

He flipped the remainder of the steak into the bin and began to wash the dishes. His hands looked very strong, but he moved them lightly.

– You will have to work hard, she will make you.

I didn't like the sound of this. Until now, housework had been something I had done without question or complaint. But from Raju's wiry frame I guessed that when he said *Work Hard*, he meant it.

Raju finished the dishes and washed his hands with a scowl of disgust. We left the kitchen by a side door which led us outside to the left of the house. We turned and walked behind the house, and entered a small flat-roofed bungalow. The gardens stretched out into the distance behind us. It was dark, but I had a feeling the gardens were very beautiful.

We were in a small room lit by a single oil lamp that burned on the table in the centre, next to a pot of food. There was only one window and the room was stuffy and smoky, but it seemed comforting after the house's funereal air-conditioning. There were four steel plates on the table, stacked in an unsteady pile, and next to them was a plastic bottle full of a milky liquor, the kind drunk in villages (Ravi used to buy it when he didn't have money for whisky). Over a gas flame in the corner was another pot in which food was bubbling.

Two men sat around the table, and they looked up as I came in. Sitting on the floor, next to the food, was an old man and a very old woman. Raju smiled at the men and they greeted him enthusiastically. He knelt down beside the woman and gripped her hand, talking loudly into her ear. She passed a leathery palm over his face, gripping his skin tightly, and asked him an endless stream of unintelligible questions. The old man was sprinkling a tobacco leaf over newspaper, but when he saw me he rose and put some tea on the stove. This was a Ravism coming true. Ravi had told me a thousand times that all anyone drank in the north was milky tea, boiled with sugar until it became a paste.

Raju released himself from the woman's grip and introduced me to the men around the table. The biggest one was called Manu. He was the driver and was very hairy and fat. He didn't say much, but he kept nodding and beaming. The other man was the gardener, called Arun. He was much less friendly, with narrow slits for eyes and thin lips that curled into a perpetual sly smile. He offered the bottle to me and then laughed. The light from the lamp crept up one side of his face and I could see that his skin was heavily pockmarked and rough, and that his eyes were flecked with blue.

As Raju passed him Arun grabbed him by the arm and tried to force the bottle into his mouth. Raju wrested the bottle from him and put it on the table, holding him by the jaw and giving his face a little push. Arun became angry and rose to his feet. He was obviously drunk, and the whites of his eyes had a wild, reddish glow. Raju laughed and took a swig from the bottle before giving it back to him. Arun slammed it on the table, and then seemed to forget, sinking back in his chair and staring vacantly.

The old man poured me some tea into a steel tumbler and took my hand and clasped it between his palms. He said that his name was Ishaq, and that I would be his daughter while I was here. I had seen him before, in the kitchen with Raju, but he seemed much older now. The old lady explained that she couldn't get up on account of her back, and that she couldn't see very well. Her name was Ambika, and she swept the first floor and the kitchen. All of them spoke in Hindi, which I had trouble understanding, especially when it came to the old lady whose voice was very weak and hoarse. I blamed my father. If he hadn't taken me out of school I would have understood every word they said, but I hardly think he'd anticipated this situation.

I took my tea and sat at the table next to Manu, as far away from Arun as possible. Raju explained that I would sleep with Ambika and the other maid, Maneka, who had gone out, in the adjoining room. The men slept on the roof, except for Ishaq who slept on the floor beside the gas stove.

Manu continued to smile at me and, not knowing what else to do, I either smiled back or looked around the room, watching the moths as they rushed towards the oil lamp, stunning themselves senseless against the glass and then getting up for a return attempt. Manu asked me if I was married and I said no, and he smiled approvingly again. He told me if I ever wanted to go for a ride anywhere in the car, then all I had to do was ask. And then he launched into an incredibly comprehensive description of Mrs Marceau's Mercedes, most of which I didn't understand. He told me he had his own telephone in the car, and that whenever anyone needed transport he would come to fetch them, *Driving like a Wind*.

He asked me if I liked movies, to which I answered yes, and he then explained which were the best movie houses and which had the most comfortable seats. After that he fell silent because he had apparently exhausted all his conversation topics. The silence appeared to irritate him however, because after a few minutes he asked me if I had any children, which, given that he had already asked me if I was married, was a grossly insensitive question. Ishaq, from the floor, politely told him to shut up, which he did, taking a swig from the bottle and looking up at the ceiling.

While I was talking to Manu I noticed that Arun was listening carefully to everything we said. He made me very uncomfortable, and every time our eyes met his perpetual smile became a little tighter, and he would jerk his head questioningly, as though he and I had some dark, cynical complicity. Sometimes he would look at Manu and laugh a wet, bile-soaked laugh. At other times he would look at me, as though I were doing something terribly shameful, and then look back at Manu and laugh. His eyes were sharp, and whenever he looked at me I felt he was penetrating straight into my thoughts, seeing only those I tried to conceal, ignoring the rest. The more I tried to avoid his stare the more keenly I felt it.

Raju had not said anything all this time. He took a plate from the table, washed it outside from the tap, and spooned food on to it from the pot in the centre of the table. He ate hungrily, absorbed in his meal, and only occasionally looked up, his glance shifting from Manu to Arun.

When he had finished eating he took all the plates outside and washed them, and then told me that if I wanted to meet the guards then I should come with him now because they would go home soon. I could sense he wanted to get away, and I immediately rose, smiled vaguely at everyone, and followed him outside. As we left I heard Arun mutter something, and then heard Ishaq very angrily tell him to shut up. I could still hear their voices, raised in argument, as Raju and I walked away.

As we neared the gates I realised something was going to happen. *The Guards* were the same men I had met when I arrived. The fat one, to whom I had freely given about three thousand rupees, was leaning against the gate smoking. The orange glow of his cigarette made his moustache gleam wildly, like a bonfire in the centre of his flabby face. I fell behind Raju, not sure how to act. It seemed clear that my earlier judgement had been somewhat rash. I asked Raju for how many years these men had been here and he said he didn't know, they had been there before he came. This put me in a difficult situation. The guards must have thought me deranged, or else extraordinarily generous; how many maids habitually gave three thousand rupee tips? But then what was I supposed to have thought? I wasn't used to seeing men who looked like contract killers strolling around in front of houses.

Raju introduced me and the men looked amused. They stood around me, saying very little, but listening attentively to everything Raju told them. All of them were grinning from ear to ear. Even Raju seemed puzzled, and when we left them to their watch I decided to come clean, and I told him what had happened. He looked bewildered at first, laughed when I told him I had taken them for hired thugs, and then looked serious when I revealed I had given away three thousand rupees. He told me to wait by the bungalow while he went to talk with them.

I stood, looking out into the gardens, wondering how far they penetrated into the night. I wished I could dive headlong into that blackness, to retreat into the impersonal warmth of the unseen, but I turned and watched Raju as he talked with the guard, his cigarette bobbing up and down as he nodded his head. Presently Raju returned, looking less than triumphant.

– He says he has already given the money to his brother. His brother might have spent it, but if he hasn't he will bring it tomorrow. He is an honest man. If he has it, he will give it to you.

– All right.

– Be careful with your money, yes? Give me what you have. I will keep it for you.

I had left my bag in the bungalow.

– All right.

– We should sleep now. You start work at six o'clock.

I nodded. I was used to sleeping and dreaming whenever I wanted, but I supposed the cleaning wouldn't take that long, which would leave me the rest of the day free.

We went back into the bungalow. Manu and Arun were already on the roof, and Ishaq was snoring in the corner, his head covered with a rough blanket. The lamp was still burning and Raju extinguished it between his finger and thumb. I checked my bag. The rest of my money was still there.

Raju asked me if there was anything I needed. I couldn't think of anything, so he said goodnight and went around the house to climb the stairs that led to the roof. I walked into the adjoining room. It was pitch black, so I went back into the other room and lit the lamp, bringing it with me. The room was very small and hot. I could dimly make out Ambika's sleeping form on the floor. She too was snoring, as gruffly as a man. She had a clay statue of Shiva by her head.

There was a bed a few feet away from her and I put my bag underneath it, reminding myself to give my money to Raju in the morning. I undressed and folded my clothes and got into the bed. Just as I was putting out the lamp, Raju stuck his head around the door.

– Do not worry about anything. I can promise you your father will never find you here.

I smiled, a little weakly, and he left. At that moment the idea of my father cascading through the door, brandishing his belt, was quite welcome. I had resisted brushing my teeth. I didn't want yet another horrible premonition to come true, not after Ravi's chillingly accurate description of The City and its inhabitants. Perhaps this was indeed the real world, a world where all my worst fears would come to pass with clockwork predictability. If that was the case, then I didn't see what difference it made whether I stayed here or went home to the horrible man.

I wondered what Holly Golightly's first days had been like, after she left her ranch in Texas. I wondered if she had felt like I did. Of course she had! It took hard work and dedication. I wouldn't be so foolish as to think that stardom would come right to my door! I would have to persevere, take French lessons, accept drinks from men who disapproved of me . . . anything it took. And if I had to work as a maid for a while, in this place, with that woman, then so be it.

But then *Breakfast at Tiffany's* only started *after* she was a star, desired by millionaires of every nation. Nobody really knew what came before, and I don't think anyone cared. Wives of Texan horse-farmers weren't interesting. And this was the uninteresting period of *my* life. I didn't like this part. I wished I could move directly to the movie, but the real world didn't seem to work like that.

The grandfather would be proud of me. I had learned a most important lesson. I would have to write and tell him.

The room was getting hotter and hotter. I heard Ambika roll over in her sleep, muttering something. A mosquito unleashed his soprano wail in my ear. I was used to nets. I didn't like the idea of a thousand insects buzzing around my head. At home I would have Ravi next to me, snoring peacefully, dreaming his hidden fantasies, living his fears in his sleep.

I wished I could talk to Ravi, if only for a few minutes, just to tell him not to worry, not to give up. Everything was so simple at home. Even Ravi's unhappiness had a reassuring simplicity about it. Perhaps if I had stayed . . . perhaps my father was just waiting, fighting against his pride. Perhaps if I came home he would be so relieved that he wouldn't make me marry the horrible man. I would stay at home and sleep and dream and drink coffee and be lectured at by Ravi and watch movies.

I wished I had the television here. Life was terrifying without the television. At home all I had to do was switch it on and everything would disappear and I would be safe. And *Majick Movie House* was only a few moments away. *Majick Movie House* . . . I missed my seat. It was vacant and would be lonely now. Maybe someone else would come and sit in it. After all, it wasn't my seat any more.

I thought about going upstairs to find Raju, just to have someone to talk to. But he would be asleep. He also had to work hard. *Work Hard*. At six o'clock tomorrow. With that horrible Mrs Marceau screaming at me. I had been so full of certainty four days ago when I had sat in that chair watching the flies. I tried to imagine my mother was in the next room, banging her pots. What would she do, if she were here?

The effort was too great. I couldn't see her. She didn't belong here. All I could see was the half-drunk liquor bottle sitting on the table. How could my mother be in the same room as a liquor bottle?

I tried hard not to cry. It wouldn't help. No one would see the tears. No one would know. I would just cry and the tears would harden and cling to the sheets and in the morning they would be gone and I would have to get up at six o'clock and *Work Hard*. And I wouldn't see Ravi, and I wouldn't see my mother, and I wouldn't go to *Majick Movie House*, I would just come back to this room and start all over again and the tears would dry and I would get up and go to work. So I wouldn't cry. Maybe that would break the cycle and stardom would come quicker, though even the word *Stardom* made me feel sick inside. The word seemed so cold now, so lonely. *Stardom* meant being alone in a room with my toothbrush, with a toothless old woman snoring at my feet, without Ravi, without my mother, without *anything*.

Against my will I did begin to cry, very softly, so as not to wake Ambika. And then I heard the door open. I was glad Raju had come. He must have sensed I was feeling bad. He came and sat on the edge of my bed and I smelled his breath and knew it wasn't Raju. It reeked of liquor. A hand reached out and touched my face leaving a thin trail of sweat clinging to my cheek. I tried to push the hand away but it was too strong, so I left it on my cheek, trembling, trying not to move.

– You like me?

It was Arun. His voice swayed under the weight of liquor. I started to shake my head but the hand pressed heavier on my face, pinning it against the mattress. I tried to call for Raju, but the hand stifled my shout, forcing a trickle of saliva from my mouth and on to my chin.

– You want fuck?

The next few moments were prolonged, as if in a dream. The

door opened and I saw a girl standing in the doorway, her face illuminated by a lamp. The lamp cast a dim pallor across the room and I saw Arun's face, covered in sweat, his eyes red and unfocused. The girl shouted something and Arun released me. Then she put the lamp down and gave him a few quick slaps with the back of her hand. Arun muttered something and she hit him again as he tried to shield his face with his arms. Ambika sat up from the floor, rubbing her eyes irritably, and Arun stumbled to the door, almost falling. He spat and left, leaving the door wide open.

The girl walked outside and then came back in and shut the door. Ambika had gone back to sleep, pulling the blanket even more firmly over her ears, and the girl came and sat by the side of my bed.

– Hello. I'm Maneka.

I couldn't find my voice. I lay back in the bed, looking at her, shaking with fright. She stroked my face. Her hands were very warm.

– It's all right. He does it all the time. He won't remember in the morning.

She moved her hand to my hair, smoothing it against the pillow.

– You're in my bed. But that's all right. I don't mind.

I looked towards Ambika. She was fast asleep.

– You're from the south, aren't you? So am I. I'm from Kerala. I've been here for a year.

She said it very proudly. She had a round face with big eyes and long eyelashes. Her skin was very dark.

Maneka lifted up the blanket and climbed into the bed beside me. I moved a little to give her room. She also smelt of liquor, but it was a nice smell, untainted by tobacco, very sweet.

– Raju told me you were coming. I clean the top two floors. I do most of Ambika's work too. Her back is finished so she can't bend, but we don't let *her* know.

When I finally found my voice it sounded like a child's. Maneka's face was very girlish, but I felt much younger than her.

– How old are you?

– Fifteen. How old are you?

– Eighteen.

I felt guilty for saying it, but Maneka didn't react one way or the other.

– Have you met Manu yet?

– Yes.

– He's so stupid, isn't he? But he's very sweet. He does anything you ask him to, it's very funny.

– I've never been a maid before.

– It's easy. You just have to make everything *look* clean. They only look at the floor really. And you don't have to bother with places where there isn't much light. Just try not to finish too early, or that bitch will have you running around like nobody's business.

I had joined a world where I was the only child.

– Raju said you ran away from your parents. Did they beat you? Mine did. I used to wake up with bruises all over.

– They beat my brother.

– But not you?

– No.

– Then why did you run away?

– They wanted me to marry a man, but I didn't like him.

She seemed to be considering this. I wished I had said *Hated* him.

– I want to marry Raju. But he's already married. His wife isn't here, but he's very loyal. That's why I want to marry him.

I smiled. Maneka spoke earnestly and her face gleamed as though fanned into flame by her own words.

– Shall I put out the light now? It's very late. The guards have gone home so I had to climb over the gate. There's a dog, but he's very friendly. If I leave here I might come back and steal something. It's really easy.

She put out the lamp and wriggled around until she was comfortable. She pushed her face close to mine and sighed a couple of times before falling asleep. I lay awake for a while, listening to Ambika snore, and then fell into a heavy sleep, the exhaustion in my limbs finally reaching my head.

I dreamed I was lying on the sofa in the house, my head on Mrs Marceau's lap as she stroked my ears. Maneka and Raju sat opposite me, lost in conversation. Arun was in a cage in the corner, but everyone ignored him. Ambika and Ishaq were asleep and there was a crocodile wandering across the floor, dangerously near to them. I sat up and shouted, but nobody heard. When I caught Raju's attention he just smiled and nodded at the crocodile as though happy I was amused by such simple things. I called out to Maneka, but she was absorbed by Raju.

Mrs Marceau had stretched herself out, her legs on my knees, and I watched as the crocodile padded over Ambika's sleeping body, his feet lightly gripping her face. She kept on snoring, and then Ishaq awoke and shooed the crocodile away. He came plodding over towards me, and when he reached the sofa he stared at me without blinking, opening his cavernous mouth wide and showing me his teeth.

I screamed and Raju and Maneka turned their heads, and then seeing the crocodile they laughed affectionately. I heard Raju say something about how he was always bored, and the crocodile turned away from me and went over to Raju who stroked his head, never taking his eyes from Maneka.

I went into the corridor and found Mr Aziz mopping the floor. He looked at me angrily and I took the mop from him and he wiped his forehead and walked away. I looked down the corridor but I couldn't see the end, only a limitless expanse of cold marble. I picked up the mop and started to clean the floor, trying to shut out the voices from the living room.

I was alone and the sun was screaming through the window. Ambika's blanket was neatly folded on the floor and the room smelt of incense. Her statue of Shiva had pink and yellow flowers next to it. There was no sign of Maneka, though the bed still smelt of her.

I got up and crossed to the window. I could see the back of the house. The windows were very dark but the white paint reflected the sunlight in a callous glare.

I found my toothbrush and passed through the other room, which was bare and well swept, and walked outside to the tap. As I brushed my teeth I looked at the gardens. They were as big as I had imagined, dancing with flowers of every colour. The grass looked very soft. I could hear a dog barking and the air crackled with the sound of insects. There was a pond in the centre, surrounded by leafless trees, and in the distance, squatting over an orange flowerbed, I saw a man in overalls. It must have been Arun. I washed my toothbrush and went back inside.

I couldn't see any way of bathing. I wondered if they brought water from the outside tap, but I couldn't see any bucket. I couldn't tell if the stove had been used, but I doubted if they heated the water. At home the water was heated over burning wood. You could hear it crackling as it touched your skin, becoming a part of you. I wondered if I could get away with using the shower in the house; I had never used a shower before. I would ask Maneka.

I dressed and brushed my hair. My skin was sticky with yesterday's sweat, but this didn't bother me. After having slept in a strange bed with a strange girl, and having been molested by a very strange gardener, habit had a much fainter pull.

I crossed to the side of the house and entered the kitchen. Raju was sitting on the floor with Ishaq, drinking coffee. They looked up but didn't smile. Ishaq poured me some coffee, taking it from the stove and straining it. That was another Ravism broken. He had sworn that coffee didn't exist in The City. I was relieved and felt less uncomfortable at the silence. Eventually Raju drained his cup and stood up.

– It is seven o'clock, but *she* is still sleeping. Aziz will not notice.

It felt like he was telling me off. My face must have revealed this, because Raju smiled and thumped me on the shoulder.

– Good, you slept. I did not want to wake you.

They seemed in no hurry to start work, and I was still wondering if I could use the shower.

– Where do I take my bath?

– There is a bucket on the roof. You have to fill it from the tap and carry it up. Go now, there is still time.

I left, disappointed. I didn't want to go back to the bungalow while everyone was working. I couldn't help feeling the others might be just a little annoyed with me.

The stairs to the roof were around the back of the bungalow. I walked up, feeling the wood creaking beneath my feet and the sun burning my neck. The roof was flat and covered with tar that was sticky from the sun. There were three blankets, all neatly rolled up, some cards, and some washing strung out to dry. The bucket was there with a hard cake of soap. There was a patch of vomit beside it. It was quite dry from the sun, and the few solid particles had turned a weary yellow.

I looked out at the gardens and saw Arun looking at me. He was much closer now, carrying a pair of shears and flinging sweat from his forehead with his fingers. He waved and then returned to his work. I wondered if he would see me if I bathed behind the washing line. He might, if he looked closely.

I decided not to bath on the roof, thinking I might risk the shower without telling Raju. I climbed down the steps and went to the tap, throwing handfuls of water over my face. The water was hot, and my face was dry by the time I stood up. I splashed some over my arms and feet, but it didn't make much difference. If there was such a thing as dry water, then this was it.

I looked back across the garden, looking for Arun, but I couldn't see him. I thought I saw a shadow coming out of the pond and for a moment it looked like a crocodile, but there was nothing there. I stood for a few seconds, swaying a little, not sure what was happening. Snippets of the dream came back to me, but the sun was so hot that I couldn't concentrate long enough to remember it all. Shaking my head, I returned to the kitchen.

Raju had gone but Ishaq was standing by the oven, pushing something inside. He turned and smiled and spoke very loudly in halting English. I liked the way he spoke. Each word was accompanied by a toothy smile, as if to show that he didn't resent the difficulties I was causing him.

– You – bath?

– Yes.

– Aziz. Aziz. Waiting, waiting.

He pointed to the dining room and I smiled as I passed, trying to hide my anxiety.

Mr Aziz was reading a newspaper and didn't notice me. I stood near the door until he looked up.

– Ah, good morning.

I smiled, and went for reckless amiability.

– Good morning, *Uncle*, how are you?

This was a wild strategy. I remembered my success at calling him *Uncle* the previous evening. Perhaps the disorder wreaked by this wanton act of subversion would be enough for him to forget how late I was. But Mr Aziz didn't seem to notice.

– It looks as though the government may fall. There is a no-confidence motion in three weeks.

I didn't know how to respond to this. I knew nothing about politics. I smiled shyly.

– That's good, isn't it?

Ordinarily I wouldn't volunteer my opinion on a subject I knew nothing about – what was a *No-Confidence Motion* anyway? – but the need for a diversion was urgent. Mr Aziz put the newspaper down, grimacing.

– Not really. If those bastards bring the government down all hell will break loose. There is only a certain amount of governments a country can take.

I nodded my agreement with conviction. Too many governments was a dangerous thing. *Those Bastards* had better be careful. I was about to say so, but that subject could prove as volatile as my lateness. I had seen men argue about politics before.

– Are you going to work now?

It was asked in all innocence. I wanted to keep the subject in his corner, anything to distract attention from the unswept floor, but Mr Aziz's face made me regret the question. He looked troubled.

– Got to work, every day. Can't stop.

– Why not, Uncle?

– My son has college fees, still not paid. My wife has her needs.

– But aren't you rich?

I considered running from the room, putting my head in the deep freeze, and then coming back, but he probably found my behaviour strange enough already.

– We could have been rich when we were in Hong Kong. They told me, *Buy Property*, but like a fool I didn't.

I couldn't think of anything to say to that. His wife was the other conversation topic that was strictly forbidden. It was dangerous enough for us to be talking at all. But talking about her? If she found out she would kill us both.

Mr Aziz returned to his newspaper and I realised that not only did I like him, but that he was a likeable person. Raju came into the room with a gigantic grin.

– Saar, the cat is dead, saar.

– Good God! Which one?

– Moustache, saar.

Mr Aziz shook his head and then cupped his head in his hands, staring at the table so hard that I thought it would break.

– Do not tell madam. She will be up in a couple of hours and is going out for lunch. When she gets back, tell her the cat is at the animal hospital. Understand?

– Yes, saar.

Raju left and Mr Aziz looked at me, scratching his head. I got the feeling he wanted my help, but I rather cruelly shared Raju's amusement. I was looking forward to seeing Mrs Marceau's face. But then I thought of Holly Golightly's dismay at losing Cat and I tried my hardest to think tender thoughts about that poor soul so recently ejected into a furry afterlife.

Mr Aziz interrupted my efforts, which weren't looking too successful.

– Sit down, sit down. Do you want coffee?

– Yes please, Uncle.

– And croissants?

– What?

– Croissants.

– Yes please, Uncle.

Mr Aziz shouted to Raju while I prayed that these *Croissants* weren't made of boiled beef. I was still suspicious after Mr Aziz's offer of *Condolences* had turned out not only to be inedible, but to contain a shock that took me completely unawares. But to make up for thinking such cruel thoughts about the cat, and out of sympathy for Mr Aziz's plight, I decided to swallow every morsel of whatever these croissants turned out to be.

Raju returned with a tray and put it on the table. I felt terribly guilty about being served by Raju, but he didn't seem to mind. He was probably still celebrating the death of Mrs Marceau's recently deceased companion. I wondered if there would be a party in the bungalow tonight.

Croissants turned out to be intriguing things, and I was relieved they contained no meat. Mr Aziz chomped on the delicate pastry like an elephant painting his nails. An acceptable quantity went into his mouth, and the rest disintegrated and fell in flakes on to the floor.

As Raju entered with more coffee, I decided to address the subject of my work. Even if Raju didn't mind me sitting there while he was working, Ishaq might. I tried to steel myself for this wild act of nobility, slamming my cup into its saucer, which caused Mr Aziz to look up, startled.

– Uncle, I am sorry I woke up so late. I was very tired and –

He dismissed it with a wave of his hand.

– Not at all. Not at all. Why should you work on your first day here? Go enjoy yourself. You can work tomorrow.

Mr Aziz seemed to be under the impression that I actually *wanted* to work, but I wasn't altogether happy about his generosity. I couldn't help thinking about Maneka and Ambika upstairs.

– But what about Maneka and Ambika?

86

– Maneka who?

– They are working upstairs. Shouldn't I also be working?

Mr Aziz seemed perplexed. He clearly had no idea who Maneka and Ambika were, which surprised me. When he spoke his tone was mildly disdainful.

– Well, if you want to work then of course you may. But I did think it would be best for you to rest today. You must be tired after your journey, and of course things have been very difficult for you lately.

Of course! His *Condolences*. I had forgotten about them.

– Well, I would like to see The City.

He looked at me encouragingly.

– I can drop you on my way. Is there anything you particularly want to do? Any shopping?

I didn't have to think about this one.

– Well, I would like to see a movie?

Perhaps this was an unwise confession. I didn't want Mr Aziz to think I was a frivolous sort of girl.

– You like movies?

He had suddenly brightened.

– Yes, Uncle, very much.

– Which actor do you like?

He didn't wait for an answer but said with finality, *Raj Kapoor is My Favourite*. He had a look of such hopeful insistence that I didn't dare contradict him, and agreed heartily that Raj Kapoor was the greatest of all time.

– He had such style. And he was a gentleman too. Not like some of those effeminate types today . . . all those gyrations and vulgar things with the pelvis . . . no style, no style. Movies are for all the family.

He was shaking his head so vigorously that I worried for the few remaining strands of his hair.

– My father also likes Raj Kapoor.

He looked at me quickly, with sudden sympathy, and I remembered my father was supposed to be dead. I affected a suitably tragic look.

– These things take time. The death of my father was a very difficult thing to bear.

I looked at the ground. I hated this lie. I couldn't bear to see him look so troubled while, in all likelihood, my father was cutting my photo from the family portrait as we spoke.

– Yes, Uncle.

There was a solemn silence, for my benefit, and then Mr Aziz rose, brushing croissant flakes from his stomach. He grabbed his briefcase, holding it as my mother would hold a fish, if she ever had reason to hold a fish.

– Well, it is time I left. Have you had enough to eat?

– Yes, Uncle.

– Are you ready to leave?

– Yes, Uncle.

We left by the front door. I hunched my shoulders, but we didn't meet Raju or Ishaq. Manu was waiting in the car, fast asleep. He awoke as we approached. I had seen drivers do this before. It was clearly a profession that required an acute sixth sense. Manu touched his head to his forehead and looked at me with surprise. I just smiled, embarrassed. Manu dusted the passenger seat and held open the door, smiling at me. Mr Aziz waved him off.

– No, Manu. My wife will need the Mercedes.

I followed Mr Aziz outside the gates where another car was parked on the street. It was an old Ambassador, but Mr Aziz seemed very proud of it.

– This is my car, you know. A very good runner. Very reliable.

I nodded. As we pulled away I looked back to see if Manu had watched me get inside, but I couldn't see him.

Mr Aziz drove like a man heralding a new dawn for humanity. He granted other drivers the right of way with a noble flick of the wrist. He sped down narrow lanes and glided around roundabouts with split-second precision, humbling the meek with his superhuman example. As we entered heavier traffic he leaned back contentedly, allowing lesser souls, trapped inside samskara, to overtake him. As we neared the city centre we became caught in stationary traffic, and Mr Aziz flicked on the radio with a cavalier stab at the dashboard. His eyes misted over, lost in the music. When he finally spoke his voice was hypnotically calm.

– Have you ever had the good fortune to visit Kashmir, beti?

Beti! Driving had an *extremely* subversive effect on Mr Aziz.

– No, Uncle.

– It is a wonderful land – deep, plentiful valleys, high, ice-tipped mountains, crystal clear waters. Yes, Kashmir is where Allah takes his holidays. It is my dream to return, when the fighting stops, and when I've earned my blasted retirement. I shall end my days with the Qur'ān and the valleys of my youth, oh yes.

He fell into a reverie as the traffic started to move again like a centipede. He didn't seem to see the road, and when the drivers behind him began to hoot and shout menacingly, I worried he might have fallen asleep, but I didn't dare disturb his dreams of the valleys of his youth. Eventually the mist broke behind his eyes and he shook his head as though re-entering a world of pain and torment.

I was beginning to have second thoughts about the movie. There was nothing I wanted more, but the thought of *Majick Movie House* had reduced me to tears the previous night, and I didn't think I was ready to face a foreign movie house. I thought of an alternative that was almost as good.

– Uncle, is there a zoo here?

– What's that, zoo? Yes, beti. It's a little out of my way –

I looked at him imploringly.

– but all right, all right. You don't want to see a movie?

– I think I would prefer the zoo. I want to be outside.

– Outside? It's so hot, beti, you should be careful.

– It's all right, Uncle, I like the sun.

– All right, up to you. Now let me see . . . zoo, zoo, zoo.

He went on repeating the word like some sort of ridiculous mantra, his face knitted with concentration. I realised that if I was careful not to overdo it, Mr Aziz could prove very, very indulgent with me.

The zoo turned out to be quite a long way away, but Mr Aziz handled the journey with skilful concentration, as though it were a pilgrimage to a new land. As I climbed out of the car he explained which bus I had to catch to get back. His instructions were extraordinarily comprehensive. He seemed to think I was exceptionally incompetent (which is a word I *refuse* to use about myself), but perhaps all of this was part of his *Condolences*. I watched him drive off, feeling quite pleased with myself.

There were very few people at the zoo at such an early hour. I had the place almost to myself.

The first cage was zebras, which I found boring. I wanted to see monkeys which are by far my favourite animal. In my search I visited the snake house, which I didn't like. Snakes didn't scare me. I just didn't find them interesting.

I found a sign that read *Primates* and headed in the direction indicated. Along the way I came to the *Cheetah Park*, but the cage was so small that even an Olympic cheetah couldn't have reached more than a canter. I supposed they justified the word *Park* by the few stray shrubs wilting by the edge of wire. I talked to the three cheetahs for a while, asking them how they were and what they were doing, and was pleased to see two of them wander over in my direction.

A group of men were standing by the other side of the fence and were throwing pebbles (I should really call them rocks, but that would be too horrible) at the cheetahs. They laughed with delight when one of them pinged off a spotted head. The animal became elegantly annoyed and prowled towards the men, snarling. This only aroused them further and they giggled and threw more stones. Eventually, the cheetah sauntered to the furthest corner of the cage and sprawled in the sun with a dignified yawn. Embarrassed at having been outwitted by an animal, the men walked off, laughing just a little too loudly, their arms around each other's shoulders. I walked away, pleased at the cheetah's victory.

The next cage was elephants. I felt an immediate flutter of

excitement, but, as this was childish, I forced myself to approach the cage at an appropriately adult speed. I loved elephants. They were the most philosophical of all the animals. There was only one elephant, and although he looked big and healthy, his ears drooped and he made little attempt to conceal his obvious depression. His tail had been cut and was frayed at the end like a piece of rope. But it was his eyes that made him look so sad. He hung his head as though he were ashamed to be seen. I had seen unhappy animals in zoos before, but his moist eyes went straight to my heart and I felt a lump in my throat.

I was trying to think what could have reduced him to this pitiful state when I saw a rusted chain around his front leg, which explained his slow, limping gait. The poor creature was unable to walk even ten steps without the chain digging into his flesh and cutting him short. There was no one else around, but the elephant didn't appear to have noticed me. I felt too dismayed to talk to him, but I decided to try, and whispered a few soothing words. He didn't respond, but just lumbered around in a lazy circle.

I walked away, hating myself for it, but unable to do anything for him. As I walked I couldn't resist one last glance, just in the hope that he had suddenly become happy. Inevitably, he was still plodding round and round in that never-ending circle, his head hanging low. I continued walking, thoroughly disheartened.

With some relief, I reached the monkeys. I pushed the elephant from my mind and prepared to be entertained. There were monkeys near our house and I used to feed them nuts and bananas whenever I could. I could never understand why everyone else hated them. Ravi always called them *Nasty Little Buggers* and would take it as a very serious insult when they pulled his hair and stole his things. They were always respectful with me, or as respectful as monkeys can get whilst still being monkeys. The more mischievous they became, the more I loved them.

Ravi's eternal crusade was to prove he couldn't possibly be humbled by a mere monkey. They sensed this and made him suffer for it. The more he protested the more they would bully him until he became completely wild and thrashed around madly.

Poor Ravi. Some day I would have to tell him the story of Ravana and Vali.

One day Ravana spied Vali from the air on the east shore of the Ganga, and landed to greet him. Vali was absorbed in his ablutions and didn't notice Ravana's arrival. Offended, Ravana caught hold of his tail, but Vali didn't notice and leapt into the air, his tail lashing around Ravana's wrist. Trapped, Ravana flew with him, trying to attract his attention.

Vali continued his daily routine, splashing into the Ganga on the opposite shore, taking off for the Himalayas for more prayers, and then making a final dive into the river on the south shore. Ravana was still trying to free himself when Vali landed in the city of Kishkinda. For the first time, Vali heard his cries, but he could not see the unfortunate King. Every time he turned around, the voice reappeared from behind him. *Where are You?* shouted Vali, and Ravana would shriek, *Here! Here!* After a while, Vali concluded that someone was trying to make a fool of him. Remaining still, he demanded to know who was there. Ravana howled that he was caught in his tail and, astonished, Vali freed him. He couldn't believe his eyes when he saw the mighty Lord of Lanka! Ravana just sighed and explained that it was an accident. Vali showed him generous hospitality, and after an acceptable length of time Ravana explained that he should be getting back to Lanka. He flew off, having made a friend and learned a lesson in humility.

This made me recall a serious contradiction in Ravi's behaviour. I had seen him, on more than one occasion, prostrate himself before Hanuman! My brother was too complex for his own good . . .

The horrible men were nowhere to be seen. I was alone with the monkeys. There were two cages side by side. The first enclosed six black monkeys with long tails, and the second, by an extraordinary stroke of good fortune, contained a gorilla. I went to the first cage, wanting to save the gorilla for later.

The cage was medium-sized and had two trees with broad branches that hung parallel to the ground. There were four baby monkeys inside, chasing each other. The smallest one, who I decided was my favourite, was always being picked on. They would push him off the branch he was sitting on, and he would turn and twist and grab the branch below him where he could swing and dance in relative security. I couldn't stop laughing at the baffled face he gave each time he found himself falling, and the air of defiance he assumed whenever he gave his pursuers the slip.

The monkeys gave up chasing him and ran up the sides of the cage, twisting in the air so that they could land on each other. Although they played very roughly, they had none of the malice that irritated me about boys. They were simply convinced that the world, including each other, had been created for their own personal amusement.

Two older monkeys sat behind in silence, chewing and scratching, watching the youngsters. Though their faces registered disapproval, I was certain that underneath was a mirth that parental responsibilities forced them to conceal. After all, a monkey with no sense of fun is not a monkey.

The smallest monkey catapulted himself on to the branch where his mother sat meditating, and clambered towards her. He sat next to her, imitating her pose, and demanded a banana from the bunch beside her. She gave him one and took one for herself. She peeled hers and turned to see what he was doing. He was trying to stuff the entire thing into his mouth, without bothering about the peel. His mother sighed, and then shrieked as, insulted, the baby made to throw the offending banana over his shoulder. She took it from him and removed a little of the peel before giving it back. He seemed to get the general idea, but insisted on squeezing the insides out like toothpaste. Eventually his mother gave him a gentle slap and he tumbled off the branch, the lesson being over for the day.

I turned my attention to the gorilla. He was a magnificent fellow, proud and mighty. He prowled around, crawling on his knuckles, saying *I am Master of this Cage . . . You may Watch Me if you So Wish . . . I Permit It*. He rose on to two legs and looked in my direction. I didn't know how to react. I had never seen a gorilla before. He tilted his head to one side and scratched his temple, in the caricatured pose of the thinking man, and then looked at me once more, intrigued. I stammered something, and then, collecting myself, introduced myself in as confident a voice as I could manage.

– Charming, isn't he?

Startled, I looked around to see who had spoken, and saw a boy with a bunch of bananas in his left hand and a pleasant smile. I didn't reply, but he seemed not to mind.

– I was just about to give him his afternoon snack. Would you like to help me?

I shook my head and he smiled again. Pulling two bananas from the bunch he handed one to me, and tossed the other to the gorilla who extended his arm a fraction of an inch, and caught it. I threw mine into the cage, but much too hard, and it went sailing over his head. I blushed, but to my amazement the gorilla jumped and plucked it out of the air. Forgetting my shyness, I took two more bananas and was delighted to see the gorilla display two more feats of agility, with an arrogance that said that, even if I was impressed, he considered this to be elementary stuff.

I looked at the boy, and was a little ruffled to see him smiling at my excitement.

– The orang-utans are performing on the main stage now. May I take you to see them?

I shook my head, but smiled this time in case I had offended him. But he just said, *Well, Enjoy Yourself Then*, and walked off.

As soon as he was out of sight I ran as fast as I could in the direction of the stage, from which I could hear laughter. I sat near the back and watched an orang-utan amble on to the stage, pick up two chairs in one hand, a table in the other, and then a hat-stand and four hats, all of which he balanced on his arms. He bowed with considerable showmanship, before exiting the stage.

A man replaced the orang-utan and said that the show was

over and thanked everyone for coming. They all clapped and clambered to their feet. I sat until everyone had left, and then began to cry. I couldn't help it. I deserved to have some fun.

– At least you saw the gorilla.

It was the boy with the bananas again. I covered my face with my hands, but then lowered my arms. There was no point, he had already seen me crying, and he had such a matter-of-fact expression that I didn't feel embarrassed.

– Wasn't the gorilla nice?

I tried to smile, but tears came instead.

– I wanted to see the orang-utans.

I waited for him to laugh, but he didn't even smile. He just tilted his head and scratched his chin in exactly the same pose as the gorilla.

– Why are you laughing?

– I'm not laughing.

– Yes you are, I can see you laughing.

Tears were still running down my cheeks, but I had to admit I was laughing.

– Are you laughing at me?

– Yes.

He seemed pleased, but confused, and reverted to his gorilla pose.

– Do you find me silly?

– Not all the time.

He was trying to look offended, but a smile curled around his lips.

– My name is Ashok.

– Hello.

I didn't know what to say after that, and this time we both laughed and we had to force ourselves to stop. He smiled and I thought of something to say.

– What is the gorilla's name?

– Ravana.

– Ravana!

– Yes.

I didn't want him to ask me any questions, so I thought of something else to say.

– Do you work here?

– Only in the mornings.

– What is your favourite animal?

I liked this question. I used to ask everyone their favourite animal at school, and I rarely guessed incorrectly.

– I like Ravana better than anyone else in the zoo, but he and I are friends so that's not really fair. I like elephants a lot, but I hate the way they treat them. Elephants need to be free, but all anyone wants to do is put them to work.

He looked upset, and for a moment I thought he might cry, but then he brightened.

– What's *your* favourite animal?

– I like monkeys, especially . . . orang-utans.

I must have looked miserable again, but then I saw his face which was so full of tenderness that it startled me. He smiled, and I smiled back.

– The orang-utans will be here next week, but I could take you to see them now if you like.

There was nothing I would have liked better, but I decided I'd had enough childishness for one day. The morning had ended, and Ambika and Maneka would still be working.

– No thank you, I have to go home, to my mother.

– Well, maybe some other time.

I could feel myself blushing. I wasn't used to lying so readily, and I dipped my face a little, hoping he wouldn't notice.

– May I at least walk you out of the zoo?

– All right.

As we walked I wished I had said yes to seeing the orang-utans, but it was too late now. We walked past the elephant and I looked at Ashok. I could see him trying not to look, but his face was very sad. He stopped suddenly and I saw his fists clench and unclench. He was staring. I followed his eyes and saw the horrible men standing on the other side of the cage. They were throwing peanuts so that they landed just out of the elephant's reach. He charged towards the peanuts, but his chain cut him short and he trumpeted in frustration. The horrible men starting to throw stones instead and, mistaking them for peanuts, the elephant sucked them up in his trunk and put them in his mouth before spitting them out in frustration.

Ashok was trembling. I was also very upset, and told him so.

– Make them stop!

– I can't.

– Yes you can. Tell them to stop!

– I'm not supposed to . . . tourists come first.

– Before the animals?

– Always.

I stamped my foot at the injustice of it all and Ashok strode off towards the men. In a loud voice he told them to leave, but they only laughed. He pushed the nearest one to him, leaving him sprawled on the grass. A voice bellowed from behind me, *Ashok! In my Office!*

I turned and saw a fat man with dark glasses wearing a shirt and tie. Ashok walked off, his movements stiff with anger. He winked as he passed me, and then followed the man. I watched him go, hoping he wouldn't get into too much trouble.

I left the zoo and waited for the bus, unable to think clearly. The last few days had become a confused jumble in my head, like the recollection of the recollection of a dream. The sun was fully awake now, and the road was a haze of dust and heat. Even the shadows looked hot, like black, relentless stares. A woman and her son were also waiting for the bus. He looked about three, and he stood next to her with a very serious expression. From time to time he hid his face in her sari, but I doubted if that gave much respite from the heat. We waited and waited. Every time a shadow loomed on the horizon I looked at the woman expectantly, but she just shook her head with a smile. Even the boy seemed amused by my fidgeting.

When the bus finally did arrive I practically leapt into the air with joy and the mother and her son stepped aside to let me on first. I leant my head against the window and sighed, stretching out my arms and legs with a yawn. They sat behind me, the boy next to the window. Neither of them showed the slightest sign of relief.

When we started moving my head was thrown back by the unexpected lurch and the steel rim of the seat burned the back of my neck. I heard the mother making some sympathetic clicks, and I turned around, glad to have made some contact. She took a bottle of water from her bag and I gratefully drank some. She explained that the water was for my neck, and I dabbed a little there, thinking this wasn't really necessary. Her son livened up and he told me he would now read all the signs that we saw from the window. He said it like an acrobat announcing he was going to swallow fire.

With considerable ceremony, his face glowing with excitement, he began to babble at tremendous speed, *Pepsi, Pepsi, Pepsi, Pepsi, Pepsi, Pepsi, Pepsi, Pepsi, Pepsi* . . . sadly, there wasn't much variation on this road, but the boy felt compelled to continue . . . *Pepsi, Pepsi, Pepsi, Pepsi* . . . I applauded, desperate to release him from his terrible obligation. He seemed very pleased with my response and stopped. I was grateful. My head was starting to ache.

His mother told me that she had taken him to the zoo for a special treat, because he had just been to the dentist. I asked him which animal he had liked best, and he said the snakes and made all sorts of unpleasant hissing sounds. I smiled and asked him if he had seen the orang-utans, and he said yes and started giggling, and gave me a garbled explanation with so much excitement that it was impossible to understand anything he said. I knew I shouldn't feel jealous of a three-year-old, but I felt like telling him to shut up. The mother seemed to notice and told him to be quiet, but he didn't listen and went on yapping. She smiled and let him be. I was annoyed that she was giving her son free rein to torment me, but then he *had* just been to the dentist.

The boy had also sensed my irritation, and so, of course, he intensified his description, using graphic gestures and appropriate noises, jumping up on to his seat and swinging his arms. His mother watched, smiling. When I tried to ignore him he began his running commentary again, *Pepsi, Pepsi, Pepsi, Pepsi, Pepsi,* I knew he could keep this up for ever, *Pepsi, Pepsi, Pepsi, Pepsi, Sachin!* I looked out of the window and saw a billboard for some music system, endorsed by the world's finest batsman (or so every man I had ever met informed me – cricket was never a big interest of mine). The boy started miming cricket strokes in the air, hitting me quite painfully on my ear with one of his more exuberant shots.

I was grateful when we reached my stop. I said goodbye to the nasty little boy and his mother as sweetly as I could. Manu was still waiting inside the gates, leaning on the car and looking up at the sky. He grinned when he saw me. I tried not to look at the guards.

Raju came out of the kitchen. I smiled at Manu and half ran towards Raju, wanting to get as far from the guards as possible.

– Manu said you went with Mr Aziz.

I nodded. Raju looked tired and serious. We went into the kitchen. Ishaq was cooking. Raju gave me something wrapped in newspaper.

– The guard brought this for you. It is not everything. He says he will try to get the rest next week.

It was just over a thousand rupees.

– Where did you go?

– I had some things to do in The City.

Raju didn't reply.

– Have you eaten?

– No.

Ishaq ladled some food into a plate and I sat, looking at Raju. I wondered if he was angry with me, though I was getting tired of disapproval.

I finished my food while Raju and Ishaq bustled about, cooking, cleaning, setting things in order. Raju took a bullet-shaped cylinder of bread from a cupboard and cut it into thin slices. He put them on a plate and took some strips of meat from the fridge, and then poured a bottle of beer into a glass. He looked a little disgusted as he carried them into the dining room, keeping his nose as far away as possible.

As soon as he left I wandered into the corridor. I wasn't sure where I was going, but Raju had annoyed me for some reason. He wasn't being very nice, although I couldn't see any reason for him to be nice to me. After all, he was *Working Hard*, which left little time for niceness. Even so, I felt it was about time that *someone* was nice to me. Ashok had whetted my appetite.

I walked down the corridor, heading for the bathroom. I decided to have a look at the shower, maybe to switch it on, just to persuade myself that my world wasn't really as narrow as it seemed.

– Where were you this morning?

I hadn't expected this. Somehow I had convinced myself that the house belonged to Raju and Ishaq, at least in the daytime. I had forgotten about Mrs Marceau.

– Mr Aziz took me to the city.

– *Why?*

Her words were like sword thrusts. She didn't want answers to her questions, she just wanted to inflict as much damage as possible.

– I went to the zoo.

– *Madam.*

Madam? I looked at her, perplexed by such deference.

– I went to the zoo, madam.

I felt like one of her cats, being house-trained.

– Sorry.

I should have said *Sorry, Madam*, but Mrs Marceau didn't notice. She was too busy preparing her next attack.

– From now on you start work at *six!* Mr Aziz doesn't know anything about the house. You do not listen to Mr Aziz. And tonight there is a party, so you have to work. Start at five o'clock. Ask Raju what you have to do. *Raju!*

Raju came running. He looked at me very quickly, and then looked at Mrs Marceau. I noticed he held his head very straight when he talked her, and he made himself as tall as possible, looking her in the eye.

– Have you fed the cats?

– Yes, madam.

– Where is Moustache?

– He went out after lunch. He has not come back.

– Went out?

– Yes, madam.

– Moustache does not go out.

– He went out, madam, to catch mice.

I could see the laughter in Raju's eyes. Mrs Marceau looked so full of hate that I thought she would rip his face to pieces. Instead she just turned and smouldered upstairs. Raju looked amused, but angry. He was looking after her, probably thinking equally violent thoughts.

– Should I start work now, Raju?

It was two o'clock. I had still seen no sign of Maneka and Ambika. I couldn't believe they were still working.

– No, no. It doesn't matter. Do not let her frighten you. She cannot do anything. She sleeps all day, she talks to the fucking cats, and she gives us orders. Aziz is good, but he is not a man. No man would let a woman talk to him like that.

Raju spat on the marble, and then looked at me. For a minute I thought I had to mop up his spit, but he immediately brought a cloth from the kitchen and did it himself. After that he became more relaxed and laughed.

– Cat is dead. She does not know. Aziz says do not tell her. Ha!

He went on laughing, but his laugh worried me. I had never seen anybody this angry before, and I had never seen anyone take so much delight in a dead cat.

– She told you about the party?

– Yes.

– Party is hard work. No need for you to do much work. Watch what we do, so you know for next time.

– All right.

101

Raju smiled. His anger had left him for the moment, but he still seemed tired.

– You saw Maneka yesterday?

– Yes.

He laughed.

– Good, good. She is a nice girl, but foolish. She drinks, and goes to all sorts of places. You should not listen to everything she says.

Raju seemed to like talking about Maneka. He couldn't stop smiling.

– Raju, last night, Arun –

He frowned.

– Yes, Arun. He has a lot of problems now, lot of problems. His son is dying, he may be dead by the end of the week.

– Oh.

The front door opened and I heard Mr Aziz's voice. I wondered if it was all right for us to be standing about in the corridor, but Raju didn't seem worried. He greeted Mr Aziz respectfully, though in a clockwork sort of way.

– Ah, hello, Raju. Hello, my dear, did you enjoy the zoo?

I blushed. Raju didn't respond one way or the other, but my confidence had increased after learning that he wasn't angry with me.

The next moment was one of those that spin against the natural orbit of time. I don't know exactly when our eyes met. The world had turned full circle before gravity once again rested in my heels. When I was ready to face the world he was still there, and I was relieved.

– My dear, let me introduce you to my son. This is Armand.

I didn't say anything. I couldn't. But my lips involuntarily cradled into a shy smile. He smiled back and I hoped no one would notice my heart floating several feet above their heads.

Mrs Marceau came down the stairs, her heels ricocheting like gunfire against the marble. She barked a couple of orders at Mr Aziz, and then at Raju, who left to go into the kitchen. He moved very slowly, as though to provoke her, but I hardly noticed, I was still staring at *him*.

With a start I saw that Mrs Marceau was looking at me in a terrifying way, and I concentrated very hard on the light bulb until I couldn't see anything, but his smile still danced before me. To my amazement, Mrs Marceau kissed him lightly on the cheek and ruffled his hair. I couldn't help wondering if her lips had burned through that silky skin. She turned her attention to Mr Aziz, who seemed to be steeling himself for trouble.

– Now, chérie, most of the arrangements are made. But there are one or two problems.

He took her arm, or rather, her arm took him, and they went into the living room with Mr Aziz making excuses, though he hadn't said what his excuses were for yet. Mrs Marceau's skirt swung behind her like a military flag, and then the door closed, and I was alone in the corridor, with Armand.

I waited for him to say something, but he seemed embarrassed, uncertain. I tried to think of something to say. *I Love You* seemed appropriate, but nobody said that when they first met.

– How are you?

He looked surprised, and then he smiled again and disappeared down the corridor and up the stairs.

I had disgraced myself. That was hardly what Holly Golightly would have said. *You look a Little like my Brother Ravi, do you Mind if I Call you Ravi?*, or, *You don't have to Worry, Darling, I've Taken Care of Myself for a Long Time*, but not, *How Are you?* I had been waiting for this moment for so long, training myself, all those movies, all that dreaming, and when the moment had come, I had blown it. I could have said anything. *Anything!* After all, we had already spent almost twenty years without speaking to each other, so there was plenty to say.

There was a statue to my left of the head and shoulders of a lady with long, sweeping hair. I felt like picking it up and throwing it at the wall. *How Are You?* No film star asks a man how he is! They ask for money for the powder room, or they talk about themselves, or they light cigarettes and don't say anything, but to humiliate themselves like that, asking such silly, childish questions! *Never.*

And that had been my big chance. Maybe Mr Aziz had done it deliberately, because he liked me and called me *beti*. Maybe he had wanted me to *marry* Armand. Maybe I was supposed to say, *Of Course I'll Marry You, I've Never Been Married Before*. I looked at the painting. *The Coronation of Emperor Ravi*. I could imagine what Ravi would say. *Don't be Foolish, yaar . . . You and your Incompetent ideas . . . Film stars are Rich . . . We are Poor . . . Film stars are Born Stars . . . You were Born a Girl . . . Film stars are Beautiful . . . They can Kill a man Just by Looking at him . . . How many Men have you Killed? . . .* And then I realised. It wouldn't have made any difference what I said, that wasn't the problem. My mistake was that I was living in the wrong movie. Hadn't I learned that yesterday? *Breakfast at Tiffany's* begins *after* Holly Golightly is a star. I hadn't reached that part yet.

But what about *Sabrina*? It was so obvious. Sabrina is the chauffeur's daughter and lives with the servants. She watches David, but David doesn't notice her.

I sighed, relieved at having identified the problem. If Armand was David Laraby and I was Sabrina, then I would need some trick to get him to notice me. Sabrina had gone to some sort of cooking school in Paris and had learned to speak French and wear make-up and do all sorts of things, but that didn't really seem practical for me. I would have to think of something else, some way of getting Armand to notice my star quality.

Nothing came to mind. It would need some serious thought.

I wondered how my mother and father met. Did they sit opposite each other, drinking coffee, ignoring the jibes of a senile grandfather and an unhappy brother-in-law? Did she look into his face and know that in forty years she would have a daughter who would run from her as though she carried a plague in the hollows of her eyes?

It made me sad to think of all the things my mother had missed. She would die of shame if she learned of my recent employment, but the possibilities . . . the limitless possibilities . . . these had evaded her. But here I was, in the centre of life, waiting for stardom. And tonight, the party? That was when the movie would begin.

By five o'clock the house was full of excitement. I knew what I had to do; stand by door while the guests arrive, take coats, smile, look like I'm enjoying myself. Put coats upstairs. Serve champagne before meal, carry tray, refill glasses, smile, look like I'm enjoying myself. Stand at doorway while meal is served. Watch for empty glasses. Give white wine if they say *White*, red wine if they say *Red*. If they ask for beer give beer, but Mrs Marceau disapproves of beer at the table. After meal serve coffee and clear plates. Look like I'm enjoying myself. Reconvene in kitchen for further instructions.

I was looking forward to taking the coats. I hadn't been upstairs yet (and Armand's room was upstairs). The guests would start to arrive at five-thirty. Raju looked pleased with himself. Either he had produced a spectacular dinner, or he was gloating over the tragedy shrouding Mrs Marceau's ex-cat. Maybe he had combined the two and cooked the cat!

He and Ishaq had laboured in the kitchen for two hours. Arun and Manu were helping, and Ambika and Maneka were dusting and tidying. I stayed with them, watching and helping where I could. Every so often, in various states of undress, Mrs Marceau would thunder downstairs and scream at someone. She smelt surprisingly good. Whenever she came in I closed my eyes until I imagined she was some divine apsara, come to shine beauty and life upon this cruel world. But her voice always spoilt my efforts. *Don't Break the Clock! What is this Stain? Where are the Napkins?*, like some kind of pubescent parakeet.

As yet there was no sign of Mr Aziz or Armand. I had given myself an alternative set of instructions, for private reference only. Stand straight, smile coquettishly, pay extra special attention to *his* wine glass, consider tasting the champagne, look like an actress playing a servant. I hoped he didn't notice Maneka. She was pretty.

Maneka was also excited about the evening, though she seemed to take her work seriously. She was very protective of Ambika and would run around doing the most strenuous jobs before Ambika could get to them. In fact, Maneka did 90 per cent of the work, but she was careful to ensure that Ambika didn't realise this. I helped where I could, but Maneka did everything so quickly and efficiently that most of the time I found myself standing around, looking confused. I didn't berate myself for this; after all, I was a film star training for the part of trainee maid.

So far I had avoided Arun, but he hadn't paid much attention to me either. Raju hadn't liked it when I had tried to tell him about the night before, and I noticed, with considerable surprise, that everyone seemed to like Arun. He bounded about, making jokes and clowning around so everyone laughed. Ambika kept slapping him as though he were a lovable buffoon. Even Maneka laughed when he pinched her bottom and tried to lift up her sari. I didn't like this. I distrusted him as much as ever.

Ishaq was the most serious one. He took orders from Raju and did his work very conscientiously, as though to make up for his deficiency in youth. Manu was the least cheerful. He dropped things and broke glasses and put things in the wrong place. Maneka laughed at him and Raju lost his temper once or twice. Manu looked embarrassed, as though aware that things would move faster if he were outside, washing his car, but this only made him more persistent and more of a liability, much to Raju's annoyance. Arun was quite nice to him and slapped him on the back and swept up his broken glass. I wondered if he was trying to make up for the previous night. I tried asking Maneka. She assured me he didn't remember anything, but I wasn't convinced.

At exactly five-thirty the guests began to arrive. I took their coats and bags to the upstairs drawing room. I could hear Armand moving about in the next room, but no matter how much I lingered he showed no sign of emerging. When the last guest arrived, I decided I would try some sort of ruse. I took a glass of champagne from the tray in the kitchen, went upstairs and knocked on his door, my hand trembling. He said *Wee*, which

I found odd, and I entered. I couldn't find my voice but I gave him the champagne, spilling a little, almost crying with embarrassment.

He was sitting at the dressing table, looking into the mirror. The room smelt of perfume. His hair was floppy and long and black. It fell loosely on to his neck and as he tilted his head it curled on to the silk of his collar and arched outwards like a wave. The contrast with Ravi and his pools of coconut oil was unimaginably huge. Armand's eyes were brown and playful. His skin looked soft, with very little beard. He spoke and his voice sailed across the air, rising like evening mist.

– Thank you. Has everyone arrived?

– Yes.

I looked at his bed. It was pink, like a girl's, and was big enough for my whole family to sleep on and still feel less cramped than at home. The surviving cat was asleep on the bed.

This was as far as I had planned. I hoped he would lead things from here, but he just looked at me, amused, while I felt flustered and stupid.

– Thank you for the champagne.

I turned the same colour as the bed, walked to the door, opened it, walked out, tried to shut it but missed the handle, and then went downstairs. Not exactly Holly Golightly, but I was flushed with excitement and felt quite pleased with myself. I resolved to consult Maneka about it later, assuming she could be trusted as a disinterested confidante, something I would have to verify first.

I went downstairs to the kitchen. Raju was there, looking very tense. He handed me a tray of champagne glasses which I carried into the living room.

Everyone was milling around, talking and laughing. All the guests were white, and they seemed to be wearing the entire contents of the zoo. The sight of so much fur made me think of dead cats, which made me smile. No one smiled back. In fact, I don't think anyone saw me. I had always imagined European dinner parties to be full of tremendously beautiful people, but I was starting to feel a misconception twitching at the base of my spine.

Mrs Marceau glared when she saw me, probably wondering where I had been. I pretended not to notice. She was balancing a glass of champagne in one hand and some carefully selected anecdotes up her sleeve whilst scanning the room with that omnivorous glare designed to stun husbands, servants and young frightened (trainee-film-star) girls into submission.

I located Mr Aziz. He didn't smile, but beneath that mask concealing terror, concealing a good heart, I detected a conspiratorial loyalty. He was busy playing cat and mouse with a tall, milky lady who was asking him to drink from her glass. He kept refusing and looked to Mrs Marceau, and then to me, for help. I left him to his own defences.

I spied Maneka at the other end of the room, serving and smiling, and I decided to leave the safety of the doorway. We were the only ones who were to serve drinks, Ambika being too old, and, although nobody said it out loud, too unattractive.

Serving champagne proved quite easy. Most people smiled when I showed them the tray, and many made some kind of remark, like *Ooh, if you Insist*, or, *Another! Well, why Not, why Not?* The glasses went pretty quickly and I returned to the kitchen for a second round.

Raju and Ishaq looked as though they were in hell, running from one smouldering pot to the next, turning down flames, stirring soup, opening bottles, bumping into each other. I smiled sympathetically, but neither of them noticed me.

As I was crossing from the corridor into the living room, Armand came down the stairs in his dinner suit and floppy bow tie. When he reached me I gave him a champagne glass, holding on to the trembling tray with one hand. He smiled, with his eyes and his lips, and took the glass from me, brushing my hand with his, and then went into the room. I leant against the wall for a moment, perspiring, and congratulated myself for not dropping the tray. I looked around, saw nobody, and took a sip from one of the glasses. I was surprised by how much I liked it.

After a couple of deep breaths I went back into the room. Armand was the centre of attention. Men clapped him on the back and women kissed him, including a very pretty girl who kissed him on both cheeks. He seemed to like her, and looked into her eyes very confidently. I marched up and pushed the tray in her face, standing between them. After she had taken the glass, Armand had gone. I gritted my teeth, trying to suppress a victory smile.

By the time everyone was on their third or fourth glass my work became easier. People weren't drinking as quickly, and most of the time I was just standing around. I listened to the conversation, which was dominated by Mrs Marceau.

– Hong Kong was so different to India. Don't you also miss Hong Kong, Francine?

– Very much. Most of all I miss the Chinese, so much more honest than the Indians. I hope you don't mind me saying so, Mr Aziz.

– I am Kashmiri, Francine.

– Oh, of course, I keep forgetting . . . so you must agree completely.

Everyone laughed. Francine looked simultaneously delighted with her joke and with her knowledge of petty South Asian squabbles.

– I have to say, Mr Aziz, now that there are no Indians present –

What about Maneka and me? And the surviving cat, assuming he hadn't been imported.

– I have never really liked Indian people. Of course they have a very interesting culture, very ancient and spiritual, and of course they live in terrible squalor and poverty, but I have always found them dreadfully unreliable, and, well, dishonest, and lazy, to be frank. I have already had to let two servants go for stealing, and a third for drilling through my bedroom wall so he could watch me changing. Honestly! A Chinese maid would never steal –

Mrs Marceau interrupted.

– An Indonesian might.

– Yes, of course, but a good Filipino, never. Rutger, I believe you only have one servant?

– Yes, only one, and she doesn't live in. I can't get used to the idea of someone else cleaning after me, and Elke isn't quite ready to give up cooking.

Elke giggled neurotically.

– You see, Francine, I didn't realise how much I liked cooking until it became something I could give up. I should feel the same about cigarettes if they ever make a nicotine-free brand.

Laughter. Mrs Marceau laughed loudly and then stopped short, as if to say that wit was all very well, but terribly rude when the hostess had something important to say. She opened her mouth, but Raju came in and announced that dinner was ready. Mrs Marceau glared at him, and everyone filed into the dining room.

As ordered, I stood by the door next to the wine bottles, and then, as Raju started serving the food Maneka and I circled round with a bottle in each hand. Red when they said *Red*, white when they said *White*. It was all easy stuff, and no one asked for beer. As soon as the first course was served Mrs Marceau resumed her sentence. It sounded as though she hadn't drawn breath since Raju interrupted her.

– Yes, I can see how it might be difficult for someone new to Asia. Asians simply do things differently, Rutger. Everyone has servants here.

At this point Raju did a most unexpected thing. I don't think he even decided to open his mouth, but the words came fluttering out.

– I don't.

Silence. Mrs Marceau fought to rescue the party from proletarian insurrection by laughing affectionately at her servant's wit, and throwing him a glance that would have castrated a lesser man.

– I also prefer the Chinese; reliable, hard-working, very direct. They never lie and they never cheat. You know, I think I even prefer Chinese people to Europeans.

Rutger looked astonished, but Francine gave a knowing nod.

– You see, in many ways Chinese people are very similar to Western people. They don't eat with their fingers either!

More hysterical cackling.

– They respect money and they're prepared to *work* for it. Look at this country! People sleep in the sun all day long and then talk about poverty!

Mr Aziz was twitching. I counted to ten. On three, he interrupted his wife. I would have lost all respect for him had he taken any longer.

– Now chérie, that isn't fair.

– Of course it is. Do you think we are here because of luck? Do you think Raju doesn't have servants because of luck?

Raju looked suitably humbled, but I could see a dangerous smile running from his fists to his face. I hoped he would come to his senses before it reached his tongue.

– You worked *hard* so we could have all this! You worked hard so Armand could go to Oxford. You worked hard for us to have cars and servants. If you want the life, you have to *work*!

– But darling, India has produced four world religions, and poetry and music, and –

– and people *complain!* All right, I am not saying there should not be poetry and music, if it's what people want. But if they want poetry and music then they shouldn't complain when others have more material things.

– But darling . . . India's constitution carries a commitment to equality and to development, and that means development of the arts as well. When Nehru was with us he used to say –

– I don't care what *he* said. If you want money, then study law or engineering or business. If you want art, then fine, read your books, but don't complain if your children don't go to Oxford, Harvard, Yale.

– But there are good universities here, darling, and in Pakistan.

Mrs Marceau snorted.

– Tell me, would you be happy if Armand was at the university of . . . of Calcutta?

– Now darling, it has quite a fine reputation and –

– Does it compare to Oxford?

– Well, yes, there are professors there with similar –

– How many movies were filmed in the university of Calcutta?

Mrs Marceau ejected successive clusters of laughter through her nose and out into the fast thickening air. Her face bore down on her now uneasy guests with the sort of reassurance a cat gives a juicy mouse. She won the battle of wills easily, and the room collapsed into socially appropriate hysterics. But Mr Aziz wasn't completely finished.

– Chérie, all I am saying is that India cannot be judged by the same standard as Hong Kong. Hong Kong was still a British colony until recently, and India was formed as an independent socialist state and –

He had gone too far this time. This wasn't the sort of party where such language could be used, particularly after Mrs Marceau had so narrowly aborted Raju's attempted revolutionary coup.

– *Ha! Socialism!* Indians always talk about socialism. I don't know much politics, but socialism seems just envy of rich people.

Mr Aziz fell silent, vanquished by this incisive contribution to contemporary thought. Mrs Marceau didn't want her death blow to seem too obvious.

– Cantonese people simply aren't like that. You will laugh at this, but Armand and I became so close to Chinese people that they accepted us as one of them. They used to say they found it difficult to talk to expatriates, but that somehow we were different. And I love Cantonese food, pure Cantonese that is, and I like ginger, and Europeans rarely do. But you know, really I think it's because in our family we don't talk. I don't like constant chatter. It hurts my head. Chinese people are like that. When they have nothing to say, they keep quiet. They don't waste time *blowing wind*.

I nodded my acknowledgement. My mother was just the same.

I was delighted to see that Mr Aziz wasn't vanquished at all, just resting in his corner.

– Chérie, Indians don't blow wind. We like to talk, talking is a way of showing affection. Why are we all here today after all . . . ?

It was daring of him to address Mrs Marceau's constituency like this.

– we are here to talk, and to enjoy each other's company.

– But Indians will talk all *day*, and say *nothing!*

In a way, this applied to my mother. On the other hand, judging from the skirt lengths and relentless babble in the room, it did seem that my theory was slowly proving itself.

Mr Aziz tried a jab. It was a little wild this time, and definitely below the belt.

– But Europeans can chatter all day long as well, chérie.

– What did I *say*? We are not typical Europeans. We are not typical expatriates. Most of them come for two, three years. We were in Hong Kong for seven, and we could have stayed even longer . . .

Unfinished sentences have a sting in their tail that can snap back at any moment. She knew she had shut her husband up with that one. I could have finished it for her . . . *If you had Bought Property when We Told You to.*

The soup was going cold. For a minute there was no talking and everyone slurped. Maneka and I left to fetch more wine.

In the kitchen Maneka almost collapsed with suppressed laughter. She seemed to have been enjoying herself enormously, and like me she'd been backing Mr Aziz all the way. She gave me a detailed description of all the guests, telling me everything she knew about them, which was quite a lot. Maneka appeared to take these parties very seriously, giving them the same attention as Ravi gave *The Bold and the Beautiful.* When we returned they were still slurping in silence. Armed with the information Maneka had given me, I took the opportunity to get the measure of the table.

At the far left was Francine. She was quite pretty, though Maneka had said she was very nasty. Next to her was her husband, François. The only thing Maneka had said about him was that he was ugly. I agreed. Perhaps not everyone would have described him as ugly, but I hate big, hairy men. Next to him was Armand (slender and with very *soft* skin) and next to Armand was

Francine's daughter, Marie. She was a problem. Maneka had said she came to the house quite often, and she was the one who had kissed Armand on both cheeks. I wondered if she had her hand on his leg under the table so I dropped a couple of things to take a look, but Mrs Marceau glared at me and, in any case, I couldn't see anything through that thicket of knees.

Opposite François were Elke and Rutger. Rutger was slim and blond. His features were fine, though a little cruel. He was virtually hairless except for his head, and his eyes were a clear blue, perhaps too clear, which was where the cruelty came from. Elke was plump, red-faced and not unattractive. Maneka said she was very stupid, and I found this easy to believe. She must have been a good twenty years older than me, but I quietly thought of her as a child.

Opposite them were two Germans, Frauke and Manfred (*Germans, from Germany!* as Maneka had said). They were big and, according to Maneka, thoroughly obnoxious, though completely unaware of this. In my opinion, this made them not quite as repellent as they should have been, and even potentially likeable. They had seemed completely at ease until now, eating and drinking and laughing at anything anyone said. They laughed during the serious parts as well, but nobody paid them much attention.

The other two were English (*Britishers, from Britain!*), Jeffrey and Donald. Donald was Jeffrey's son. Maneka had never seen them before, but she had been watching them closely. She said she thought Jeffrey was important. He didn't say much, and it seemed to me that he made everyone uncomfortable.

Raju served the main couse, announcing *Garlic Snails, Pigeon Breast, and Saladd Nisswas*. I think he enjoyed doing that. As soon as the soup was cleared they all started talking again, about snails.

– Really, Mrs Marceau, I must congratulate you. These escargots are superb.

Mrs Marceau beamed, while Raju smouldered.

– Escargots are not an Indian dish, are they Mr Aziz?

– I don't think so, Frauke.

– But I wonder if Indians eat them. After all, I know an Indian gentleman who loves Chinese food.

So did I as it happened. To my alarm, as I was filling her glass, Frauke decided to test her hypothesis.

– My dear, do you also like escargots?

Mrs Marceau jumped in before I could disgrace myself.

– She is a vegetarian.

– Oh how *charming*, whatever for?

Raju came to my defence, at great risk to his personal safety.

– Because it is cruel to eat animals.

Maneka giggled and Mrs Marceau glared, either because of Maneka, or because Raju had graciously informed the room of the innate barbarism of their culture. Either way, it seemed she was losing control of her staff. Frauke seemed interested in my opinion of carnivores.

– Do you really think so?

Mrs Marceau silenced all of us with an imperious glare, sweeping the room with her eyes.

– I've tried to tell her, Frauke. She thinks she is eating her ancestors, you see.

Jeffrey raised his eyebrows.

– Not at all, Mrs Marceau. Most South Indians are vegetarians. Neanderthal man was originally vegetarian, you know.

Apart from the comparison with Neanderthal man, I was quite grateful for this unexpected support. Mrs Marceau made the mistake of taking him on.

– People here are not nourished properly. People need meat.

Frauke's social conscience made a rare, but undeniably profound, entrance.

– I feel so bad about it sometimes. Children are starving on the street. It teaches us how lucky we are. My father brought me up like that, he told me never to leave food on my plate because there are children in India who'd be grateful to have it.

Jeffrey pricked up his ears again.

– I believe, Frauke, that the boy who served us this meal is from a village . . .

Raju looked delighted. I suspected it was years since he'd been called a boy.

– and he could tell you of the people who grew and harvested this food for us with their own hands . . .

How do you harvest a *pigeon*?

– Perhaps theirs is the real tragedy.

Personally, I thought the real tragedy was that these people actually liked eating slugs and pigeons!

Mrs Marceau said nothing else on the subject and bit her lip. Her pride had taken a tumble after her tussle with Jeffrey. She seemed desperate to recover her stature. Inevitably, her chosen victim was Raju.

– I am thinking of sending for my old Filipino. Indians know very little about food, and I miss my Cantonese food terribly. This boy's smile irritates me.

Elke, good-naturedly, decided to leap to Raju's defence.

– I think he's lovely.

She gave Raju a playful little smile. I wondered if it crossed his mind that, had he wanted to, he could have taken Elke upstairs and taught her about Khujarao amidst the coats. Mrs Marceau seemed annoyed.

– Filipino maids are honest.

Raju's eyes flashed like distant thunder. I could tell he'd had enough, and I had a feeling he'd been swigging the brandy in the kitchen. He seemed to be searching for a suitable retort. I prayed it would be one that would keep him his job.

– Madam. Moustache is dead.

– What?

– Poosy cat. Is dead.

– What are you talking about?

– The elephant ate him.

– What are you talking about? There are no elephants here.

– It is true, madam. The elephant scooped him in his nose and crunched his little bones.

Raju made appropriate gestures. Mr Aziz came to his defence, though I felt it was too late.

– It is true, darling. I'm sorry, I didn't have time to tell you, but I bought you a beautiful kitten.

I hoped Mrs Marceau would cry. But at this stage her pride was more wounded than her heart.

– There are no elephants here. Raju is lying.

Jeffrey, like an insatiable encyclopaedia, chimed in.

– There are elephants to be found all over India, Mrs Marceau.

She rose and stared at Jeffrey with an almighty vengeance. This was entertaining stuff, but Raju was still bristling with fury.

– Madam, poosy cat is not dead. Poosy cat ran away because you shouted at him.

He spat the words with a viciousness I hadn't seen in him before. I had no idea if it were true. I was pretty sure the cat hadn't been murdered by a homicidal elephant, but he could have been slaughtered by an irate servant. I think this occurred to Mrs Marceau as well. She stifled a shriek with her napkin and, throwing the cloth over her plate, she left the table, close to tears. Mr Aziz called after, *But I Bought you a Beautiful Kitten*, but she ignored him and thundered up the stairs. Raju said nothing and carried her plate to the kitchen.

The rest of the evening passed quickly. Mr Aziz tried to salvage what was left of the party. Armand disappeared upstairs to comfort his mother. Maneka giggled. Frauke and Manfred tried to be funny, but only sharpened the already razor-edged atmosphere. Elke flirted with Raju who, boiling with rage, only narrowly avoided telling her to shut up. Francine tried to talk about maids, but nobody was interested any more. Jeffrey and Donald were completely silent and seemed to be enjoying the evening immensely.

I was not at all happy about the incident. I was worried about Raju. At best he would lose his job. At worst Mrs Marceau might strangle him on the roof in the middle of the night.

Eventually, without having coffee, everyone made their excuses and solemnly exited. I hurried upstairs to get their coats. I could hear Mrs Marceau screaming in Armand's room. It was the most chilling sound I had ever heard and I practically ran downstairs.

Mr Aziz was in the process of saying goodbye. He apologised for the drama and then went to join his wife. Armand reappeared and accompanied the guests outside to their cars. Maneka and Arun began to clear the plates and Raju went to the kitchen with Ishaq.

I slipped outside to watch Armand. I wanted to make sure that girl wasn't kissing him again, but eventually I decided this was undignified and returned to the kitchen. Raju was sitting around the table with Manu, Arun and Ambika. They were drinking what remained of the wine. They didn't bother with glasses but passed the bottle around the table, each taking a deep swig. Everyone was quiet and worried. Ishaq came in and sat down with a few reassuring words for Raju, but everyone knew his chances didn't look good. Ishaq suggested they take the wine back to the bungalow. It was after midnight and it didn't look like Mrs Marceau would show her face again till the morning.

I went to help Maneka. She was sitting at the table, drinking brandy and crying. In the time it had taken me to spy on Armand and then decide against it, she had succeeded in becoming very drunk. I took the rest of the dishes to the kitchen where Ishaq was washing up by himself, and I told her not to stay in the dining room in case Mrs Marceau found her. She said she didn't care. I was torn between helping Ishaq and, out of solidarity, staying with Maneka. I decided to stay with Maneka. I had never been in such a tense house before. The grandfather would be proud, this was serious *Experience of Life*.

– That bitch will make him go. I know she will.

She was sobbing loudly, which made me nervous.

– Mr Aziz won't let her.

– *Him!* Didn't you see? He is almost a servant himself!

– Maybe her son will do something?

She looked at me as though I were crazy.

– Why?

– I don't know. He might.

– Raju will have to go home if he can't find another job.

She descended into floods of tears, her head on the table.

– I could talk to him. I already talked to him once today.

This wasn't an entirely altruistic offer, but Maneka wasn't listening in any case.

– I'll never see him again.

Somehow I coaxed her to leave the dining room and we went into the kitchen where Ishaq had finished the dishes and was cleaning up. Maneka was hysterical now, and was still clutching the brandy bottle. Ishaq tried to take it from her, but she started flailing her arms about and shouting, so he gave up. In the end I persuaded her to go into the garden, thinking that it wasn't a good idea for her to confront Raju in such a condition. Ishaq muttered something, and went on cleaning.

Maneka disappeared into the blackness with the bottle. Women didn't usually drink brandy, so perhaps Mrs Marceau wouldn't notice, though it wouldn't have surprised me if she marked the bottles every morning. I decided to worry about Maneka later. She could take care of herself, and if she didn't return by sunrise then I would go to look for her.

I didn't want to go in the bungalow either. Somehow I felt my presence wouldn't be welcome. So the only thing to do was to talk to Armand, for Raju's benefit.

Armand was still outside, saying goodbye. Ishaq came from the kitchen. He asked me what I was doing and I said I wanted some air. He didn't press me, and walked off towards the bungalow. I sat on the step by the kitchen doorway, watching Armand. Ishaq had turned the lights out, so I was sure he couldn't see me. I couldn't help thinking how much like *Sabrina* this was, the dreamy servant girl, watching the dashing gentleman from afar. Of course, Sabrina had watched from a tree, but I didn't think climbing trees was practical in a sari.

I watched as Manfred slapped him on the back and he walked some distance away from the others with Marie, beyond the gates. I don't think she kissed him, but I couldn't be sure, it was too dark. Armand came back and I heard him shouting for

Manu. And then he saw me. I was certain that by now Manu would be in no state to drive, but I scurried off to the bungalow. Everyone was on the roof, so I climbed the steps and found them sitting in a circle around an oil lamp, still passing bottles of wine around. They were discussing the situation, but when they saw me they fell silent and looked up. I went to Raju and told him that Manu's services were required. Manu's eyes were red, but he said he would give it a go. Nobody questioned his judgement.

I walked back down the stairs with Manu, glad to leave the roof. He was singing softly under his breath, but he managed to walk in a fairly straight line towards the car. I returned to the kitchen step, while Armand waved goodbye. When the last car had gone he walked towards me. I recognised this as my opportunity and stood up. He looked surprised and smiled. I thought he was going to walk past me, but when I stopped, as though to speak to him, he stopped too. He looked tired.

I didn't know what to say and for a while I entertained the possibility of various Holly Golightly one-liners, but then decided to get straight to the point.

– Will Raju lose his job?

This directness astonished him. He walked inside through the kitchen door. I stood in the darkness, wondering how to salvage the situation, when he leaned outside saying, *Come Inside*.

I went. The thought struck me that perhaps, by saying what I had said, I had also put my job in danger. Inside Armand was bending in front of the refrigerator, searching for something. Finally he emerged holding a bottle of champagne. He went into the dining room and returned with two glasses. *You like Champagne?* he asked, undoing his bow tie. I nodded and, taking an oil lamp from the kitchen table, he asked me to follow him into the garden.

This was it! I had willed myself inside the movie! David Laraby. In the tennis court. Except there wasn't a tennis court. Champagne. Two glasses. Not in his back pockets because movies evolve with time, and David had learned his lesson.

We walked in silence. I tried to stand between him and the

bungalow, from where I could hear voices. I looked for Maneka but I couldn't see her. I hoped she wasn't lying in a pool of vomit somewhere at the bottom of the garden. That would spoil things.

When we reached the pond, Armand set the lamp on the ground and we sat on the bench. There was no breeze and the lamp sent a warm, orange glow running across the grass and the water. The moon was reflected in the water, pale and emaciated, thin strips of algae hanging across its face like a wreath. The sky was a watery purple and there were plenty of stars.

Armand opened the champagne and the noise startled me, making me suddenly conscious of the unstoppable rush of events that had flung themselves, one upon the other, to fashion this situation. The movie was running and the lights had dimmed, and now I was conscious that there was only me, enveloped by sound and colour, like in *Majick Movie House*.

He poured the champagne and it slithered into the glass with stuttering protests and gasps. I took the proffered glass but didn't drink. I could see light from the roof of the bungalow. I wondered what Ravi was doing.

– My mother is selfish, but she likes her cats. Sometimes I wish I were a cat.

I related to this. My mother wasn't selfish, but she would have loved to have been a cat.

– Why?

– Wouldn't it be nice? To eat and sleep all day long?

I hoped he wouldn't ask me to dance. I didn't know how to dance.

– My brother eats and sleeps all day.

Armand laughed, but it wasn't a nice laugh.

– Well, he used to work, but he's sick now.

That was a scripted line. I knew the movie had started but I only remembered Holly Golightly afterwards, *He wasn't Dotty, just Sweet, and Vague, and terribly Slow. He's in the Army now. And it's really the Best Place for him, Until I Get enough Money Saved.*

I wondered if Armand was the *Ninth Richest Man in France under Fifty.*

– What's your favourite animal?

That one took him by surprise.

– We like cats.

I drank some champagne. It fizzed in my nose and I held my breath, trying not to sneeze.

– I like monkeys.

– Monkeys scare me.

– Cats are selfish.

– That's why you can trust them. They don't pretend to be loyal.

I hoped we would move on from animal psychology soon. But I thought I was doing well. I drank some more champagne. It didn't get up my nose this time, but I could feel the bubbles rising to my head.

– Will Raju lose his job?

I wasn't thinking before I spoke any more.

– I think so.

– Can you stop it?

Armand laughed.

– Why? You like him?

I wasn't sure what he meant by that.

– Yes.

He laughed again. There was a faint echo. I shook my head and the echo spread to my eyes. Armand's face was shimmering, blurred. I liked that.

– I'll talk to my mother.

Cross your Heart and Kiss your Elbow. It was in the script but I didn't say it. My glass was empty. Armand filled it. His hand was very steady. His movements were graceful. I liked the way he gave the bottle a neat, swooping twist at the end.

– Where do you sleep?

– There.

I pointed to the bungalow from where I could still see a dim light. He looked very quickly, his eyes narrowing like hard, shiny marbles.

– Do you all sleep there?

122

– Yes.

– All together?

He laughed.

– No. The men sleep on the roof.

– Even the driver?

– Yes.

He laughed again, through his nose.

– The driver is funny, isn't he?

Maneka had said just the same thing. I didn't find him funny, *Just Sweet, and Vague, and Terribly Slow*, but I had already used that one so I didn't answer the question.

– My father says it isn't easy to find servants you can trust. That's why he keeps him on.

– Oh.

– My father is depressed.

– Why?

– He wants to retire. He wants to read. We keep telling him, but he doesn't listen. If he works hard for a few more years then he can retire. We have a house in Spain, in the mountains. He can live there.

– Not Kashmir?

– Spain is much nicer.

– But what about his family?

– Oh, Maman will go too.

– But his Uncles and Aunties? And his parents?

– He isn't very close to them. He sees them maybe every three years, then he leaves and they gossip about us. Indian families are like that, aren't they?

– Yes.

He laughed. I didn't like the way he laughed, but I knew Europeans laughed differently from us.

– My father told me about your parents.

I gulped more champagne. I knew the script, I just needed the courage to say it.

– It isn't true.

– What?

– I ran away from home because they wanted me to marry a man I *hated*.

Hated. I had got it right that time. Armand looked interested.

– What do your parents do?

This was the question I had been waiting for. My answer was all prepared. I looked at the ground, concentrating.

– My father is a software engineer and my mother is an actress. They live in Bangalore.

I was perspiring, but my voice had been a still monotone. Software engineer was a good one. My father had a friend who lived in Bangalore. His son was a software engineer, his daughter-in-law was a software engineer, his nephew was a software engineer, and his nephew's wife was a software engineer.

– An actress?

– Yes.

Well, this was more or less true.

– An Indian actress?

– Yes.

This seemed to amuse him. I wished I had said *No*, but it was too late now. I hoped he wouldn't tell Mr Aziz. Then I'd be in real trouble.

– Please don't tell Mr Aziz.

The script was disintegrating. I drank more champagne but it didn't taste of much. I felt like running towards the light from the bungalow.

– I won't tell him.

His hand was in my hair, brushing it back over my ears. He was looking very carefully at me. Not a visual autopsy, much smoother, gentler. I could feel my face shaking. I was having trouble looking at him.

He leaned forward and I couldn't see his eyes properly. They looked big like ponds. I felt his lips brush my cheek, his hair on my face, and I jerked backwards, my glass turning horizontal and spilling over my knees where his hand was. He drew backwards in surprise, wiping his sleeve, and I stood up. I felt sick. I could taste the champagne in my throat. It tasted like stale, sunclotted sugar. I walked in the direction of the light.

It felt like there was a bucket of water sloshing inside my head. I looked back but I couldn't remember where the bench was. Everything was black with silver shadows. I wanted to vomit, but I walked on towards the light. The grass felt thick like treacle. The evening heat had balled inside my head, laughing.

The script was long gone. It had slipped from my fingers and the leaves were floating around in the sky, giggling above my head. Ravi would be laughing, or would he be disgusted?

I reached the bungalow and went inside. The moon was bright and I saw Ishaq sleeping on the floor. I went into the other room. I heard Ambika snoring from the corner. I almost fell on to the bed. I felt Maneka's face, hot and sticky, and I crawled in beside her. She mumbled something and moved closer to the wall.

I tried to shut my eyes but I felt sick and kept them open. There was some light from the window and I tried to focus on it. The effort was so great that I couldn't think. The only thing that mattered was that I didn't vomit. Nothing was still. The window kept shifting, teasing me, swaying so I had to keep moving to look at the light. I tried closing my eyes again and this time things were less chaotic. I pressed my face against the pillow, concentrating on the blackness, and sank into a tangled, spiralling sleep.

It was eight o'clock. Maneka and Ambika were gone and I was late, again. I tried not to worry about it. There were so many things to think about, so much had happened and I deserved a little time for reflection.

The room was pleasantly warm. Ambika had left fresh flowers by her statue of Shiva, and the musky smell of incense clung about the sheets. I remembered what had happened, though it seemed a long time ago now. If only I hadn't drunk so much champagne . . .

Just as I was wondering whether Armand would ever talk to me again, he walked in through the door, followed, interestingly enough, by his mother and Mr Aziz. I knew I was in serious trouble. He had repeated my awful lies, and they had believed them, in place of the awful lies the grandfather had told them. And I hadn't shown up for work, and I was still in bed, casually sniffing the morning breeze. And maybe, maybe Armand had told them about last night's drama, or some version of it. Maybe he was so hurt by my behaviour that . . . but they were all smiling, and smiling at me! It could have been a smile of vindictive pleasure, but it didn't look like it.

Armand sat by my bed and put his arm around me, his mother and father watching. Mrs Marceau and Mr Aziz had linked arms, which was infinitely more disturbing. Armand smiled and smiled, his eyes singing with excitement. Mr Aziz spoke first, *We are So Proud of You, Beti, You're Going to be Very Famous*. Mrs Marceau confirmed this with a nod, *Yes, It's True, It's all Settled Now*. What was settled? Armand smiled and kissed me on the cheek. His lips felt warm and fresh and my head was light and clear now. *My First Film Star Wife!* he said. *First?* Had he been married before? I doubted it.

But What about Raju?, I said, and Mrs Marceau laughed. I had never heard her make a sound like this before, so light, so musical, practically fragrant. *Oh, That's All Old News. He's Waiting for You, with Maneka. But we Wanted to be the First to Congratulate You, After all, We're Family Now*. Mrs Marceau came and sat by Armand and kissed me. There were tears of gratitude in my eyes. I couldn't say anything. I just lay back, with my head against the pillow, smiling from one happy face to the next.

My head hurt. My mouth was dry as a desert and full of caked mucus. I wasn't used to this. Snapshots of the dream flung themselves at my eyes, wet and full of feeling. Against the nausea in my throat and the stabbing, vicious pain in my head, they sickened me, pulling shame from beneath the sheets and rubbing it in my face. I pushed them away, trying to forget.

It was almost six o'clock. I couldn't see the sun, but his smile had broken the sky's sobriety into a maze of pink and yellow streaks. The room was cool, but I could smell vomit. I turned my head. Maneka was fast asleep, her hair was dishevelled and

126

her face, turned away from me, looked grey. I lifted myself on to my elbow and saw that her mouth was leaking dribble and her face was virtually floating in vomit. Fighting nausea, I got out of bed and went to the kitchen. I found a rag and soaked it in water and then returned to the bedroom. Lifting Maneka's head, I pushed her to the other side of the bed and then cleaned up the vomit, trying not to breathe.

I shook her, but she remained comatose. Ambika's blanket was folded on the floor and there was an unlit stick of incense by her Shiva statue. I lit the incense, holding my head over the fumes and breathing deeply. I hoped it would clear the smell. I didn't like leaving Maneka sleeping there, but I didn't think I would succeed in waking her.

I found Raju in the next room. He was boiling coffee on the stove. Ishaq was sleeping. Raju's back was turned to me, but I had the feeling he was crying. When he turned around I could see that he wasn't. He was transformed. His face was a black sunset of pride and fury, stretching powerfully into the distance, shining with an irresistible force, straight from his blood, straight from his liver and stomach. He said nothing, but his look passed through and into my body, making me tremble and smile. He handed me a tumbler full of coffee and inevitably I spilt most of it on the floor, but this pathetic display didn't dampen his demeanour. I raised the coffee to my lips and drank, and as the scalding liquid rasped its furious whisper inside my throat, a deep, fearless laughter shook my body. Raju laughed too, and I felt his laugh rising from over the horizon, roaring high above our heads.

Raju was a small man, and so dark that he usually seemed to slip inside shadows, the coarse, unruly net of his eyebrows dimming the blaze of his eyes. But now, his furrowed skin threw out a brilliant, black glare, flooding the room with darkness. His burnt, retreating face seemed brighter than the sun, with an intensity that cut through all sources of light, spinning them irretrievably into the background. I wondered what would happen when he met Mrs Marceau. Would her shrinking alabaster frame be shaken and spun out of the house and across the ocean? Would her skeletal hand melt into snow when it slapped his face? The thought terrified me, but curiosity propelled me forward.

Arun came inside and pulled up a chair. His face was a matted mess of concentration. His eyes were burrowing inside his tangled head, parting leaves, crawling through moss and lichens. He hadn't noticed Raju's blazing presence and scarcely looked at him when he was handed his coffee. He sipped at it with a grimace. I could imagine it spitting in his throat, burning in the cauldron of his stomach. Arun seemed angry, but his face was as impenetrable as the steel shell of his coffee cup. He remained locked in a furious silence, staring at the time-spun knots in the wood of the table, and then he looked up, his eyes boring into the walls. I could hardly follow what he said, but he seemed defiant, in a Gandhian kind of way. When his eyes, like unaimed gunfire, encountered mine, he gave me a self-absorbed sigh of exhaustion, as though to draw me into his cobweb of frustration and impotence. I didn't care. I refused to look at him.

Raju's brilliance had softened slightly. He made no attempt to outshine this cloud that had passed across the sky. The greyness made me weak, but Raju seemed unperturbed. He sat opposite Arun and looked calmly, quietly, into his eyes. Arun sputtered protests and Raju listened, and then Arun thumped his fist on the table, upsetting his coffee. Raju softly picked up the tumbler, but left the brown liquid lying glibly on the table. He rose, and put his arm around Arun, gripping his shoulder tightly, dispelling the cloud in soft, powerful waves. Arun cried. I stood and watched him. His eyes were closed. He seemed lost in his own reality, clinging stubbornly to the greyness even as it frayed around him.

I noticed that Ishaq had sat up from the floor, watching the scene unfold with pursed lips. Eventually he asked Arun, in a voice so serious that the cloud immediately cleared, where everyone else was. Arun said that Ambika and Manu were on the roof. Ishaq told him to call them and Arun grated his way out of the room. I filled my tumbler with hot coffee and left to fetch Maneka. I felt Ishaq wanted to be alone with Raju.

Maneka was awake. Her head was on the pillow, facing me; her eyes were open, cold and painfully clear. She made no effort to smile, but looked at me with a pallid entreaty. I sat next to her on the bed and gave her the coffee. She could hardly hold it, so I took it from her and helped her to sit up. She didn't resist, and allowed herself to be pulled into a sitting position. I gave her the coffee and this time she drank a little before giving it back to me.

– Where is Raju?

Her voice was pathetically weak, a childish whimper. I realised that Maneka was little more than a girl, but a girl who was used to men and their world, who had accepted it. I wondered if she was happy, but decided she was too young to know.

– Everybody is meeting.

– Now?

– Yes.

Maneka got out of bed and dressed, very slowly. I could practically hear the screaming of her joints and the enraged ringing in her head as she moved. I waited until she was ready, making sure she drank the rest of her coffee, and then we both went into the other room.

Everyone was there. It was the first time I had seen Manu without a big, hairy grin plastered to his face. I sat down on the floor, next to Maneka, whose body was shaking ever so slightly. She looked about to cry, but this could have been for any number of reasons.

The conversation was mainly in Hindi, but Raju would occasionally lapse into Kannada, or would turn to Maneka and myself and explain parts in English. He announced his intention to resign before Mrs Marceau could get to him, and this was met with consternation and outrage from all corners of the room. Manu was adamant that Ishaq should resign instead, because he was older, but I couldn't follow this logic at all. Manu seemed to want to turn Ishaq into some kind of human sacrifice, but in any case, as Raju laboriously explained, it would take nothing less than the slaughter of a thousand live virgins to appease Mrs Marceau. Manu then turned on me, which I hadn't expected at all.

He reminded me that I had hardly eased the situation by letting Raju come to my defence by explaining that non-vegetarians were cruel, heartless people. I couldn't think of a response, but Raju dismissed this idea as ridiculous. The issue was Mrs Marceau's ex-cat, not cross-cultural dietary practices. I eagerly wanted to know if Raju *had* killed the cat, but of course I said nothing, and no one else raised the subject.

Arun became wild. He was outraged by anything anybody said, denied everything, contradicted everyone, and seemed unwilling to accept any possible solution except for the instant metamorphosis of this embittered planet into a fairer, happier, freer world. Maneka's protests were sporadic and tearful. She declared that if Raju left then she would go too. Raju quietly explained that this was pointless, but Maneka said her mind was made up.

I didn't say anything, but then Ambika, who had been equally silent, turned to me and asked in her coarse, croaking voice if I had anything to say. I said that perhaps we should try to talk to Mr Aziz first. Arun spat, and Manu said that I should talk to him, seeing as we were such good friends. This was clearly intended as an insult, but I replied that I would do exactly that, and Manu was silent.

By the time they finished arguing, a decision was made. If Mrs Marceau threatened to fire Raju, then everyone would refuse to work. Everyone would threaten to resign. This decision was made over Raju's head. He found it laughable. He said that Mrs Marceau would fire the lot of them, and there was no point at all in such quixotic proofs of solidarity. In any case, he said, he didn't want to be a servant any more.

After a while a strange thing happened. Everybody, excepting Ambika and Ishaq, stopped listening to Raju. It was as though the object of the discussion had shifted from an attempt to better Raju's fate, to a voicing of our collective hatred for Mrs Marceau. It was no secret that all of us, myself definitely included, hated Mrs Marceau, but everyone seemed determined to demonstrate this. As I looked from Arun's face to Manu's to Maneka's, I could see each of them, inward-looking, eyes gridlocked on a point frozen inside their pasts, shifting stares, grating desires, fighting for lost adulthood.

It was well after seven o'clock. I still hadn't done a proper day's work yet, but no one seemed in a hurry to go anywhere. And just as Maneka was declaring her intention to burn herself alive there was a knock at the door and Mr Aziz entered. He stood in the doorway but didn't come any closer. Raju, who was standing, offered him coffee but Mr Aziz shook his head. He explained, in a mixture of Hindi and English, that Mrs Marceau insisted Raju should go, and that her mind could not be changed. Before anyone could say anything he added that he would begin looking for another position for Raju immediately, and that he was unhappy about everything, but that there was nothing he could do.

Raju nodded, and Arun announced that none of us would start work until Mrs Marceau changed her mind. Raju patted him on the back, but said that he would leave at once. Mr Aziz said that there was no need for that, and that he could stay until he found somewhere else to live, but Raju explained that he wanted to leave at once and that there was no cause for worry.

Mr Aziz left after generously assuming responsibility for all the wrongdoings in the world, and thereby absolving himself from blame for anything. Raju ordered everyone to get back to work.

Mr Aziz's unexpected visit acted as a release for Manu and Arun. Inner conflict was abandoned for the time being and they did as instructed. I doubted that Arun would do much in the garden, and I doubted that Mrs Marceau would require Manu's services that day. Maneka refused, point blank, to go anywhere near the house. But eventually, after much coaxing from Raju, she changed her mind.

There was one unpleasant incident. Just before everyone left for their respective duties, Manu turned on Ishaq. I couldn't understand everything he said, but the general idea seemed to be that Mr Aziz should have sacked Raju *and* Ishaq, but had let Ishaq stay on because he was Muslim. Ishaq just stared. He didn't seem angry, but he did seem surprised, and more than a little hurt.

Eventually, Ambika and Arun told Manu to shut up, which, as seemed to be his habit, he readily did. But the incident stayed in everyone's memory for some time. It made me unhappy. I liked Ishaq, though for some reason I spent most of my time feeling sorry for him.

Raju didn't say goodbye. He said he would be back soon and no one doubted this. But he did take me aside for a few private words. He said that he was sorry about all this, and that he didn't like leaving me alone, but clearly he had no choice. He said that Ishaq and Ambika would look after me. And then he told me, with some amusement, to look after Maneka, and explained that when he was settled in another job we would see each other as often as possible. I thanked him and told him not to worry about me, and then I went with Ambika and Maneka to start my first day of work.

Without it being said, it was decided that Maneka should go upstairs and do something resembling work while Ambika showed me what to do. I was glad of this. I wasn't sure if I could handle Maneka's hysterics, and I had plenty to think about myself.

My work turned out to be much harder than I had expected. The floor was to be swept and mopped, rugs were to be taken outside and beaten, brass and wood were to be polished, *everything* had to be dusted, anything broken or torn or scratched was to be mended, curtains had to be cleaned, the outside of the house was to be mopped and scrubbed, and toilets had to be cleaned, which I was not happy about at all, though I did it. Afterwards, there was washing and ironing, and, Maneka and Ambika both assured me, on a usual day there would be hundreds of other errands. It seemed that Mrs Marceau spent her days sleeping, eating, talking to the cats, and dreaming up new backbreaking jobs for us to do. The cleaning took until two o'clock, but by then the day had only just begun.

Maneka had been right about Ambika. She worked very slowly, though she had a resilient strength and was able to beat rugs and polish floors with more venom than I had thought possible. She muttered to herself constantly, reminding herself of what she was doing, what she had still to do, and what she had done already. She reminded me, at regular intervals, that few people could do this work better than her, and that nobody in the village knew how good she was at it. She seemed very annoyed at this. In fact, this seemed to be what prevented her from collapsing with exhaustion, what gave her that vengeful rug-beating style. I wondered if Maneka would turn into Ambika one day.

I was unused to such work, and I was forced to concentrate so hard that my head began to shake, as though a waterfall were raging through my ears and into my brain. As we sat down in the kitchen to eat, Ambika continued her monologue. Ordinarily I would have found it impossible to follow, but my powers of attention had become unusually acute and against my will I listened to every word. Ambika told me what fools everyone was in the village, how they had sent her to The City because there was no place for her there, and how, in all her years as a maid, she had never broken or scratched a single thing. She then told me, in a hushed tone, how Maneka was a good girl, but how she drank and occasionally stole from *madam*. She told me that in her last job she had been ayah to three Parsi girls, and had cooked for them, and held them on her lap, but how after they had grown up they had become resentful and hadn't cared for her any longer, and had treated her like a donkey. She said that her eyes had been better then, and that she had been learning to read until she had been sent to work for Mrs Marceau.

She said that her last bai had been much kinder than Mrs Marceau and had understood that sweeping is easier for a younger woman than for an older woman, without her having to tell her. She lowered her voice again and said that she wanted to tell Mrs Marceau this, but was afraid of losing her job, and that if she did lose her job she would have nowhere to go to because of the fools in the village. She became incoherent at this point, or perhaps my concentration finally faded. It seemed that she had returned twice to her village, but something had happened the second time that had prevented her from ever going back. She told me she was happy that I was here, and that I listened to her, unlike Maneka. But that I shouldn't blame Maneka for this because Maneka was a very good girl, except that she drank and occasionally stole things, which could get both of them into trouble, and that she was sexually rather loose. At this point Ambika stopped, as though she had gone too far, and then laughed. She said that she had been just the same in her younger days, but that she had got into all sorts of trouble and that the fools in the village had never understood, and although her father was a very honest man, he had never understood, although it wasn't his fault, though she blamed him for the death of her mother, who had been under far too much strain.

She then asked me why I didn't pray in the mornings, and told me that God was very important and not someone to be neglected. I didn't answer the question, but I understood that Ambika was very religious and was taking it upon herself to see that I didn't pick up any of Maneka's loose ways. This was a privilege I could have done without, but I couldn't see how her attentions would prove more than a minor irritation. She told me that she would take me to temple and that she knew that I hadn't had my bath today, and that that was bad, though she didn't say this in a disapproving way. She then told me that her sister used to take her bath in very dirty water, and that she was certain that her sister poisoned her younger brother, though she couldn't prove it. She then told me not to drink, and that Arun was a good boy when he didn't drink, though she didn't look me in the eye when she said this.

Ambika didn't seem bitter exactly, but she seemed to have crystallised her opinions on life, and everyone and everything in it, a long time ago. The things she said didn't seem real at all. Her past didn't seem to be something that had actually happened; it was just a collection of faded photographs, or rather, the memory of a collection of photographs, most of them being lost. She seemed to live partly in these memories and partly in the present, but I wasn't sure that her connection to either of them was very strong. She wasn't very good with names either.

She kept confusing Maneka with her sister, whom she evidently hated, and kept confusing me with her grandfather, which I found strange, and a little disconcerting. I decided that I would listen to Ambika, but not too carefully.

As I finished eating Ishaq came in to give me a letter. He seemed distracted, probably he was upset by Manu's behaviour in the morning. I used the letter as an excuse to get away from Ambika and went into the garden to read it. I couldn't see Arun, but a potential Arun was better than an inescapable Ambika. The letter was from Vijay Kumar's grandfather.

To my dear young friend,

I shall not waste your time with pleasantries. These are testing times and there must be many things that you are eager to know and I shall try my best to satisfy your curiosity on all fronts.

I have seen your mother twice since you left. She misses you and is terribly afraid for your wellbeing. Please write to her and assure her that you are well. If you like, you may post the letter to me and I shall see that she finds it. She will not speak much about the matter, but I am sure of one thing, she is secretly very happy that you did not marry that terrible man. Your father is dreadfully angry, even though now, well, matters are different.

The day after you left, your intended bridegroom was murdered by a young Muslim boy. It seems that this was an act of vengeance for the rape of this boy's sister. Do not think too much about this. What is done is done.

Your sister cried for two days after you left. I did not realise she possessed such emotional reserves. Ravi was attacked by monkeys and also misses you terribly.

That is all. I also miss you very much and my thoughts are with you constantly. I know Mrs Marceau is a hard woman. I have never met her before but have heard bad reports. Mr Aziz is a decent fellow. I have not seen him for over ten years now. I am sure that Raju is taking good care of you.

I have little advice to give. Follow your heart. You are a woman now and have embarked on a difficult journey. Only a fool would turn back from the road to truth once he has begun, and I know you are not a fool.

Your friend,

I agreed that my mother hadn't wanted me to marry the horrible man, and I doubted whether his murder had caused her much grief. My mother had had no education. She hadn't even had a childhood by modern standards. I don't know exactly what it was that my father did to her on her wedding night, but she seemed to carry a shadow of disappointment wherever she went. The first half of her life had been lies. She had been taught only that her husband was a god, and this had turned out to be substantially untrue. And now, she had lost a son to failure, a daughter to Vijay Kumar, and another daughter to – to what? – to a terrifying city, to champagne, to the zoo, and perhaps, though only time would tell, to David Laraby. All this grief, and all this drama, because a man had lost control of a controversial and (everybody agrees) essential function at a critical moment. But there could be another reason . . .

What was the last thing she had said to me? *Go, Go Now. After you Come Back from Your Walk then We Will Talk*. What did that mean? Had she wanted me to go?

It was impossible to say what lay beneath her watery silences, but I imagined whirlpools and rocks. Until now I had seen the grandfather as the sole agent of my freedom, but perhaps my mother was a puppeteer even more skilful than he. There was no way of telling. The best puppeteers keep their mouths firmly shut.

I knew my sister even less than I knew my mother. Of course, we had grown up together, making faces from opposite ends of the room. But as we grew older the faces became increasingly strange, until mine aroused only disapproval and hers just bored me, blended into the greyness of the walls. She may have been jealous, but even this didn't seem so likely.

I had known since I was a child that Ravi was a failure. He had been born, he had made a few whimpers and soiled a few floors, then he had learned to talk, painfully late, and then everyone, simultaneously, on some auspicious day, had pronounced him a failure. Failure wasn't my word, but if Ravi was a failure then so was I. And just when I'd had a chance to redeem myself, I had disappeared. So my sister wasn't crying for me, or for herself, she was crying from shame. That wasn't nice. I wanted her to be happy, I wanted Vijay to try his hardest not to be the monster his father had created, but I didn't want her pity.

My sister's problem was that she only listened to people who talked. And she believed everything they said. Of course, a person could hardly be blamed for not listening to people who didn't talk. But, like my father, she refused to listen to herself, and that was probably a mistake, though I couldn't be certain.

I had a feeling my sister hated me, hated me because I never spoke. And now I had taken all my thoughts, and all my dreams, and had put them as far out of her reach as possible. But this wasn't my fault! I was a girl, or so everyone told me, and if I was a girl, then it wasn't my job to fill the emptiness in my sister's head, or Ravi's for that matter. But Ravi was a different case. He didn't understand monkeys, and I didn't blame him for this, but it was sad that everyone and everything attacked him. I could imagine Ravi sitting in a room, rain spitting on the glass, birds scratching at the window, the wind slashing at his ears. And Ravi just sitting. And in the background, my father's voice. Shouting at him. Telling him, *Drive them Away! No Son of mine Sits Cowering in a Room! Some Things Have to be Done!*

The whole world wanted Ravi to be Vijay Kumar, including Ravi, for what it was worth. But that clearly wasn't going to happen.

The sun was at his hottest. Thinking about Ravi demanded good weather. It was terribly unreasonable to expect a young girl to think such bleak thoughts under baking heat. I folded the letter and put it away. I would write to the grandfather that night, and send a letter for my mother. There wasn't much to say. I would tell her I was fine, but not too fine, and tell her not to worry, though that was unreasonable. My only hope was that quietly, secretly, her inner voice would tell her the truth. Of course, no one would ever know.

Maneka and Ambika had come out to look for me. I could see them in front of the starched, white exterior of the house, squinting into the garden, afraid to go any further. When they saw me Maneka waved me in, as though there was nothing I would like more than to get back to work. Perhaps they thought I had got lost.

I went inside like a dutiful goat. Maneka explained that there was washing to be done, and that she didn't expect Mrs Marceau would remain so quiet for ever. We picked up the clothes and went outside, and for an hour or more we beat the clothes senseless, flinging every trace of human odour from the cloth. I quite enjoyed this. Ambika was fierce, relentless; Maneka was perfectly competent, but rather too graceful for such a vicious job; and I just did my best. I worked much slower than the others, partly because I was unused to the job, and partly because I was tremulously aware that this shirt that bled its soapy mush between my fingers had very recently swayed to the rhythms of Armand's breast. That was a nice thought.

I was glad of Maneka's company. I couldn't help noticing that, despite our three years age difference, she was much more of a woman than I. Plump would not be fair, but there was so much more than the seamless drop that I saw when I looked beneath my chin. Her breasts were constantly moving as she worked, drawing attention to themselves, and she hadn't the slightest trace of self-consciousness in this. Her face was flushed with effort, sweat stood unabashed on her forehead, and as she wiped the moisture away she gave a controlled, cheerful sigh, awash with self-knowledge. She and Ambika shared an understanding which I would be for ever denied.

As Ambika squatted, clutching the soap in a wrinkled hand, her knees forced themselves out to squint at the sunlight. They were hard and charred from the sun, and I found it impossible not to stare at them. And it wasn't that Maneka didn't notice, but she noticed without staring. Ambika's withered, twisted body was nothing remarkable to her. It was as ever-present as the aged face of a rock, or the gnarled scowl of a tree stump. But I couldn't help watching, enthralled and terrified by Ambika's withered breasts, by the time-defying fact that this washed up slab of chewed, congealed misery, was nevertheless a woman.

I wondered, not for the first time, how I appeared to them. I felt timid, precarious, as though the slightest scratch would send me reeling like a stalk in the wind. Ambika just muttered, as though this muttering would cure me of my dread of life. But when Maneka looked at me, or came to my relief when I couldn't do something, she seemed interested in my ineptitude. I think she saw me as terribly exotic because I was so unused to this heat, and to this life of endless work and exhaustion. I think she would have preferred it had I stood by her side and watched her while she did my share of the work. Perhaps she realised, quite correctly, that I wasn't a maid at all, but a film star in training. And this caused her to see me in a certain light of reverence. And in turn, this made me feel uncomfortable, and guilty, which was not something I was used to.

I wondered what Ambika had meant about Maneka being sexually loose. The meaning seemed obvious enough, and was commensurate with those perpetually moving breasts, the way the cloth wrapped itself around her hips, creasing in countless places, and with the wide-eyed, unflinching smile of her belly-button beneath her blouse. But this morning Maneka had seemed such a child as she shuddered away from her coffee, her face pale and drawn against the pillow. I decided that it couldn't hurt to ask her.

Mrs Marceau was shouting for Ambika. Maneka told her to stay where she was, and I ran to answer madam's bidding. Mrs Marceau was standing in the kitchen, and Raju was standing in front of her. When Mrs Marceau saw me she told me to call the guards. Raju, without looking, told me there was no need, he was leaving, and called Mrs Marceau a dog. She trembled with anger and slapped him hard. Raju lifted his hands above her head and she stumbled backwards, but he only spat, and then left.

Mrs Marceau turned towards me, livid and shaking, and again told me to call the guards. I left and went to the bungalow. Raju was there, collecting his things. He saw me and smiled. I smiled back. I told him she had sent me to call the guards, and he told me to go back to the garden, he would send the guards himself.

I did as I was told. Maneka and Ambika were still there, still washing. They asked me what was wrong and I said, *Nothing* and turned away from them, picking up a shirt and wringing it as hard as I could.

I could scarcely believe what I had seen. It was as though the walls of the house had teetered and fallen. I felt safe, here in the garden with the washing, but I didn't want to go back inside the house.

We washed until five o'clock, and then we *had* to go inside to hang out the washing, away from the sun. No Mrs Marceau in sight, but the kitchen echoed with her presence. Ambika took out the ironing board and unfolded it. The rusty legs of the board creaked discordantly with Ambika's own rusted joints. Maneka took out a heavy, black iron and set to work. I passed the clothes, and folded them when she had finished, and Ambika sat on the floor, muttering to herself, or muttering to us, it was hard to tell which.

Ironing was definitely Maneka's strong point. Her slender arms hefted that hunk of metal with surprising fluidity. I watched her work, slightly envious. I had heard of women who did things to other women, but I was pretty certain I didn't fall into that category. In any case, I was a girl, not a woman, and I didn't do things to anyone. That was why I had run away from home. But this knowledge didn't stop me from watching with doubled interest when Maneka slammed that scalding iron up and down Armand's trouser legs. Steam sighed from the cloth, rising up to the dipping curve of Maneka's neck, and Ambika went on muttering. I was starting to feel dizzy. I blamed it on the heat.

The ironing was finished after seven, and Ishaq began to make the dinner. No Raju any more, so Maneka and I helped him. Well, Maneka helped him. I got in the way most of the time. This kitchen confused me. Nothing was in the right place, and everything was easy. Pots and pans were easy to lift, flames were easy to light, taps were easy to turn, knives were sharp and came in every size. I found it all tremendously difficult.

Ishaq didn't have any objection to cutting up squirming lumps of flesh and Maneka watched him do it quite happily. I tried not to look, but ended up watching most of it; watching Ishaq wipe his bloody hands on his apron, watching him flick away unwanted scraps of offal with his fingers, watching him sink a murderous meat cleaver into a quivering, pink carcass, watching it writhe and scream as the steel gasped through bone and cartilage. He wiped the knife on his apron, sweating. I felt sick and went outside.

I hoped I wasn't going to vomit. That slab of meat had looked so vulnerable, and the knife had come down so hard, so mercilessly. I was certain I heard it cry out, an involuntary shriek. And Ishaq's hands were so big, and so bloody. And he had been sweating like an animal. His skin was red. I tried to imagine plunging that knife into my own hand, or my leg. I wondered if my own flesh would be so pink. The blood hadn't gushed or flowed, it had just lain there, too thin to be a pool, clinging to the chopping board as though clinging to life. To Ishaq it was just another job, just another part of the day to get through.

It was dark now, but still surprisingly warm. My clothes were sticking to my skin. I heard a car door slam. It must have been Mr Aziz, back from work, hungry for his meat. Tomorrow he would put on a clean shirt, neatly starched and ironed, drink his coffee, march across that polished floor, the guards would open the gates, Manu would start the engine, and off he would go. And we would work all day so he could do the same thing the next day. And the next day, and the next, until we were all dead. Ambika and Ishaq were more than servants, they were like internal organs. But replaceable, as this morning's drama had confirmed.

I heard footsteps behind me. It was Maneka. She said Ishaq had told her to go, he would serve the meal. I had wanted to help him, Armand might be at the dinner table and I wanted to see his face. I wanted to see if he was angry, to see if he had told them. I doubted he had. He seemed to live in his own, carefully stylised world, and it was that world that I wanted to enter. I was certain that everything I was looking for was there. It would be like jumping into a movie. And so far, no movie had started, except for those few, longed-to-be-forgotten moments in the garden when everything had gone wrong. So far I hadn't succeeded in crawling out of the real world. In fact, it had got worse, more real and more oppressive, enfolding me in its acrid breath. But I was sure that Armand's shiny eyes, and his long, floppy black hair, contained a universe so expansive, and so colourful, that if I could only find a way inside it, the real world would crumble into dust.

Maneka and I went into the bungalow. It was after eight o'clock and I felt ready for bed. I hadn't eaten dinner, but I wasn't hungry. I was just exhausted, and the longer I stayed awake the longer I would have to accept that this relentless world was indeed the one I inhabited.

I slept like a mummy for two hours. I think Maneka tried to wake me to tell me to eat, but I might have dreamt it. I was so tired that the musty odour of the sheets didn't frighten me, and the air, awash with flies and dusty, sticky heat, didn't repulse me. I just pulled the sheet over my head and crawled inside, too tired to be aware of what I was doing. As sleep arrived I realised, with relief, that I could leave this world as easily as I could the one at home.

I dreamt of a dog I had seen at a bus station. A wheel had crunched over the tar and cut open his stomach and he had run around yelping, protesting at the injustice of a world he hadn't created. Some women had made sympathetic noises, and he had run around, hopping with pain, looking for a shadow where he could spill his guts in peace. The flies had gathered, ecstatic at this unexpected gift, and the dog had run off and the women, with churned stomachs, boarded the bus, dissatisfied with life, but not their fault. I couldn't see the driver. He would have heard the commotion, he would have seen the flies hissing in delight, and he would have shaken his head, dissatisfied with life, and gone on reversing. It wasn't his fault, buses didn't wait for dogs, and didn't he know that the coolest place to sleep isn't always the safest? Not the dog's fault, but not his fault. The wheel was painted with entrails and blood, but the wheel was grimacing too, not the wheel's fault.

I awoke as Maneka was squeezing herself between me and the wall. It was after ten o'clock. I was used to being awoken from strange dreams at strange times, but it took me a while to remember where I was. Even when I was certain, and called her by her name, I still felt that something was wrong, that this was Ravi, cleverly disguised. I couldn't see her face, but the warmth of her shoulder against my cheek was reassuring, like a soft glow in a dark room.

– Aren't you hungry?
– No.
– You should eat something.
– I don't want to.
– Eat something, just a little.
– I'm happy where I am.
– All right.

I couldn't see her. I hoped she wasn't angry. As so many people did, she might take it as a personal insult that I refused to eat food she hadn't cooked. But I doubted it; she was just being herself. I was thankful for this, otherwise there would have been little point in my leaving home.

– You'll get used to it, the work.
I hoped not.
– I hope so.
– Raju is gone.
– I know.
I wondered if she was crying.
– He didn't say goodbye.
– He'll come back.
– He was my best friend –

She was crying. I couldn't hear it in her voice, but I could feel tears against my forehead.

– but you're here now, so it doesn't matter.

I wondered if this was a good time to ask her about her lack of morals. I was still burning with curiosity and I felt rested, and the room was much cooler.

– Maneka, do your parents want you to marry?

– Oh no, that's why I'm here.

– Oh.

– I know I can't marry Raju, he's already married, so I just enjoy myself.

Aha!

– *How* do you enjoy yourself?

– What do you mean? You don't know about *It*?

– No, not really.

Not at *all*.

– You never liked a man?

– Not really, I don't know, maybe.

There. I had articulated my emotions as clearly as I knew how.

– So you've never done *It*.

– No, of course not.

The *Of course Not* wasn't really necessary, but even though I had raised the subject, I was determined to make it clear that this wasn't something I *wanted* to talk about.

– Why not?

I remembered the grandfather asking the same sort of question.

– I don't know. It's bad for you, isn't it?

That was the truth. Everyone had told me *It* was bad for you, diseases and babies and that sort of thing, and I had never questioned this.

– No, not really . . . not at all.

My mother had done *It*, hadn't she? It didn't seem to have done her much good, though perhaps this wasn't *It's* fault. It probably had something to do with my father, and my father, thankfully, had *nothing* to do with Armand.

144

– I like Armand.

Quelle confession! There was no turning back now.

– Who?

What did she mean *who*? The one with sunshine in his hair! David Laraby! The walking, talking, godlike, perfumed, ambassador of perfection. *Who?!*

– Mr Aziz's son.

– Mr Aziz's *son!*

Her voice reeled with astonishment, even outrage. I hoped I hadn't said anything wrong, but I decided that this was a good time for honesty. I felt more confident now, now that I had done a proper day's work.

– Yes.

She didn't say anything. I felt she was going to slap me, or storm out of bed and wake the others. I wondered if it was too late for me to pretend it was all a mistake. I had meant someone else. Or I was still dreaming, or drunk, or completely insane.

– That will be difficult.

There was a latent admiration in her voice, but her tone was very serious, as though evaluating a business proposal.

– I spoke to him yesterday, in the garden.

– I know. I saw you. I thought you were talking about Raju.

That sounded like an accusation.

– We were, but, but I drank some champagne, and he tried to kiss me.

– He *tried* to –

– Yes, but I ran away.

– Why?

– I don't know.

I felt like crying, but this was time to be an adult. *Experience of Life, Damn It!*

– If Mrs Marceau finds out she will kill you.

I could believe that, after what I'd seen in the kitchen.

– So, do you think –?

– With him, you will *have* to do *It*.

– Why?

– No question about it. That is what he wants.

– No it isn't.

Now, admittedly, I didn't have this information on any authority.

– Why do you say that?

I didn't like her talking about me like that.

– I don't like you talking about him like that.

– Don't be silly. There's nothing wrong with *It*, that's just how boys *are*.

– I don't think I want to do *It*.

– If you want him to like you, you'll have to.

This was serious stuff. I had never considered myself to be the sort of person who did *It*. Even thinking about *It* seemed wrong. It was as though someone else were thinking these thoughts and had put them in my head as a cruel joke. Either that, or it was just gross self-indulgence, the sort of thing a silly girl does when her parents aren't there to police her.

Maneka was different. She actually did the things other people thought about. But she was even lower than me in the great chain of being, or she cared less about herself. Or she was braver, less afraid. Perhaps that was it.

Perhaps she was already living her movie.

My dreams were complicated, confusing.

I was praying to God. Armand was praying to me.

Praying for me to do *It*.

And I was trying to find out if I should.

Raju came in and distracted me, refusing to pray. I should have been angry, filled as I was with divine fervour, but I wasn't, because Raju was a child. This didn't seem strange, this being a dream.

So this child ran around the temple, throwing the flowers about and laughing.

The priest frowned, but Raju was a child so he didn't do anything.

But then Mrs Marceau came in, and the priest shrank and

kept on shrinking till he was a squeaking mess on the floor. Mrs Marceau kept spitting, swiping at the air like a cat.

The priest was far too small for her. (She couldn't eat him alive or gouge out his eyes.) So she ran, scratching her way around the temple.

Gods leaned towards her, eternity spinning in their eyes, an anger infinite and consuming.

They would lurch towards her, staring deep inside, and she would scream and twist and run in the other direction. Wherever she turned, they were there. (What did she expect?)

So Mrs Marceau went careering around that temple, faster and faster, whipping the air, ensnared, hysterical fear.

I kept praying, but I was afraid of those claws landing in my back, tearing my flesh.

And there was Raju (who hardly seemed to notice Mrs Marceau). He kept running around with those tiny legs and his curly, moondipped hair. And when at last, inevitably, their two paths collided, caged beast and frolicking child, Raju smiled, sweetly, irresistibly, and laughed his gurgling, bubbling, crystalpure laugh.

And Mrs Marceau didn't scratch out his eyes, didn't rip his lungs from his chest, but turned and went writhing off again, running from eyes, running from swords, running from Hanuman's mace, running from the gleam in Rama's smile.

I wanted to pray, but with all these distractions . . .

Outside now. Far from the temple, far from Raju, far away from Mrs Marceau.

Sitting on a sofa with Maneka. She wore pearls on her neck, diamonds in her toes, rouge on her cheeks, smoking a thin cigar.

Her legs were bare
so were mine when I looked down
elasticlace on skin

I looked around worried – what if someone saw me? – but I took the proffered cigarette, burning in its holder, and inhaled – sweet like perfume

looking down
moonskin, soft and pale
arms snake smooth
the lace of my blouse, strung like time
forced with a secret
A terrible timefree laughter
Maneka and me
drunk in Space
legs entwined, alabaster vines
a song to make reality dance.
I turned to her and laughed and her eyes were oceanblue,
drowning history.

4

The sun had finally cracked. One day he had risen, violent and furious, and the next day his head was bent over the clouds so everyone could see his greying hair, his infirmity and depression. I was pleased. It hardly seemed right to delight in Surya's personal problems, but here in The City my old respect and reverence had turned into sickly frustration. I still wasn't convinced that this sun, with the rage of a demonic child, was the same smiling face I had come to love at home. So his downfall, if it could be called that, was my triumph, although I knew better than to think his retreat had anything to do with me. Anyway, the air was tolerably cool and the days moved faster, spurred by lighter feet.

Raju was long gone. No new cook had arrived, but it would only be a matter of time. I had a mental picture of him; fat and ugly, with an apron covered with grease and blood, fond of drink, fond of teasing girls. I already hated him, and Maneka was ready to split his head in two as soon as he tried to set foot in the bungalow.

Such changes meant nothing to Ambika. She went on muttering and praying, cleaning and belching. Ishaq had become even quieter, I think because Manu was relentlessly hostile, glaring at him across the table. Once I even saw him kick him while he was sleeping, and then pretend it was an accident. I didn't like this, but there was nothing I could do.

I hardly saw Arun. I was less afraid of him now, but I hadn't forgotten that night. He seemed unhappy, frustrated, and he stayed in the garden even later than he was required, which was a phenomenally long time. I don't know what he did there. I think his son had died, but I didn't ask him and nobody mentioned it. I still didn't think that Arun's problems excused his terrifying behaviour on my first night, but it was an unwritten law – no one was allowed to mention what Arun did when he was drunk. I saw him drunk again, on more than one occasion, and he was equally unpleasant, though he never ventured into my bedroom again.

I was two thousand rupees richer. The guard had returned my money. I think Raju was responsible for this, but I became friendlier with the guards. I smiled once or twice, and I even talked to them once. They were very curious about why I had entrusted all my worldly assets to their safekeeping, and I told them, which took great courage. They laughed for a very long time, and then all of them clapped me on the back. I think they liked me. I was better at talking to people now, or rather, better at not talking and getting away with it. The instant repulsion I used to arouse in others had lessened; at times it was even replaced by something close to acceptance.

I wasn't completely happy about this. This was all good *Experience of Life*, but I didn't want to forget why I was really here. I was a film star in training, not a servant, but nobody seemed to realise this except for Maneka. Maneka and I never talked about *It* again. She could tell I didn't want to.

Work was the same, except that Mrs Marceau recovered her ferocity after she was sure that Raju was well and truly gone. I understood what Maneka had been talking about now. The trick was to make the cleaning and washing and ironing last all day, and then to make a big fuss in the kitchen, running around as though the meal would never be ready on time without our help. Otherwise Mrs Marceau would pounce on any spare body, putting it to work, creating the most inventive and strenuous jobs she could think of.

On one occasion the kitten got stuck under the piano. Actually, he didn't get stuck, he was just too terrified to come out. But the official job description was *Removal of Stuck Kitten*. The piano was raised on legs off the ground, just high enough for me to crawl under. Now it must be emphasised that after Raju's exit, this kitten had become the victim of all Mrs Marceau's fury. The kitten, as an intruder from Outer India (that is, from outside the house), and as Mr Aziz's peace offering, had come to symbolise all Mrs Marceau's frustrations. So it was hardly a surprise that he was hiding under the piano.

I didn't like being selected for this job. Kittens scratch, and as I advanced towards him, crawling on my elbows, my face was perilously exposed. Mrs Marceau was watching, her hand on her hip, but as I crawled further under the piano her face receded from vision leaving only her legs. I quite liked it under the piano. I felt a quiet solidarity with the kitten, the two of us cowering in this dark cave with the evil witch's legs sealing our escape.

The kitten shrank further under the piano as I advanced. I sighed. I was certain I wasn't going to come out of this unscathed. I could hear Mrs Marceau barking instructions in her tense, military voice, and I reached out my hand, making a few soothing noises. The kitten swatted my hand, thankfully without his claws, and then dashed past my face, pitter-pattering over my body and across the room. I sighed and sank my head into the rug. I could hear Mrs Marceau yelling, but for the time being I was safe in my cave.

I was trying to decide on the most dignified way of getting out from there when I heard Armand's voice. I think he was asking what was happening. He sounded very amused. After all, he could see my legs sticking out from under the piano, with the kitten probably making faces behind me.

This was going to be difficult. Every time I tried to reverse my sari lifted higher and higher, and there was no room for me to lift my arm and pull it down. I stopped, paralysed. I would have waited until he left the room, but I had a feeling he considered *Removal of (Un)Stuck Kitten* to be some sort of spectator sport. I wasn't enjoying the situation at all. My face was pressed tightly against the rug, bits of fluff had found their way into my mouth (admittedly, that was my fault – I was supposed to have cleaned the rug) and, with every movement I made, Armand could see more and more of my legs. Even from where I was I could sense Mrs Marceau's frustration increasing. I hoped she wouldn't drag me out by the feet. That would be unpleasant. She kept barking unhelpful comments like, *What are you Doing?* and *Are you Going to Stay there All Day?* To make matters worse, Armand kept laughing. I didn't like that, and it only served to prick Mrs Marceau's temper even more. This didn't look good.

Armand came to my rescue by lifting up the end of the piano. I reached down and covered my legs, and then exited with as much dignity as possible. He smiled and I blushed. He could have done that *earlier!* But I suppose that would have spoiled his fun.

The kitten was under the sofa now. The thought crossed my mind to take a long broom and swing the handle around, but I don't think even Mrs Marceau wanted him dead. Another dead pussy cat would be too much for a woman of such acute sensitivity. To make matters worse, Armand announced that the kitten had left me a present under the piano, so my next job was pretty obvious.

Eventually I had the idea of bringing a saucer of milk from the kitchen and placing it in the centre of the room. The kitten went for it and Mrs Marceau scooped him up and put him outside. When she returned I looked at her, trying to conceal my pride behind a show of modesty, but she said, *Why didn't you do that First of All?*

My patience was fraying. Armand laughed again and I lowered my head, fighting every instinct that gripped me. I was torn between exploding at her, slapping him, running outside in a huff, or just screaming. But I did none of these and just stood there. She told me to clean up the kitten's mess and I went to fetch a cloth and soap.

Armand caught up with me in the kitchen.

– Congratulations, with the kitten I mean.

This was the first time we had spoken since *That Night*.

– Thank you.

– I'm sorry for laughing at you, but you did look very funny.

I was still embarrassed, and I hoped he couldn't read it in

my face. I didn't say anything, my voice would have given me away.

– The other girl has the day off tomorrow, so you will have to clean my room. Is that all right?

– Yes.

I looked at him, trying to keep my eyes as low as possible. I wished I could wear a veil or something, it would make talking much easier. I kept thinking about doing *It*. I wondered if that was really what he wanted. I knew what Maneka would say if I told her about this, but I wasn't going to tell her.

– Good.

His eyes were gleaming. He smiled and walked past me, his hand brushing against my hip. I sat down for a while, trying to control my runaway breathing, and then went back to the living room with a bucket of soapy water, cursing the kitten.

The next day the kitten was sacked. Mrs Marceau had Manu dispose of him. I'm not sure how he accomplished this. I hadn't the heart to ask. Mr Aziz grabbed my arm as I served him his croissant, speaking in his now familiar conspiratorial whisper.

– So, the damn kitten had to go, eh?

– Yes, Uncle. Manu took him.

– Shame, shame. I want to buy my wife something. She is angry with me, you know. I need to make amends. Do you have any suggestion?

– For a gift?

– Yes, a gift.

Cyanide was the only word that leapt to mind.

– I don't know, Uncle.

– I was thinking of a ring, from silver, maybe with sapphires. I was thinking you could come with me, to choose.

– Of course, Uncle.

– She is a difficult person to buy gifts for.

– Why, Uncle?

Mr Aziz often gave me very interesting information in these conversations.

– Well, once I bought her a book, a collection of Urdu poetry, translated into French, and she put it in the bin. She said I should have known better. She said a gift should be something *she* wanted, not something I wanted her to have.

That sounded more like protection money than a gift.

– Last year I bought her emeralds, to make a necklace from, and she put *them* in the bin as well. She said she didn't wear emeralds and I should have known. But it was my fault. I *should* have known.

– Uncle?

– Yes.

– Where is Raju?

Mr Aziz immediately assumed the position of a hunted squirrel, hunching his shoulders and nibbling while twitching his head from left to right. He got up and closed the door then brought his chair closer to me.

– Mrs Marceau must never learn of this.

I nodded, trying to conceal my excitement. This was a tremendous victory.

– I am looking for another position for him, and . . .

He resumed the squirrel position for a moment and then regained his composure.

– and I have been sending him money, for his family. *Sshh!*

I hadn't said anything.

– Don't tell her, all right?

– Of course not, Uncle.

Of course not.

– I like Raju, beti, but there was nothing I could do. You must understand.

– Yes, Uncle.

– Though I wonder whatever did happen to that cat.

– Do you really think he ran away?

– It's possible. He was the sensitive type and . . .

Squirrel position.

– and she could get very mad with him when he misbehaved.

– Or maybe the elephant ate him?

154

– I don't think the elephant ate him.
– Why not?
– There is no elephant here, that I can think of.

He knitted his brow, searching his memory for local cat-killers. I was enjoying this immensely. I was now convinced that Mrs Marceau's diamond-studded friends had been sipping pussy cat soup at the party.

– Mrs Marceau was very attached to the cat, wasn't she, Uncle? Squirrel position.
– Oh yes. She . . .

He lowered his voice and turned his head sideways to get a clear view of the door.

– she lives for those blasted cats. Talks to them all day long.
– But she does other things, doesn't she?
– She shops. Oh God, she shops. Do you like shopping?
– No.

Shopping was hardly a leisure activity in our family. He might as well have asked if I liked breathing.

– Neither do I. But she and Armand, for days . . . nothing but shop. Every time in Hong Kong, all the time, shopping, shopping, shopping.
– And what do you do?
– I stay in the hotel sometimes and read. And sometimes I just take it.

He smiled. Poor Mr Aziz. I could picture him, dragged along on a leash from shop to shop, cheque book in hand.

– Anyway, beti, today you and I are going shopping for sapphire rings. You promised.
– Definitely, Uncle.

Definitely.

– Well, shall we go?
– I have to dry the floor, Uncle, it's still wet.

I left and went into the corridor. When I reached the living room door I stopped. I could hear Armand and Mrs Marceau talking very loudly in French. A hand touched my arm. It was Mr Aziz.

– I wouldn't go in there, beti. They are fighting.

– Why, Uncle?

– Because of money.

He sighed.

– It seems Armand has been rather too free with his mother's credit card.

– Oh.

– Well, let them fight it out. It doesn't really matter. Let's go.

In the car I decided to explore this matter further.

– Do they often fight, Uncle?

– Oh yes, all the time. Sometimes they shout so much that neither of them can speak above a whisper for the rest of the day.

– Really?

– Oh yes, beti. Those two can get really angry. It was worse six months ago when Armand came back from Oxford. My wife had withdrawn all his money from his bank account and spent it in Hong Kong. She took him for a shopping trip to compensate, but he still wasn't happy, and then . . . bang!

He raised his hands towards the sky with heavy melodrama.

– He was shouting and crying and screaming, and she turned white as a sheet! Really, quite white! But she bought him a watch in the end, a gold watch, quite lovely, and they didn't fight after that, not for a while anyway.

Mr Aziz burst into a loud guffaw, but then, realising his laughter wasn't fooling me for a minute, he gripped the wheel and looked at the road.

– You see, beti, they don't really operate as you and I do. They explained it once. They said they are naturally less relaxed than us. They said that Indians are very relaxed and Latin people aren't. It is simply a question of . . . temperament.

– Latin people?

– Ah yes, well, you see this is a question of anthropology. Armand and my wife are French, and my wife and, er, my son, like to call themselves Latin people. Anthropologically this is rather a

156

tricky matter, but, er, there we have it. After all, identity is rather a matter of self-perception when all is said and done. You see?

I understood completely. I saw myself as a film star.

– Anyway, to complete this little explication, Armand and his mother are of, erm, highly strung temperament. And so, or at least this is the way they explained it to me, when they lose their temper with each other, or with me, I am not to take it badly. Otherwise I would be guilty of . . . erm . . . racism.

I nodded, completely confused.

– Yes, yes. But I just wish they didn't shout so much. I get headaches very easily you know, beti, and . . .

He didn't finish the sentence. He seemed to be running out of energy, even his driving lacked its usual aplomb.

– Well, I suppose Latin people are like that, Uncle.

It wasn't my habit to be so cruel, but Mr Aziz's air of quiet resignation somehow drew it out of me.

– Quite right, beti, quite right.

He wiped his head with his handkerchief and then dabbed at his eyes a little which made me feel terribly sorry for him, though not wholly repentant.

– You see, beti, sometimes I feel the two of them are playing a game, just playing some game.

– Yes, Uncle?

– Yes, yes. I don't really understand you see. It's all so, well, so damn confusing . . .

We had arrived. Thankfully, Mr Aziz never completed his eulogy on the mysteries of domestic psychology.

We spent most of the morning going from one jeweller to the next. I liked it. The shops were bright and cool and everyone was polite and friendly. I had hoped that at least one of the shops would look like *Tiffany's*, but they all fell short of the mark.

Mr Aziz didn't find anything suitable. In each shop we were shown a selection of rings with stones of various sizes. Mr Aziz would enquire about the biggest, heaviest stone, and would divide the price by three. He assured me that this method always gave the true value. Each time he would shake his head sadly, thank the jeweller, and then we would leave. I was concerned for his plight.

– Perhaps we should think of a cheaper gift, Uncle?

– No, not cheaper, not cheaper.

– But then –

He smiled.

– Those damn stones were *too* cheap, beti. Sapphires are always cheap here, although she can't know this.

– Well, maybe we could get something more costly. What stones aren't cheap?

– I don't know, diamonds perhaps. But she already has plenty of diamonds.

– Well, maybe you could buy two rings?

– Then she would *know* they were cheap.

This was a serious problem.

– What about something else?

– Like what?

– What about a pen?

– What would she do with a pen?

– Well, she could write letters with it. Does she ever write letters?

– I think so. She wrote me a letter once. I had to go to Australia for a project and she decided to stay in Hong Kong. We hadn't seen each other for a month and she wrote me a letter . . . in beautiful handwriting . . .

His eyes went a little misty.

– actually it was more of a shopping list than a letter. And I'm not sure if she wrote it herself . . . it could have been Armand. But damn it all, what makes you think my wife would want a pen?

– I saw some pens in the last shop. They looked very expensive.

– Yes, I saw them too. I still think jewellery is a better idea, if only she didn't already have so many wretched diamonds.

In the end we chose a gold pen, inlaid with diamonds. This

seemed a good compromise. It cost the price of two rings. Mr Aziz was happy, but nervous.

– I hope she uses it. I think she'll like it. She hit a shopkeeper once for not having a pen. She wanted to write a cheque and he gave her a pencil from behind his ear. She slapped him, said it was covered in oil. He didn't know what to say, he kept apologising and she slapped him again! In the end he sent his son out to buy three pens. I don't know how she gets people to do these things for her.

He pursed his lips in thought.

– But I think she'll like it. The diamonds are very big.

He took it from its case and held it up to the sunlight. I was terrified that someone might steal it, but there was no one around.

– Next time I buy a pen for you, eh?

An interesting idea. I wondered what Ravi would say if he saw me with a diamond-studded pen behind my ear.

– You like diamonds, beti?

He was teasing me, but I had waited years for someone to ask that question. I delivered my line with great accomplishment.

– Well, Uncle, diamonds are tacky for a woman under forty.

– Eh, what's that? Tacky? Well, yes, I suppose so. Quite right, beti.

He laughed and patted me on the head. His spirits were high and he drove off in his usual apocalyptic style. He was sweating like a hippo and kept repeating as he drove, *An Excellent Gift. Excellent. She Will Like It. She Will Like It.*

I wasn't so optimistic. I fully expected to wake up and find him at breakfast with the pen sticking out of his eye.

Mr Aziz took me to a hotel for Pepsi, as a reward for being *Such a Good Little Helper.*

The hotel was very Holly Golightly, and I tried my best to look important. Two European women were standing at Reception with cameras around their necks. A tousled-haired man came up to them, and almost fell at their feet before asking if they needed a taxi. They seemed mortally offended and, ignoring him, continued talking. This irritated the man and he repeated the question, much more loudly. They looked at each other, seething with indignation. The resilient driver repeated the question a third time and followed it up with a barrage of the destinations he could take them, *At the Fastest Speed Possible.* They seemed unimpressed, and one of the women, without taking her eyes from the ceiling, proclaimed that they didn't require any taxi. The driver explained that he was very competent, knew the city very well, and was certain that the ladies were in direst need of transport. The women had had enough by now, and left the hotel in a huff, announcing, *They Shouldn't Let them in Here!* We all saw them climb into a taxi outside and disappear.

The driver turned to us and exclaimed in exasperation, *Those Damn Gorah Women don't Know What they Want! If a Taxi runs away Down the Street they Chase after It, but when it Comes to their Bloody Door and Bites them on the Backside they tell it To Go Away!* I gave a shy smile. He definitely had a point. Mr Aziz, surprisingly, was most sympathetic. He offered to buy the driver Pepsi as well.

We sat for a while and Mr Aziz and the driver talked, each complaining about their respective wives, sons, clients, jobs and lives. It was engaging stuff.

After a while, the driver said he had to get back to work. He offered to drive us home, but Mr Aziz explained that we had a car, so he wished us luck and left. Mr Aziz was on his second whisky and looked sad to see the driver go. He paid for the drinks, and after a last look at the diamond-studded gift, we drove off.

The next day Mrs Marceau left for Paris, and I received a letter from the grandfather.

To my dear young friend,
    I have seen to it that your mother received your letter. I left it in the kitchen among the vegetables, where she would be sure to find it. On my next visit she told me how astonished

she was that it had magically appeared in her house. She does not suspect my involvement. After all, I am a senile old fool to most people. She was very happy to know that you are well. I suspect she is secretly glad that you ran away, I cannot be sure of course, she says so little.

Your father still acts angry most of the time. He behaved very strangely when he learnt of the death of that awful man. He cursed you, as though it were your fault. I think he finds it hard to believe that a man he selected so carefully could turn out to be so low. But as you know, he finds it hard to be flexible. He believes there is a right way to do things and a wrong way, nothing more. He finds solace in whisky, and cards, on which I understand he wins and loses quite a lot of money. Despite his failings, I firmly believe that your father is a good man, though this does not necessarily make him a good father, or husband.

Ravi has built a shrine to you in his bedroom. He has placed your picture on top of your books, together with some locks of hair he collected from your hairbrush. He decorates it with flowers that he picks daily. He has become quite mad, in a very endearing sort of way. He still makes long and ornate speeches. The extraordinary thing is that there is a sort of supernatural wisdom in what he says, although I suspect he does not understand his own words. Like so many of us who speak words of wisdom, he is heard by very few. I do not think anyone takes him seriously. I wish I could think of some way to give his life meaning, but I cannot.

Your sister has given birth to a baby girl. I believe she is very happy about it. As we both know, my grandson is an arrogant fellow, and not always pleasant company. A baby will give her someone to love.

I hope Mrs Marceau is not being unkind to you. I learned from Raju that he lost his position, something to do with a cat if I am not mistaken. I am investigating other avenues for him.

Never forget that you are a woman, that you belong to life as much as life belongs to you. Never run from truth or suffering or pain. Never think with anything but your heart. I hope you have found friends, you deserve to be understood. Do not try to understand yourself, leave that for others. And do not try to understand life, life is to be lived, not to be explained away.

Enough advice! Enjoy life, drink deeply of it. Be free. My thoughts are never far from you.

Your friend,

Ravi was intriguing. Every day he became more ridiculous. If he went on like this people would *have* to take him seriously. Ravi had tried being a *Big Man* whom people would respect. He had pursued success, and failed. Then he'd tried to be a bitter, broken man, and failed at that too. It seemed to me that failure at failure equates to *some* sort of success.

I loved my brother very much, for his rudeness and ill-humour as much as for his carefully veiled affection and kindness. I had been the only real thing in his life. He used to fling all his emotion at me, then search my face for approval, or occasionally, disapproval. Now he had lost the only real component of his existence, which was dangerous for someone with so little imagination. I could picture him, clutching at air, then, as he realised air cannot be embraced, sliding lower and lower into the depths of pain. Without me, Ravi *had* to find something real, otherwise he would go . . . *insane*. I didn't like this word; it was casually tossed around at anyone who found the world a little odd at times, and made the mistake of telling people about it. But the insanity that threatened Ravi was very serious; it was the insanity of a man who finds himself floating over the more obvious scraps of reality that others nail to the ground in desperation. So when the grandfather said that Ravi was starting to talk sense, I believed him.

Ravi's speeches might have earned him a few bruises from my father. He didn't have much time for philosophy, especially not from his dumbhead son. I wondered if my father would ever stop beating Ravi. It didn't look likely. I had never stopped to think about Ravi and my mother. She always looked at him very tenderly, as though she wanted to take him in her arms and hold him, but wasn't allowed. She served him his food of course, and he greedily slurped at it while she watched him. But I doubted if they ever talked.

On the other hand, my mother and *I* rarely talked, technically. But it felt as though our private worlds had meshed, though the flow of ideas was usually one-way. I felt certain she could read my mind, while hers remained infuriatingly opaque to me. But then, hadn't the grandfather told me to live and not to try to understand. He had also told me that I was a woman now, but I wasn't so sure.

But my sister was definitely a woman. She had walked straight into it, like a lamb to the slaughter. No sideways glances, no tantrums, no bizarre personality traits – just a simple, honest, tiptoe to the knife. I doubted if she had even screamed much. It wouldn't have occurred to her.

My sister had typhoid once, when she was small. She almost died. I remembered her face, covered with red sores, her eyes, like bashful moons, peeping out at me. She was frightened, but she didn't fight it. She just lay there, shivering. I was sure she thought me very selfish. While she was shivering with fear, I was running around having a good time. But why was that my fault? How would it help her if I also curled up in bed, shaking with fright? I think my mother had found me selfish too. Ravi hadn't, and my father hadn't noticed. He was busy poring over his accounts – the medical fees had almost bankrupted him.

He was a grandfather now! I wondered how he felt about that. Probably he was proud. Vijay had done his job, my sister had done hers. Everything had turned out nicely. It wouldn't make up for my disgrace, but it was better than nothing.

I wrote back to the grandfather, telling him all about Raju and my theories on the cat. I told him I didn't like Mrs Marceau, but I made no mention of Armand. I wasn't sure how he would react if I told him I was considering doing *It*. He might tell me to go for it, *Experience of Life!*, and I didn't want to hear that. This business of doing *It* weighed heavily on my mind. *It* seemed important. Holly Golightly must have done it plenty of times. All actresses did.

If I was going to do *It*, Armand seemed the best bet. He wasn't Vijay Kumar, and he wasn't the horrible man. My father had nothing to do with him, nothing at *all*. In fact, I doubted if Armand would have given him the time of day. That was a good thing, a plus point, but there was plenty on the minus side. I didn't like blood and I didn't like screaming, but Maneka had said it wasn't like that, hadn't she? She had said it was nice. And then there were diseases and babies and that sort of thing, but probably Armand knew ways around that. Nevertheless, I didn't want to do *It* just so Armand would like me. I wanted him to like me first.

There seemed a clear logical obstacle here. For Armand to like me, I would have to be a film star. But for film stardom, having done *It* was an essential prerequisite. A solution might be to do *It* with someone else, and then to do *It* with Armand. But I couldn't think of any other suitable candidates.

Unless, what about the boy with the bananas, from the zoo? What was his name? Maybe he would want to do *It*. But he had been a very nice boy, very kind. I had liked him, which was an obvious obstacle to doing *It* (my mother would have liked him). And maybe he wouldn't want to do *It*. Maybe he was happy giving me bananas and showing me orang-utans. In any case, it wouldn't hurt to go to the zoo sometime, to see him, and see the animals again. I still wanted to see the orang-utans after all. And with regard to us doing *It*, well, I would just wait and see.

I found it difficult to tell whether it was only the *idea* of doing *It* that attracted me, the sheer excitement of thinking illicit thoughts, or whether I actually *wanted* to do *It*. In career terms, it seemed like a sound proposition, and Armand was obviously very kind-hearted. He hadn't said anything about *That Night*. And he always smiled at me. *That Night* was something I'd tried hard to forget. But now, it didn't seem that bad. It was a misunderstanding. Latin people were like that; different temperaments, different customs. And I shouldn't have drunk all that champagne. I wasn't used to it. And at least I was sure now that Armand wasn't interested in Maneka. He didn't even know who she was! There was that other girl of course, Marie, or something like that, the one who had kissed him on both cheeks. But I didn't think he was really interested in her. As I saw it, my chances were good. He had already shown plenty of promising signs, and he didn't seem offended by *That Night*. And he was kind, and very beautiful, and intelligent.

I wondered if he had done *It* before. Probably not. Well, probably yes. It didn't matter. It might be better if he had, but I didn't want to think about it.

Mrs Marceau's departure for Paris caused several changes. Mr Aziz was happier. We talked more, and he wore a kurta pyjama in the evenings and drank less. Armand was rarely seen in the house. I don't know where he went in the evenings. I think he was with his friends. He might have been with that girl, but this was another thing I preferred not to think about.

There were two other significant changes. The first was that our workload more than halved. Not only were we free from ridiculous odd jobs in the evenings, but we could start work later without anyone saying anything. Maneka explained that this was normal. Every time Mrs Marceau went on a shopping expedition, we would be given a substantial reprieve. We could take days off, get up at seven, finish at one – just so long as Mr Aziz was given his meals. Mr Aziz didn't even notice the change. And if he had noticed, I doubt he would have minded. (Armand might have, but he was hardly ever there.)

The floor didn't gleam quite so brilliantly, and there was a little more dust, but all in all this made the house a nicer place. It didn't have that glare that Mrs Marceau's military regime lent it. It became a house where *people* lived, instead of a vigilant warlord demanding eternal toil from the serfs. Since the incident I had witnessed in the kitchen, with Raju, I had lived in terror of the house. Even when Mrs Marceau was sleeping I felt her eyes in every wall, cutting into my skin. Now I felt quite relaxed. I even used the shower once, which turned out to be an overrated experience.

The best thing was that I no longer felt tired all the time. My bones didn't ache. I still worked fairly hard. It was unanimously agreed that Ambika would take a full-time holiday while Mrs Marceau was away.

The other, more startling change, was that the new cook didn't arrive, but Raju did. I learned that as soon as Mrs Marceau had left, Mr Aziz had contacted him and told him he could work until she came back. He had drawn a thick, red circle on the calendar around the date of her return. The calendar hung in the kitchen, sporting this big, angry sore. I tried not to look at it.

Everyone was happier with Raju around, even Arun. Raju was happiest of all. His triumph over *The Evil Witch*, as he called her, filled him with irresistible joy. He grinned wherever he went, whatever he was doing. And, with only Mr Aziz to cook for, he didn't have to cook steaks and pigeons, or snails in garlic. He cooked real food, and Mr Aziz was happy. With all this happiness around, I decided it wouldn't hurt to try to turn some of it to my advantage. After a few days I asked Mr Aziz for a day off. He readily complied and I went to the zoo.

I was excited and fidgeted like a child. I had gone to the stage, hoping to see the orang-utans. It was unusually hot. The sun was high in the sky and there was no shade. I sat in a plastic seat, hoping I wouldn't stick to it while it melted like an ice cream. I looked at the sky and it hurt my eyes. It ought to have been blue, but the sun was so bright that all I could see was white.

A sun-stained man with rubbery limbs led the elephant on to the stage. The elephant looked like a bloated, colourless bag of misery. His eyes were veiled with a mess of flies and his feet shuffled through the dust. He didn't look at the audience, but hung his head low, happier with the cockroaches and city-slime beneath his feet.

The man told the elephant to kneel, but he didn't react and let the sun whip his hide, watching the flies as they probed his face, looking for a way inside. The man repeated the order and gave the elephant a sharp slap with a stick. Slowly, like a moving rock, the elephant collapsed on to his knees, as though praying. He looked up at the sky, oblivious to the glare, and his trunk lay in the dust like a dead snake. The little man poked the beast to his feet and announced that the elephant would now stand on one leg. He did as he was told, and I looked at his shrivelled, helpless eyes and wondered if he was dreaming, as I used to do when Ravi would order me around. The man requested applause and the small crowd clapped with the mindless enthusiasm of people determined to have a good time no matter what.

I watched as the man tossed a pink ball to the elephant who bounced it up and down on his trunk to more applause. The sun was so fierce that I had to watch from the corner of my eye, and the elephant looked like a huge, rough stone, glinting in the light. Finally, the elephant fell to his knees again and shuffled forward with the little man prodding him in his enormous sack-like rump. The show was finished and the man explained that next week the orang-utans would be here at the same time.

I didn't move but let the sun continue its assault. It felt as though someone was holding a lighted match to the back of my neck.

– I hate the way they treat him. Sometimes he's so unhappy they have to force-feed him with a tube.

It was the boy with the bananas.

– I hate it too, Ashok.

That was his name, Ashok. When someone is a potential candidate for doing *It* names are important.

– I'm sorry you didn't see the orang-utans. I think this is their week off.

– Oh.

– I could take you to see them.

– Really?

– They're kept in a separate enclosure. Visitors aren't usually allowed in. They're the zoo's most valuable asset, you know, they've performed all over India.

– Will you get into trouble if you take me?

– No, I shouldn't think so.

– Did the man shout at you?

– Which man?

– After you pushed the tourist.

He paused, trying to remember, and then laughed.

– Oh, that. Yes, he shouted at me, but that was all he did. I said I wouldn't do it again and that was that.

I was relieved. I thought he might have lost his job, and it would have been my fault, indirectly.

– Well, shall we go to see the orang-utans?

We rose and walked through the zoo. Ashok didn't look at the animals much. He walked very quickly, with an assurance that impressed me. His unselfconscious, professional air was something Ravi had been seeking all his life. I had visited Ravi twice at his office. He had moved around as though it was his first time out of the house, knocking things over, spilling drinks, getting shouted at. I wondered if Mr Aziz was the same in his workplace.

– How many orang-utans are there?

– Six. Five males, one female, all from Borneo. They are called the Pandavas, you'll see why. They've been trained specially for it.

We reached the enclosure and walked past the man at the entrance. He smiled at Ashok and winked at me, for some reason. The thought occurred to me that perhaps Ashok regularly invited girls to come and see the orang-utans, but I dismissed this idea as unfair. I decided to give no further thought to doing It. It was a dirty, malicious thought. I liked Ashok. He was very kind. It was I who was the deceitful one, although in spite of my plunging self-opinion, I was feeling sickeningly contented.

I was astonished to see that the orang-utans were not in a cage but were roaming around freely.

– Won't they escape?

– How can they escape? They're free, and happy here. They are the celebrities of the animal kingdom, and celebrities never wander too far from the limelight.

– What are their names?

– The big one, the one walking on all fours on his knuckles, his name is Bhima. And that one over there, scratching his chin, he is Yudhishtira. The one swinging from the rope is Arjuna, and the two fighting are Nakula and Sahadeva. This one is Draupadi. Would you like to meet her?

Draupadi was staring at Ashok. He took my hand and she feigned a jealous pout. She walked over to us on two groomed, orange legs, staring ahead with a proud, defiant bearing.

– I think Draupadi is trying to impress you.

Or trying to intimidate me, though with five husbands I couldn't see why she needed Ashok as well. I clung to his hand. I had visions of Draupadi suddenly attacking me in a fit of rage.

I was amazed by how feminine she looked. Her hair was a silky, bright orange, and where the light fell it looked as though a silent sheet of flame were spreading over her body. Her lips were full and curvaceous and flickered intermittently between a pout and a grin, as though she could not quite decide how she wanted to feel. The only thing which spoilt her ladylike poise was her walk. She leaned precariously from one side to the other as she moved, and hung her enormous arms out like washing-lines to stabilise herself. She was easily a foot taller than Ashok, and when she reached us she seized his hand between her own hairy palms and pumped it up and down with gusto. Ashok told her to mind her manners.

– Draupadi, this is my friend. It is very rude to ignore a guest like this.

Draupadi turned to me and wrapped her arms around my neck and kissed my cheek, or at least pushed at it with her moist mouth. I was overwhelmed by such an affectionate greeting, and by the earnestness of this animal who had so graciously put all jealousy behind her. Ashok was enjoying my reaction.

– Don't think this is all an act. Draupadi knows exactly what she's doing, and she's very sincere. She knows what all human gestures mean. She's saying that she's sorry for giving you the cold shoulder.

Draupadi had had enough of all this talk and pushed herself between us, taking hold of my hand and his, and dragged us towards the other orang-utans. We followed like indulgent parents after a demanding child.

– She wants us to meet her husbands.

– Are they really all her husbands?

– Of course. These are the Pandavas. Can you remember which is which?

I looked. Bhima was obvious; he was the biggest and prowled with a dark, watchful intensity, keeping his distance as if to say that he found his role as muscleman tiresome, but he couldn't help it if God had chosen to endow him with such prodigious strength.

I looked at the one closest to us. He approached on all fours and held out his hand. I took it and he looked at me with cool moist eyes, as if to enquire whether I needed anything. He must have been Yudhishtira.

The animal standing behind him had to be Arjuna. He had a warrior's bearing, if that is possible on all fours, and waited until Yudhishtira had finished before holding out both of his hands, as though to offer only one would be inappropriate for someone of his greatness. I found him quite charming, but I was careful not to arouse any further passion in Draupadi. After all, in the Mahabharata Draupadi's only weakness was her partiality towards Arjuna. She had tumbled from the mountain peak because of it.

After Arjuna, only Nakula and Sahadeva remained. Before Ashok could explain which was which they threw themselves at me and hugged me so tightly I thought I would be killed with kindness. Yudhishtira pulled them back by the hair, as though to reprove them for such an indiscreet display of emotion.

Ashok seemed mightily pleased with the impression his friends were making on me.

– Yudhishtira, our guest might like some refreshment.

Yudhishtira ambled off towards a white tent. He entered on all fours and came out carrying a folded table. The others, minus Draupadi, followed and returned, each carrying a chair. Yudhishtira unfolded the table, and he and Bhima arranged the chairs around it in an untidy circle. Draupadi disappeared and reappeared with a checked tablecloth, a tray with six glasses, and a bottle of water. She threw the tablecloth on the table and dumped the tray on top of it. They all sat down around the table and Yudhishtira tipped the bottle upside down, pouring most of it into the glasses, and offered me and Ashok a glass each. We congratulated and thanked him and sipped our water, fighting back laughter.

The six of them eventually realised that there were only four remaining glasses. Bhima seized one and retired to the grass where he poured most of the water over his head and then threw the glass over his shoulder. Yudhishtira gave Nakula and Sahadeva a glass each and, before he could do anything else, Arjuna snatched the last one and sauntered off to join Bhima. Ashok called out to him, but he pretended not to hear. Ashok winked at me. Arjuna's walk slowed until he came to a halt and then turned around and headed back to the table. He pressed the glass into Draupadi's hand and, as though embarrassed by his own gallantry, bounded off and soon became preoccupied with swinging upside down from a rope. Draupadi didn't seem too grateful, and ended up throwing her water at Nakula.

Yudhishtira watched the proceedings and then, without excusing himself, began to return the chairs to the tent. After he had taken four chairs he moved to where I was sitting and gave my chair a gentle, though insistent, tug. His eyes looked very weary, as if to say that he had been very polite for a very long time, and he'd had a hard day and still had a lot of work to do, and would I please mind allowing him to get on with his duties. I stood up and he hoisted my chair on to his shoulders and wandered off into the tent.

Ashok and I said goodbye to Draupadi, the only one who wasn't utterly bored by us, and she gave me a firm, serious handshake. I was sad to leave, but the moment we turned our backs she seemed to forget our existence.

A girl almost ran into us as we walked away.

– Ashok, what the hell are you doing?

– I was taking my friend to see the orang-utans.

– Really.

– Yes.

– And the crocodile feeding?

– What about Ravethi and Amir?

– Well, they ended up doing it. Look, it doesn't matter, but you were supposed to do it. Your name was down.

– Sorry.

Ashok didn't look very apologetic.

—You're obsessed with these bloody orang-utans, Ashok. It's pathetic. Painted, performing monkeys, tramping around like walking teddy bears.

– Well, they're happy.

– Orang-utans don't feel happy or sad Ashok, they're animals. Happy doesn't mean anything to them.

– Yes it does.

– Who is your friend anyway?

Ashok introduced me to the girl, whose name was Ashwini. She talked and moved with great urgency, as though her world turned at double speed. I quite liked this trait, though I found her somewhat intimidating.

– And did *you* like the orang-utans?

– Yes.

– It's ridiculous. Completely ridiculous. The *Pandavas!* What rubbish!

I decided not to argue with her.

– We're going to have coffee now. Are you coming?

Ashok asked me if I wanted to meet the other two zookeepers. I said *Yes*, but I hoped they weren't all like Ashwini.

We went into a small wooden hut, about a hundred metres behind the elephant's cage. It was quite bare except for a table and several cups of coffee on a tray. Ashok gave me one of the cups and I sat down next to him. The other two came in. They looked exhausted and sweaty, presumably from feeding the crocodiles.

172

He introduced me to them; Ravethi and Amir. They didn't seem angry with Ashok, but Ashwini was still very excited.

– I don't know why you're so, so sentimental, Ashok. The orang-utans are slaves, just as much as the others. Maybe worse, they've been made human.

– Well look at them. They're almost human anyway.

– What are you talking about? What does orang-utan mean, Ashok?

– Man of the woods.

He sounded very sulky, almost guilty.

– Man of the woods. Do you see any woods here?

– No, that's not the point.

– Then what is the bloody point?

Ashwini lit a cigarette. I was impressed by that one. She didn't do it like Holly Golightly, more like Humphrey Bogart, tilting her head and striking the match with a quick, impatient stab.

– Ashwini, we can't stop them from being here. All we do is take care of them. But at least the orang-utans are well treated, and they have a good time –

– Rubbish! They mimic us like fools. For God's sake, Draupadi even wears lipstick. And all this crap about being celebrities. They don't know what a celebrity is. All they know is, if they do what we tell them, they get fed.

– That isn't true. They know what they're doing. They've learnt human gestures. They know how to communicate. They're highly intelligent –

– How does intelligence help them? To make fools of themselves? What about a little dignity, Ashok?

– Well, what do you want me to do, Ashwini? Break the locks? Set them free? Let them wander around the city?

– Obviously not. But nobody asked you to have these damn tea parties with them, trying to impress girls.

I think this was my cue to say something, but nothing came to mind. The reference to me broke the tension in the room. Ashok and Ashwini had been locked together by the horns, but they separated and drank their coffee. Amir turned to me.

– We fight a lot, you know. It isn't easy working in this place. The animals aren't well treated, and there's nothing we can do about it.

Ravethi, who looked extremely glamorous, if this is possible in overalls, was smirking.

– Ashok doesn't usually spend his time impressing girls, you must be a very special friend.

I blushed. Ashok sank a little lower in his seat. I didn't think Ashwini had been fair, though I could see her point.

– We've only met a couple of times. She likes orang-utans. I didn't think it would hurt for her to see them –

He threw Ashwini a sideways glance.

– there's nothing wrong with having a little fun once in a while.

Ashwini ignored him and turned to me.

– So, what do you do?

I hesitated. Everybody was looking at me. I couldn't remember if I'd told Ashok anything last time. When I spoke my voice was as quiet and bashful as always, but my words surprised even me.

– I work as a maid. I ran away from home and came here.

Silence.

– You ran away from home?

Amir didn't seem very bright. Hadn't I just said I'd run away from home? It had been hard enough to say the first time.

– Yes.

Ashok tried to silence Amir with a look.

– Why?

– They wanted me to marry a man I *hated*.

Good. That was an improvement on last time. They were all staring at me, except for Ashok who was looking away. Ravethi put her hand on mine. I didn't like this. I didn't know her and I'd managed to take care of myself until now.

– But you seem much too educated to work as a maid, there must be something better.

How did she know that? It wasn't as though I'd passed around

174

my school certificates as soon as I'd met them. Ashok glanced at Ashwini. He looked very serious.

– Maybe we could get her something here?

I didn't like them all suddenly taking charge of my life.

– I'm happy where I am.

Ravethi looked scandalised.

– As a maid! But maids work all day long!

I couldn't tell them that the master of the house confided all his troubles to me, and that I was very close to doing *It* with his son.

– It isn't that bad.

I felt guilty as I said this. I thought of Maneka and Ambika.

– What are the people you work for like?

That was Amir. I liked the way he looked. He had a boyishness about him, as though he were incapable of taking anything seriously. I gave the question some thought. This hardly seemed the time to launch into a description of Mrs Marceau.

– The man is nice, but I don't like his wife. She's French. Her son is at Oxford.

Ravethi snorted.

– Bastion of the British Empire.

I didn't reply. I was wondering what *Bastion* meant. It was a good word, very cutting. It sounded a bit like *Bastard*, which was one of Ravi's favourite words. Ravethi's scornful tone set Ashwini off again.

– Oh so what? It's good education.

– So you would want to go there?

The two of them seemed to have forgotten me.

– Ha! Not much chance of that.

– But if you had the chance?

– Yes. Why not?

– I had a friend who went there. She came back talking all sorts of rubbish about pheasants and port and God knows what.

– Oh come on, Ravethi, you can *afford* to talk like this.

– What?

Ashwini fixed Ravethi with her eye.

– You're a rich kid.

Ravethi's eyes blazed. I noticed she wore a lot of eye make-up. I quite liked the way it looked. I had never worn any make-up, although my sister had once, until my father found her.

– I'm not a rich kid.

– You don't *need* to work here!

– No, not for the money. I told you that. It's not a secret.

Amir turned to me. He looked very amused.

– Ravethi wants to be a model.

– I *am* a model! I just don't have my portfolio ready yet, that's all.

A *model!* This could be a useful contact.

– I want to be an actress.

Ravethi didn't even look at me. She was still smarting.

– Every girl wants to be an actress.

Now that wasn't fair. Not fair at all. I was about to say so when Ravethi became nice again.

– I'm sorry. I didn't mean it like that.

Amir looked very interested.

– I think you'd make a good actress, or a model.

I think the last comment was a stab at Ravethi, but the first part seemed sincerely meant. Anyway, Ashok agreed.

– Definitely. Maybe Ravethi could hook you up with someone. She knows lots of people, don't you, Ravethi?

– I could try. Do you know T.R.M. Raman?

Who?

– Not really.

– He's a major producer, only had a couple of flops. I could try to get you an audition, my father –

She stopped and bit her lip.

– I know someone who knows him.

Ashwini muttered something. I think she said *Rich Kid*, but I couldn't be sure.

– Anyway, I could try if you like.

– Thank you.

This must have been stage three: *A Passion for Cinema, Experience of Life, Knowing a Rich Kid*.

– Are you from a village?

That was Amir again, grinning away.

– No.

– Most servants are from villages, aren't they?

I thought. Maneka, yes, Raju, yes, Ambika, yes, Manu, didn't think so, Arun, didn't know, and Ishaq wasn't from anywhere as far as I knew.

– Yes, some of them.

– Are *your* servants from a village, Ravethi?

Ah, so that was the point of all of this. Another dig at the *Rich Kid*.

– Some of them. Look, I know what you're talking about. We give them jobs, there's nothing wrong with that.

– And a few good lathas when they misbehave, eh?

– No. We never beat our servants.

– Don't *we*?

Ashwini had joined in again.

– We taught two of them to read.

– Read what? The instructions on the washing machine?

Ravethi had had enough. She muttered some curse at Ashwini, I wasn't sure what, and then stormed out. I hoped I would see her again, especially if she was serious about getting me the audition. Ashok looked troubled.

– You were too hard on her. She can't help it.

– I don't care if she can help it or not.

– We've all got to work here.

– *She* doesn't have to work. She does it for fun. *She* likes playing with orang-utans too. She'll only stay here till she gets bored.

– I know, but try to be nice to her, Ashwini.

– Why?

– She's a person too. She has feelings.

– She can afford them, oh yes, terribly sensitive, one little scratch and she starts crying.

That didn't sound unlike me, although I was currently a

representative of the downtrodden. Ashwini lit another cigarette.

– What time is it?

– Almost twelve.

– Still a lot of work to be done, Ashok.

– I know.

Ashwini was cooling off. She had quite an impressive way about her. She stood up to leave.

– Well, it was good to meet you. You should come again, and look, if you really want that job then we might be able to arrange something. I have a feeling Ravethi's job will be vacant soon.

Amir burst out laughing. I think Ashok wanted to laugh too, but he didn't.

– I don't know.

– Think about it. The work is quite hard, but if you like animals you'll enjoy it.

It was the audition I was really interested in. Ashwini didn't seem to realise that she'd just bullied stage three out of the door.

– Thank you.

Amir left too and Ashok said he'd walk me out. As we walked I decided I no longer wanted to do *It* with Ashok. My mother would definitely like him. Maybe he would become the second friend I had ever had, after Maneka that is.

– I hope Ashwini didn't upset you.

My mother wouldn't like her.

– On no. She's an interesting person.

Ashok laughed.

– She was serious about the job, you know. I'm sure it could be arranged.

– I'll think about it.

– All right.

– Was *Ravethi* serious?

– About her modelling? Oh yes, she probably will end up as a model.

I didn't want to have to spell it out, but he'd left me no choice.

– Not about that, about the audition with that producer.

– Oh, I doubt it. But I could ask her again when she calms down. She probably would do something, she can be very kind that way.

We reached the gates of the zoo. Ashok said goodbye and I promised I'd come and see them all again as soon as I had the chance. I thanked him for taking me to see the orang-utans, but after Ashwini's tempestuousness he didn't seem to want to talk about it. Anyway, even if Ashwini had been right about the orang-utans, I'd still had a good time.

During the bus ride home I thought about what they'd said. The atmosphere had been very tense after I told them I was a maid. I wasn't sure what the silence had meant. I think, maybe, I was supposed to have been more ashamed than I was. Ravethi had made every effort to show that *her* silence was due to a compassion that stole all words from her lips. I was sceptical. I think Ashwini was just surprised. She seemed the sort of person who was used to sealing every aspect of life with a harsh, definitive judgement, but her powers of judgement didn't extend to domestic service and runaways. Amir's response was the best. He had also been lost for words, but after a while he saw only opportunities for amusement. I preferred that. Better to laugh than to be scandalised.

I had deliberately not looked at Ashok. But he was a kind person. He wouldn't think any the less of me. Actually, with the exception of Ashok, I think the others would have preferred it had I lied. I think they all felt immediately responsible for me and they didn't like this, having enough to worry about already. I didn't mind. At least I'd got two job offers out of it; zookeeper or film star. Not a difficult choice. Feeding on croissants was infinitely preferable to feeding crocodiles.

This business about the orang-utans had made me think. I did think Ashwini had a point, but I didn't think that painting a monkey with lipstick could take away his monkeyhood. I had developed a theory about people (which applied equally well to primates). They always come in disguises. Raju was a warrior disguised as a servant. Ravi was something, I hadn't decided what yet, disguised as a Ravi. The grandfather was my friend, disguised as an old, senile fool. Mr Aziz was a nice man, disguised as a buffoon. Armand was David Laraby, disguised as . . . well, as David Laraby. And I was a film star disguised as a maid. The problem was that we'd all been dumped inside the wrong realities. Maybe it had something to do with past lives. I couldn't be certain. But there was one thing I was sure of – disguises always slip off. It's just a matter of time.

It was like the Pandavas when they were hiding out at Virata's palace, all of them in disguise. Draupadi had worked as a maid! Bhima was a cook, and Arjuna disguised himself as a woman, a dance teacher. And, as far as I knew, Arjuna was a pretty good dancer. The name he took for himself was Brihannala. Anyway, things fell apart when Susharma invaded Virata's kingdom. Virata took his armies and charged off to meet the enemy.

It turned out that Virata had fallen for a cunning ploy. While he raced away to the southern frontier, Duryodhana attacked the northern frontier. This meant another army had to be assembled fast. The only person for the job was Virata's son, Uttara. Unfortunately, all the best charioteers had gone with his father and so Uttara wandered around the palace wailing to his wife that there was no one to drive his chariot. Eventually, Brihannala said that she wasn't a bad charioteer. Uttara was shocked. Some fluffy, dancing, singing lady! A charioteer! But Brihannala, after some coaxing, insisted that yes, she was pretty good at it. She had picked up a thing or two in her time. So Uttara said, *Why Not?* Better than no driver at all. Everyone laughed to see them go, the mighty warrior being driven along by a dance teacher, but nevertheless, they sped off to face the enemy.

Along the way, Uttara informed Brihannala of his prowess. He told Brihannala to pay close attention to his fighting technique, which he had learned from his old master, Arjuna. Brihannala, understandably, just smiled. When they reached the enemy Uttara began to tremble. He was terrified. Duryodhana and the Kauravas were a fearsome lot. He told Brihannala to turn the chariot around. Brihannala refused. She said it was the Prince's duty to fight. Uttara insisted that they leave. Brihannala said, *Nothing Doing, Let's Go for It!* So Uttara, quaking with fright, jumped from his chariot and ran for his life. Brihannala jumped down and ran after him, saying, *Where do You Think you Are Going? Come Back and Fight!* The Kauravas rolled with laughter at the sight of this woman chasing after the Prince.

Brihannala caught up with him and gave him a good talking to. The Prince said he was sorry, he knew it was his duty, but he just couldn't fight. He wasn't up to the job. Brihannala said, *All Right Damn It, I'll Fight Them Myself! But first We have to Pick up A Package.* And they rode off into the forest. Brihannala stopped at a tree and pointed to what looked like a corpse, high up in the branches. He told Uttara to fetch it. Uttara was a bit worried that he'd be defiled for touching a corpse, but Brihannala explained that it wasn't really a corpse. When Uttara brought it down they opened it and it was a bundle of weapons. Brihannala explained that he wasn't really a dance teacher, he was Arjuna, the greatest warrior in the world.

Uttara felt silly, but Arjuna forgave him for his cowardice. When they returned to the battlefield Uttara drove the chariot, and Arjuna decimated the enemy, his true self emerging after he had abandoned his disguise.

The point of the story, as I saw it, was that a warrior is always a warrior, even when he's disguised as a woman, or a servant. And a film star is always a star, even when she's a maid. The problem was that Arjuna had been born a warrior and had chosen his disguise on purpose. I had been born a girl, as Ravi kept telling me, and not a star, and I had never really wanted to be a maid.

There is an alternative interpretation. Perhaps Arjuna had been born a warrior, but deep inside himself he really wanted to be a woman, and a dancer. So when the opportunity came he grabbed it with both hands. But if that was true, then why did he go back to killing people for a living? I had a horrible feeling the answer had something to do with duty, but at the moment I wasn't interested in such things.

It was early in the afternoon when I got back to the house. I found Maneka in the kitchen with Raju. They didn't ask where I had gone, which was standard practice whenever any of us went out. I think Maneka had initiated this. She didn't want to tell anyone where she had been, so in return everyone else kept silent about their own forays outside.

I had a feeling that Maneka had been fighting with Raju. He looked very stern and didn't say much. Maneka wasn't herself at all. She seemed glum and wouldn't look me in the eye. I felt they were both willing the other to leave. So I stayed, and waited, asking silly questions and getting clipped, evasive responses. As this silent battle of wills reached its climax, the door opened and Armand came in. None of us had expected this. Since Mrs Marceau's departure the kitchen had become our territory. Mr Aziz would never think of going in there, and Armand wasn't usually in the house, and when he was he tended to stay upstairs. He saw Raju and stared at him, but didn't say anything. As far as I knew, Armand hadn't been told that Raju had returned.

Raju left the kitchen and went outside. It was too late now, but I think Raju wanted to show that he wasn't seeking a confrontation. In the end it would be Mr Aziz who would suffer for it, and Raju knew this.

Armand ignored Maneka and walked straight up to me, pinning me with his familiar dancing eyes and half-smile. I blushed a little, though not as much as usual. I knew Maneka would be watching intently.

– I want tea in the morning, not coffee. And I want *you* to bring it, seven-thirty, all right?

I nodded.

– I'll be in my room. Bring a glass of wine, please.

I nodded again and Armand swept out, humming to himself. Before I could say anything Maneka came over to me and grabbed both of my hands.

– I told Raju.

– Told him what?

– About you, and Armand.

Oh God. I wondered what she had told him. After all, there was nothing to tell yet.

– What did he say?

– He was really angry. I told him it was nothing to worry about, and he shouted at me. He told me I should have known better than to put such stupid ideas into your head. He's still angry with me. I'm sorry, I didn't think he'd be like that.

– Oh well, it doesn't matter.

– He's very angry.

I told her not to worry, but Maneka kept flapping about, getting more and more worked up. In the end I poured the wine and, putting it on a tray, gave Maneka's hand a last squeeze and went upstairs.

Armand was sitting at his table reading a letter. He didn't look up when I entered, so I put the wine on the table and started to leave, very slowly. As I had hoped, he called me back just as I reached the door.

– Why is that servant here?

I didn't know how to answer this, so I just smiled.

– Didn't my mother tell him to go?

– I think he's only here until the new cook arrives.

– I see.

– Please don't tell madam.

Armand sipped his wine, thinking about this.

– All right. I won't. Sit down.

I did as I was told, sitting on the bed.

– I'm sorry if I frightened you, after the party.

I couldn't look at him.

– I wasn't frightened. I just felt sick, because of the champagne.

He came and sat beside me, very close.

– Oh. You mustn't drink too much if you're not used to it – Thank you for telling me.

– it can give you a terrible headache in the morning.

I knew that. I wondered what he was thinking.

– You needn't work every day, you know, not if you don't want to –

I didn't reply. Neither he nor Mr Aziz understood that I wasn't the only servant in the house. Didn't they realise how bad it would look if I were the only one who didn't work?

– and you can come and see me whenever you want, if you are bored.

– All right.

– Good.

Was I supposed to leave now?

– Where were you yesterday?

– Yesterday? I, it was my day off –

– You were supposed to clean my room, remember?

– Oh, yes, I'm sorry.

As was my custom, I was carefully keeping Mr Aziz out of any of this.

– It doesn't matter. One day without cleaning doesn't matter. But don't forget again, OK?

– All right. I'm sorry.

He patted my knee.

– And tea not coffee tomorrow, all right, you'll remember?

– Yes, sorry.

Stop saying sorry!

– Good, good.

I got up and left as he returned to his table and his letter. I wasn't sure about anything now. I wasn't sure what he wanted. Did he want to do *It*? Had he ever wanted to do *It*? Maneka said that that was the way boys were, but how many boys did she know who were like Armand? I doubted if the boys she did *It* with, on her mysterious ventures into The City, had anything in common with Armand. They would surely be rougher types who saw girls as shiny toys to be spied from high and then pounced on and used up. Armand wasn't like that, though I knew the reason for this.

People like Armand would have to try very hard not to get

184

what they wanted. That was why his skin was so smooth. His face and arms weren't creased with those grimaces of frustration that wrapped themselves around the rest of us. His smile was easy, he didn't have any scowl to drive away. When he sipped his wine his hand was still, it slipped down his throat; not like Ravi with his whisky bottle, or my father. They drank with large, ugly swigs, knowing that tomorrow the bottle might be gone, they might be gone. But Armand knew he would wake up every morning in his beautiful perfumed pink bed, he would yawn and stretch, wait for his coffee (tea tomorrow, mustn't forget), smile at whoever gave it to him. He didn't need to snatch at things, they would all come to him in time.

I knew I had to become a film star fast if I wanted his soft voice and his shiny hair. Every day I spent here brought Ambika's gnarled, corrugated face closer to mine. The zookeepers had made me certain of the urgency of this matter. But I also knew that Armand had no need to make a grab for me, no need to creep up on me while I was sleeping. He could afford to be nice, to give me champagne, to say pretty, pleasant things, to make me blush and watch me with that half-smile of his. And the longer this went on, the more likely he would be to lose interest. He would start to see me as a maid. Worse still, *I* might start to see myself as a maid, and then it would be only a matter of time before my hands were as callused as Ambika's. I would never see Ravi again. I would never be a film star. I would measure out the rest of my life with idle, fleeting glimpses of people like Armand. I'd become like the rest of those fools gaping with open mouths in *Majick Movie House*, day after day.

So the onus was on me. And what had the grandfather told me that day, pinching my cheek, *You Must turn Your Dreams into Reality*. And it wasn't as if Armand hadn't given me enough chances. I had already ruined one in the garden, and then I had disappeared off to a tea party with orang-utans while Armand was waiting for me. The next time could be my last chance, and if I wanted to throw off this disguise of mine, if I wanted to show the world who I really was, then I'd have to grab it.

I went to the bungalow, hoping to sleep for a couple of hours to digest all these thoughts. Raju was there. It seemed he'd been waiting for me. He didn't look happy at all.

– Maneka told me.

– Told you?

Raju wasn't a fool, and he wouldn't appreciate me treating him like one. The next best thing was to pretend to be a fool myself.

– You know. About that boy.

I didn't say anything. I concentrated on making my face look as stupid as possible.

– Do not trust them –

His face was still, calm, but his body was radiating energy, shouting over the table and across the room towards me. I couldn't have ignored him had my life depended on it. When Raju chose to, he could fill a room like an opaque mist, his dark glare streaming through windows, keyholes, cracks under doors, bursting out and blotting out the sun.

– I know you are not a fool. You think you can use him. He will break you, as if you were an insect.

I nodded, keeping my face well hidden. It was pointless to reply. I wasn't capable of anything but lies, and lies would suffocate in seconds under Raju's gaze. Eventually he took pity on me and left the room, squeezing my shoulder with his powerful hand.

The next day I brought Armand's tea to his bed, as instructed. He told me I could visit him in the evening if I liked, if I was bored, and he stroked my hair. I didn't move while he did this, but I left the room as quickly as possible.

The day passed as usual. I cleaned the ground floor and then went upstairs to help Ambika. Ambika had given up even the pretence of working now, she would sit around, banging a rug now and again, or chasing a cockroach before splatting it with her sandal. She loved watching the cockroach as it haemorrhaged in front of her, kicking its useless legs. Ambika had become so vague that it was impossible to tell whether she was sane or not, the words didn't even apply to her. She had completely withdrawn from the world she inhabited. Perhaps she was throwing off her disguise, though not to free her true self, simply to scorn the life that had cheated her. If she had a private world, and I suspected she did, vast and ethereal, then that was where she could have been found, had anyone succeeded in finding a way in there. As it stood, no one cared enough about her to join her in whatever place she spent her days. But Maneka and I did her work without complaining. It seemed that nothing could compensate for the life that had been snatched from her at the cradle. I knew better than to dwell on it. I could spend more than the rest of my life trying to atone for Ambika's suffering, and I had other plans.

As usual we went outside to do the washing. This was my favourite part of the day, now that the sun had lost his edge. It was almost like the afternoons at home where the air was cool and pink and everyone was tired of shouting and bullying. I considered such moments to be the only time when the world was at peace, not through any sudden rush of collective enlightenment, but because of sheer exhaustion. Perhaps the day would come when the world would be so exhausted that no one would do anything except be nice to each other. I doubted it, but such thoughts would come to me in the afternoon as I scrubbed Armand's shirts.

Maneka was quiet and apologetic. Raju had refused to talk to either of us in the morning, and Maneka, quite rightly, blamed herself. I wasn't angry with her. My patience never frayed where Maneka was concerned. I saw the faults in her, that others condemned, as if they were beauty marks, soft moles breaking the landscape of shiny, laughing skin. I hoped that, wherever I was going, I would take Maneka with me. But the thing was, Maneka didn't wear any disguise. She lived her whole life as though it were a movie and I loved her for it, although she would never have understood this had I told her. Maneka was an unappreciated person, and unlike me, this never bothered her. She never sought appreciation from anyone.

As the evening approached we went inside to do the ironing.

Raju and Ishaq were starting to cook the evening meal. I wondered if Raju had told Ishaq anything. I doubted it. As soon as the clock struck six I poured a glass of wine and excused myself under the pretext, both feigned and real, of taking it to Armand. I moved quickly, but I could feel Raju watching me.

As I reached Armand's door I heard voices from inside. There seemed to be a lot of people in there, and they all sounded very confident. I thought about going downstairs, but the thought of facing Raju was too much for me. Anyway, Armand had told me to come and see him, and here I was.

I knocked on the door with a passion that would have stunned all the warriors of the Kuru-field into submission. I heard polite, embarrassed excuses, and then Armand's eyes peered into mine.

– Yes?

– I came to see you.

Armand smiled and took me inside. There were four of them, three Europeans – two girls and one boy – and an Indian boy. Armand introduced me as *A Friend of My Father* and I gulped the wine I had brought for him. I sat next to Armand and they went on talking.

– The music was so loud that you couldn't talk, and the toilets were so stinky . . .

– I hate lamb, it's horrible . . .

– So you were seeing him *before* you broke up with Fernando?

– Well, my father thought we should sue him, but I couldn't see the point . . .

– For the first week the stupid A/C wouldn't work . . . can you imagine?

– All Germans say that, they need an instruction manual for everything . . .

– I used to smoke, but my skin kept going all blotchy and my boyfriend hated it . . .

– It takes six CDs and the player is in the boot so it's a bit of a nuisance to change CDs, but it's better than only having one . . .

– A lot of Europeans like Asian girls, but I'm Asian and I like Europeans . . .

– I hate her, she's such a bitch and never talks to anyone who isn't pretty . . .

– Nobody has a fax in India, *nobody*, so I said, *What do you do when you want to send a Fax?* And he said they *had* a fax, but it was a *telex!*

– You must all come, we've got a house on the beach . . .

– He thinks he's so cool, and he drives a Suzuki! –

I was beginning to feel left out.

I decided to try talking to them. I was forewarned about Latin people and their temperaments, so I knew I had to be careful. I started by asking them who they were. Asking *how* they were might have been more affectionate, but first things first. The girls ignored the question and the Indian boy just smiled, but the European boy gave an explanation on behalf of all of them. They had been to the same *International School* as Armand, in Hong Kong. I didn't see how an *International* school could be in Hong Kong (didn't *International* mean *Between Nations?*), but I decided not to press him.

It occurred to me that they were *Foreigners*. I was pleased with this idea and asked them if they liked India. Nobody replied, until the European boy initiated the discourse and the others followed suit, as though in response to him.

– The toilets are stinky, and the air-conditioning never works . . .

– The countryside was better in Vietnam . . .

– The pavements are awful, you ruin your shoes . . .

– The phone lines are bad, not enough faxes . . .

– I like the food, but there's nothing to do . . .

– The people are rude, they should smile more, but some of them are quite polite . . .

The last one was the Indian boy's contribution. I agreed with him. In fact, I agreed with all of them, although I wasn't sure about the fax situation, and it had never occurred to me that there was nothing to do. Everyone was always doing *something* (with the possible exception of Ravi).

The whole gathering was like some kind of performing theatre troupe. I had never met people so carefully stylised. Ravi had only the window-spy to deal with, but these people! It was as though the world's press were perched at their feet! Their movements had such impeccable precision. Their every mannerism was choreographed; the way they drank, the way they smoked, the way they placed their feet, but most of all the way they talked. The girl who had shared her thoughts on toilets had used the word *Stinky* as though it were some sort of erotic mantra, casting it into the air where it fluttered in the breeze, sweeping its scent across the room. Her face had fluttered too, pouting like a lotus.

– Why don't you like Indian girls?

The *Stinky* girl was fluttering again, this time at the Indian boy.

– Well, everyone talks about how pretty they are, but the girls you see on the street don't wear make-up or anything, and they're very dark from the sun so you can't really see their faces. And of course a lot of them aren't all that clean, which is always a turn off. But in nightclubs I've seen lots of pretty girls.

Judging by their glances, I wondered if some donkey had secretly emptied his bowels over my head. My mother made that same face whenever someone said the word *Toilet*. I looked into my wine glass. I could feel the lice in my hair, burrowing into my scalp. I could smell my own body, a smell of urine and sweat. There was dirt under my nails, black and rancid. The Indian boy nodded his head.

– Indian men are just the same.

What? Something was very wrong. Indians are ugly, and he knew this because he was one. But he didn't think *he* was ugly. So this meant he wasn't Indian. Nothing made any sense. I decided to ask him.

– Where are you from?

– Half-English, half-Indian, born in Saudi.

It was as though he were giving his credentials to a board of examiners. I waited for him to ask where I was from, but he didn't. I decided to question him further. I had nothing to lose.

– Are you a student?

– Finished last year. I'm with Goldmann Sachs.

– What's that?

This was obviously the wrong question to ask. There was a chorus of nasal trumpeting. It sounded like politely suppressed laughter, but they looked like a firing squad.

– It's a bank.

– Oh, my father worked in a bank, for a while.

I wasn't sure whether to go on. My father had lost his job for using so many staples to fasten notes together that when they were removed the money had a tendency to disintegrate. My father had always been an excessively efficient man. This trait also led him to shine each strand of his moustache with boot polish, which meant he never drank directly from a cup for fear of leaving a black stain glaring on the rim.

– You mustn't use too many staples, you know, you could lose your job that way.

This was meant as a sincere piece of advice. It's always best to learn from other people's mistakes.

– What staples?

– The ones on the notes.

He seemed a little slow to me.

– I work for the Singapore branch. I'm, er, not too sure how things are done here.

I didn't like the look of him much, but I hoped he wouldn't lose his job. He would have done better to heed my warning, but he was looking at me as though *I* were the idiot. Armand looked baffled as well.

The *Stinky* girl broke the silence.

– And are *you* a student?

I gulped my wine. It was the first thing she had said to me.

– No, I work.

– Oh really, who are you with?

– I work for Mr Aziz.

– You're a trainee?

Yes, yes, trainee film star!

– No, I'm a maid, in the house.

This was deliberate. After testing out the zookeepers and meeting with quite a favourable response (two job offers), I didn't think it would hurt to drop the bomb a second time.

– In *this* house?

– Yes.

The *Stinky* girl looked at Armand. It was a look that suggested reproach, admiration, disgust, amusement, coyness and betrayal. These were complex people.

The Indian boy decided this was an opportunity for comedy. He leaned back, slapped the European boy on the shoulder, and said, *She's a Maid, man. A Fucking Maid!* The *Stinky* girl looked at Armand again, and said *Armand* . . . I wasn't sure what this was supposed to mean. The other girl just stared at me, pretending not to stare. The European boy glared at his friend and looked at me, not unkindly.

– If your father works in a bank, why are you a maid?

– My parents are dead.

At that moment, I preferred to think of them as dead. I could face my own enemies, but I didn't want the knowledge that my humiliations were automatically transferred to my mother.

– I'm sorry . . .

Why did they all say that? It wasn't his fault. It wasn't even true actually, but if it had been true it still wouldn't have been his fault.

– *my* father died two years ago.

He gave me a profound look, the sort of look Ravi would give after one of his philosophical tirades. I think he wanted me to appreciate the significance of this last comment. He had established our common humanity.

The Indian boy still couldn't get over my confession. He said again, to himself this time, *A Fucking French Maid, man.* He turned to me with a sneer.

– So what do you do? Change the sheets? Wash their underwear?

The *Stinky* girl sniggered and the European boy glared at him again.

– Don't be rude, man. It's not her fault.

The Indian boy looked at me again, still sneering.

– Sorry. I didn't mean to offend you. So what *else* do you do, any *other* services?

This time I saw all of them laugh, though I didn't look at Armand. The European boy didn't laugh with his lips, but I saw his eyes.

– Stop it, man.

– Sorry, sorry.

The girls were giggling. *Breakfast in Bed? Coffee, two Eggs and Some Head!* The Indian boy had completely lost control of himself. He kept slapping his thigh while writhing in hysteria.

I was drunk. Armand had refilled my glass along with everyone else's. I'd been enjoying it. But when the Indian boy laughed, I looked into my glass and the wine looked foreign and ugly. They had tricked me. They were laughing at me, as I had laughed at the orang-utans.

I wanted to cry, but I concentrated on sitting still, waiting for them to disappear. I kept blinking, trying to look everywhere and nowhere. I saw Armand. He was smiling at me, very gently. As I drifted backwards, inside of myself, they rose like shadows, kissing and shaking hands. I tried not to look. The European boy was saying goodbye to me, but I stared dumbly ahead.

When they were gone, Armand asked me if I had enjoyed myself. I tried to say *Yes*, but no words came out. He filled my glass again, putting his hand on my knee and watching me.

– Are you all right?

– Yes.

– I hope that boy didn't upset you. He was very rude.

– No, he didn't upset me.

– What was all that about the staples?

– What?

– The staples?

I sighed. I had expected him to be quicker than the others.

– The staples in the notes.

– *What* staples in the notes?

I explained, perhaps a little incoherently.

– So that's why all my money has holes in it?

He laughed and took hold of my hand. His eyes were full of kindness.

– Why did you tell them you were the maid?

– They asked me.

– You shouldn't have told them.

– Why not?

– It doesn't matter. I wanted to have you here, that's what matters. I don't care about them.

He squeezed my hand. I looked up with a weak smile and he leaned over and kissed me. I couldn't taste anything but wine, a sweet, perfumed taste. I wondered what Raju and Maneka were doing. I hoped Raju wouldn't look for me, though I doubted he would come up here.

– Do you feel better now?

– Yes.

– Would you like some cognac?

– Yes please.

I had become accustomed to accepting everything I was offered, *Condolences*, *Croissants*, *Kon Yak*. Armand went into the other room and I stood up. I could smell only wine. I felt like I was drowning. I wasn't sure what had just happened. Armand's friends had laughed at me, and then he had kissed me. And now everything was all right. He didn't care about them.

Armand returned with two glasses that looked more like bowls. The *Kon Yak* was good. It burned my mouth and made me cough, but I liked the feeling afterwards. Nothing seemed to matter any more, all my silly fears, that horrible boy who had laughed at me, Raju and his warnings, my father. I didn't care. My whole body was on fire. The room looked blurred but I could hear Armand's voice.

There's no Shame in being a Maid, his voice was nice, so soothing, so soft, *You Can Trust Me*, I wanted to forget everything I knew, forget how bad I had felt, forget my anxiety, forget my guilt, *There's no Shame At All*, his friends didn't like me, it wasn't my fault, *You're a Beautiful Girl*, I was crying now, *You don't Have to Work*, I had been trying so hard, fighting so hard, I was tired, *You can Trust Me*, I wanted to trust someone, I wanted to forget everything, he was laughing, I didn't know why he was laughing, but he was laughing, smiling, filling my glass, and I kept on crying, I didn't want to be here, but I didn't want to be anywhere else, I wanted my mother, but I didn't want her to be here, I wanted to forget but he was still laughing, and I was still crying.

Part Three

In exile from the warmth of your arms
and the milk of your teeth
and breath of your secret whispers in my ears
shall I not stride back to you with haste
rout all my enemies and bind the wicked husbandmen
Shall I not kneel to kiss the grains of your sand
to rise naked before you – a bowl of incense?
and the smoke of my nakedness shall be
an offering to you
pledging my soul.

From *Pledging My Soul*, by Dambuzo Marachera

5

Even though the journey took forty-eight hours, I hardly slept on the train. There was too much to think about.

Everything had happened so quickly. I passed out in Armand's room and woke up in his bed. So we didn't do *It* after all. But maybe he did. Raju said there were ways of telling, but I didn't want to know. I woke up to look into Mrs Marceau's cutthroat eyes, back home early from Paris, to surprise her son, who was sleeping next to me. She only said one word, *Out!*, very loudly. I did as I was told. Armand woke up but didn't say anything. On the stairs I ran into Raju. He didn't shout at me but asked if I was all right. I said I was, though my head hurt. Mrs Marceau came stampeding down the stairs, and when she saw Raju she stopped dead. I thought her eyes were finally going to bulge out of her head. She said the same thing to him, just one word, *Out!* Raju, also, did as he was told.

We went into the bungalow where we knew we would be safe, for a while. The others were working, but Maneka had stayed behind because she was worried about me. I knew what she was thinking and I answered her with my eyes, *No, I didn't do It*. She seemed relieved, perhaps because Raju would have killed her otherwise. We thought quickly. Raju and I would have to leave. Raju said I could live with him, but I decided to go to the zoo, to see what they had to say. Maybe I could still get that job. Raju said all right, and he told me to find him when I knew what I wanted to do.

I said goodbye to Maneka. It was all very emotional. I told her I would see her soon, but I had no idea what I was doing.

I went to the zoo, but Ashok wasn't there. I could only find Ashwini, reading in the hut. She said of course she would try her hardest to get me the job, and I could live with her in the meantime. She went out to find the supervisor and I sat down to think. When she came back she said there might be a job available, starting next week, and I could move in with her that night. I thanked her, and told her *No*, I had changed my mind, I wanted to go home. She said she didn't understand. This was a step up, not down. Feeding crocodiles was better than feeding Mrs Marceau. But I shook my head. I wanted to go home.

We talked for a while and then I left. I asked her to say goodbye to Ashok for me. I liked Ashwini, I think we would have been friends. I went to find Raju. He was waiting for me, still in the bungalow, talking with Mr Aziz. Mr Aziz said he would have to go, no question about it, but he had found a new position for him. Raju said he didn't want to be a servant, he was tired of washing other people's dishes. Mr Aziz looked surprised, and he turned to me and said he would find *me* another position. I explained that I wanted to go home, to my parents, and Mr Aziz shook his head. His wife was kicking us out, one by one, and we were going hopelessly insane.

Mr Aziz accepted Raju's explanation as understandable, though impractical, but his look suggested he found my idea of returning to a couple of corpses somewhat foolish. I told him my parents weren't dead, they were alive and well and living in torment. This upset him. He even cried, a little. I tried to tell him why I had left home, but he just kept shaking his head. In the end he gave me some money and wished me luck. He said if I ever needed him then he would be at my service, but he was hurt that I had lied to him.

Raju wanted to know why I had suddenly decided to go home. Had I decided marriage wasn't so bad after all? I said it had nothing to do with marriage, and he repeated the question again. What was I to say? I barely understood it myself.

It had all happened the moment I woke up. I had understood. Arjuna was born a Pandava, and a warrior, but his true self was Brihannala, a dance-teacher with slender ankles and rings on her toes. And where had he found his true self? In heaven. During his exile, Arjuna had visited Indra, his father, for a year, and it was there, in the land of beautiful disguises, that he had learnt to dance and sing. It was also there that Urvashi, in a lovesick fit of rage, had cursed him to be transformed into a woman for a year. So the ones who loved him most had presented him with his true self, albeit temporarily, and, for a while, under the pretext of wearing a disguise, he had thrown off his disguise. But that was all it was, a chance to have some fun. He was born with a duty. He had to fight the bloodiest, greatest war of all time. He had to face his enemies and his bow had to slip from his hand. He had to turn to Krishna, ashen and weak, and Krishna had to, well, everyone knows what Krishna had to do. The point was that Arjuna was born a warrior, but really he was Brihannala, but because he was born a warrior he had to fight. I was born a girl, but really I was a film star, but because I was born a girl I had to go home to my brother, and my sister and my mother. Not to marry, but to fight.

Arjuna had had his chance. He could have remained Brihannala for all his life. When Susharma attacked the northern frontier, he could have thrown up his hands and fluttered his eyelids and said, *Oh my Goodness! Horrible Men on the Northern Frontier. Uttara, Save Me!* But he didn't, he put on his armour and got behind the reins, though surely not without one last, wistful glance at the dancing hall. And in his heart of hearts he would always know he'd had the chance to be his true self, and had given it up. And I had had my chance. No one had made me cry. No one had made me get so drunk. I could have stayed sharp and sober and done *It* in an efficient and businesslike manner. And my life would have changed. But I didn't, and now I had to fight.

I wondered what my mother was doing. Cooking probably. And waiting for my father. I had this unpleasant feeling that her life had got worse since I left home. Even more unpleasant was the feeling that it might get worse when I returned. But I had to confront my father. It was my duty, a word that had only recently entered my vocabulary.

I wasn't looking forward to seeing him. I wondered what he would do when he saw me. Perhaps I should see the grandfather first. He would know what to do, though as much as I tried to deny it, a part of me resented him. He had made me think only of myself, to forget Ravi, to forget my sister, to forget my mother.

Freedom was a dangerous thing. I realised this after Raju was sacked. All of us had lost a week's pay because of Raju's *Insolence*. At the time I pushed this from my mind, I told myself that it wasn't Raju's fault. But perhaps it was. Perhaps Raju had thought only of his own freedom and never about the rest of us. And now, because I had thought only of my own freedom, my father would be making Ravi and my mother suffer for it. The grandfather hadn't cared about this, or hadn't considered it. He only cared about truth, he only cared about the face behind the mask. But if he couldn't see the face then he couldn't see the suffering.

The fields were starting to look familiar. I was an hour from home, at most. I tried to collect my thoughts. I would go to Vijay Kumar's. I hoped my sister would be able to withstand the shock. Even though she hated me, I was looking forward to seeing her, and the baby. Perhaps we might understand each other better now. Perhaps I could even *help* her. The new Ravi would be an interesting experience. The grandfather's letters had painted an intriguing picture. Were it not for my father, this visit might even have been fun.

I had shattered his world, and a man with little imagination whose already tiny world has been shattered is a dangerous animal. He had had months to let his bitterness fester and grow. Nursing his hatred. Keeping it sharp and primed behind bars. Saving it for me. His satisfaction at seeing me return in a decidedly less than triumphant manner could only be matched by the pleasure he would take from scaring me senseless.

My sister and I sat facing each other, with the baby asleep in her arms. My tea was scalding hot but I drank it anyway and burnt my tongue. I needed something to hold in front of my face. I didn't want her to look at me yet. She appeared to be doing the same thing. I knew I should speak if I wanted to save both our mouths from feeling like the inside of a tandoor, but I couldn't think of anything to say.

She looked more like my mother than ever. Except she looked healthy and peaceful. The baby looked in equally good shape. I admired the relaxed way she handled it, completely unperturbed that something so fragile and helpless should be sleeping in her lap. I felt she had learned how to live in the world, instead of letting it spin hopelessly around her. I didn't know what she thought of me, but she had dealt pretty well with the initial shock.

I wished I could think of something to say, but still, it was nice to be sitting with her like this. Feeling uncomfortably relaxed. The room looked very pleasant. It smelt of flowers and sunlight. The word *Homespun* leapt to mind.

– Vijay will be home soon.
– How is he?
She smiled, and I thought I could see a touch of rouge enter her cheeks.
– He's very well.
She smiled again, and instead of avoiding my eyes looked directly at me. She seemed to be trying to tell me something. I wondered if the trans-Atlantic demi-god had had his tongue cut out by marauding dacoits.
– Where are Aunty and Uncle?
– Hyderabad.
A mischievous glint crept into her eyes, but it was replaced by an exaggeratedly adult sobriety. I had never seen her wear this look before.
– But there's something I have to tell you.
– Yes?
– We didn't know where you were so we couldn't reach you.
– I know, I –

– Vijay's grandfather died two weeks ago.

The teacup started to rattle. It took me some time to realise that I was making it rattle. I wanted to ask *Why?* But that didn't make any sense. People don't die for a reason. I suddenly felt very cold. The room looked smaller now and that light, breezy atmosphere had turned stale and empty.

– Oh.

She reached out and touched my hand, but I wasn't ready for emotion. I felt very decisively alone.

I didn't know what my sister thought of any of this. All that had passed had been at the grandfather's instigation, and I hadn't expected him to desert me at such a critical moment. Had he planned for this, or was he just some crazy old man who had wanted some entertainment before he died? It was strange really, but he didn't seem at all like the sort of person who died. It just wasn't *him* somehow. Or at least, he might have died, but only when he felt like it, like Bhishma.

– He left a letter for you.

She went upstairs to find it and I took advantage of this interlude to sink my head in my hands and try to forget where I was. There were so many things I couldn't bear to think of. I wouldn't let myself think of the grandfather in anything but reproachful terms. And I couldn't think of Maneka or Raju, or Armand. Sooner or later I would have to confront them all, to recognise my failure, to face all that I had lost. But for the time being I would live under house arrest in my own head, at least until I had dealt with the immediate and very uncertain future.

My sister returned with the letter. She gave it to me and averted her eyes, as though she expected me to read it in front of her. I tucked it away for later. She seemed a little offended, but that was the least of my worries.

– What are you going to tell Appa?

– I don't know.

– You could stay here for a few days. We won't tell anyone.

I considered it. It wasn't a bad idea. But what would I do? Wander around the house beating myself with a stick for all the pain I'd caused? I had nothing in life but the job I had come to do. Dreams, movies, fantasies . . . I was too old now.

– I think I should go soon, today.

– Well, stay at least until Vijay comes. Maybe he will think of something.

Maybe *he* will think of something! Was she crazy? Only if he took time out from thinking about himself! I hoped he would be late. I needed time to figure out whether my sister was still pathologically stupid. Perhaps that was a bit harsh. I didn't know why I was always so cutting about my sister, particularly when I forgave all Ravi's idiocies. Perhaps because Ravi was beyond hope and to be pitied, whilst she deliberately and meticulously wasted her life. Perhaps she felt that by being the first of us to be truly and sincerely unhappy, she was the first to be a real woman.

– Where have you been all this time?

She spilt the words into her teacup, but nothing could conceal the hurt in her voice. It made me hate myself for thinking so unkindly of her.

– I was in The City. I went to the zoo.

I Went to the Zoo! Of all the things I could have told her, this was the most unfair.

– To the zoo?

– Yes, sometimes.

– But where were you staying?

– With a friend.

– What friend?

– A friend of . . . a friend.

– What have you been doing?

What was I supposed to say? The truth would be the cruellest thing imaginable, even if I stressed the hardships of domestic labour and relegated tales of croissants and orang-utans to the footnotes. I didn't want to think about the interrogation my father must have given her. It would have been horrible for her to admit she knew as little about it as he did. Her husband would think her doubly stupid now. Even I behaved as though she didn't exist. I had betrayed her.

– Nothing special. I thought a lot.

– I have also been thinking a lot.

This was an earthshattering revelation, but she seemed earnest about it. Or at least, as earnest as when, aged five, she told me she was going to marry Kapil Dev.

– Have you?

– I have so much to think about now. I worry about Appa a lot, and I have to finish my cooking, I have to watch baby, I have to clean before Vijay comes home, I have to buy vegetables.

– Oh.

– What did *you* think about?

– I don't know. I was scared.

– Of Appa?

– Of that horrible man. The one I had to marry.

– Oh him. He's dead. It seems he had done all kinds of bad things. I'm glad you didn't marry him.

– He's dead?

This was the worst disguise of all. As I tried to look shocked I wondered who I was beneath all this mess. I didn't know. Things had been easy when no one asked any questions. I was labelled, *Stupid, Boring, Thinks She's Clever, Thinks She Knows Better Than Us*, but no one ever *asked* me. Now there would be nothing but questions, and I had no answers, none at all; whatever I said they would hate me.

The only solution was to be like them; never leave home again, be a dutiful daughter and a loving sister, never complain, never dream, never see movies.

– I really admire you.

Alternatively, I could go back to The City and take my sister with me. The two of us could feed crocodiles together.

– I think Amma admires you as well.

That settled it. I would leave with both of them.

– But Appa is very angry. When you see him make sure Vijay comes with you.

All this talk of Vijay was starting to irritate me, but I was beginning to understand. My sister had fallen for the myth, the age-old myth that has inexplicably weathered reason for hundreds of years. She had come to see her husband as innately imbued with the divine.

– How is Ravi?

She smiled like a proud child with a secret – another sign of her headlong dash towards insanity.

– Ravi is fine. He has changed since you left.

– How has he changed? Is he ill?

Before she could answer Vijay Kumar bustled into the house. My sister jumped like a drunken chicken and rushed over with the baby in her arms. I was looking for somewhere to hide, he still hadn't seen me yet. He was busy kissing the baby and then . . . and then kissing his *wife!* This was ridiculous. *Nobody* kissed their wife. *Nobody!* Not here. Not in my family. Not in the whole town as far as I knew. Not even in movies! And it wasn't just a little dab on the cheek, *he was really kissing her!* The baby, trapped between their amorous bodies, was chuckling with delight, *and they were still kissing!* My sister made warning noises as Vijay's hands began to wander. He looked over and saw me, and *ran* towards me. He didn't saunter, or strut, or stroll, he *ran*.

I jumped up from my chair in surprise, mixed with more than a little horror. And Vijay Kumar, half-man-half-deity, connoisseur of budget chow mein, trans-Atlantic voyager, gave me the biggest, warmest, most generous hug I have ever received from anyone in my life. This really looked very serious indeed.

I collapsed back into the chair, not knowing quite what to do. It didn't matter. Vijay Kumar was grinning, oblivious to my attack of premature rigor mortis.

– I'm so happy to see you. Delighted. Wonderful. We've been so worried about you. We didn't know what had happened. You look lovely, simply lovely. If only my dear grandfather could have been here to see you today. It would have filled his heart with joy. Are you hungry? You look so tired. Has my wife fed you?

He looked at my sister and she blushed in response. He put an arm around her waist. I was still too stunned to speak.

– What's the matter? Are you ill?

– No, no, I'm fine. I'm just tired.

– Can I get you some coffee?

– Just water, please.

Vijay Kumar scurried off and returned with the water which he offered to me with both hands, as though terribly excited to be of such service. As I drank, Vijay took the baby from my sister and held her above his head, making strange goo-goo-gah-gah noises. My sister giggled. I asked for another glass of water and he returned the baby to her and hurried off again to the kitchen. I remembered reading somewhere that when you have eliminated all other possibilities, whatever remains, however improbable, must be the truth, which meant that, however improbable, the truth was that my sister and Vijay Kumar were in love, assuming the possibility of a vicious insanity cluster had been eliminated. Most of the water dribbled down my chin this time, but Mr and Mrs Domestic Bliss didn't notice. They were too busy smiling at each other.

– Vijay, what do you think she should tell Appa?

He immediately began to pace up and down the room, looking very serious and absorbed.

– Yes, this is a difficult question. He is still angry, isn't he? I think perhaps we should all go together, with baby as well, he's always in a better mood when baby is there. Perhaps we could tell him she was abducted by terrorists, but escaped and found her way home.

I wasn't sure if he was serious or not. Probably he was, judging by the expression of awe on my sister's face.

– I don't think he would believe that.

I said it as icily as I could, but Vijay remained unaware of how surreal I was finding all this.

– Yes, quite right, quite right. A silly idea. Quite stupid. *Stupid!*

– No Vijay, it was a lovely idea.

I was starting to feel sick.

– Thank you, my love, but no really, I am very stupid. Stupid, stupid, stupid.

– How can you say that, Vijay? Of course you're not stupid. Appa isn't stupid, is he?

The last question was directed at the baby, who sadly lacked the power of speech.

– Well then, perhaps you could tell him the truth. What is the truth, if you don't mind me asking?

Another difficult question. Well, seeing as I had discovered my sister was basking in delirious happiness, I supposed I could risk telling them one or two things.

– I worked as a . . . as a maid, in The City. But things became difficult and I came back.

I couldn't help but say this as though I were talking to children. It must have been all the goo-goo-gah-gah noises.

– As a maid?

– Yes, for a while.

– That must have been very tough.

– It wasn't that bad.

– But things became too difficult for you?

– Yes.

I gritted my teeth. I wasn't going to let the trans-Atlantic demi-god interrogate me, even if he had reformed.

– Well, I suggest we discuss it in the morning. It sounds like you have suffered a great deal and had a hard time. You should take some rest. Sleep. And in the morning we can decide what to do.

This sounded like a good idea. I really was very tired, and too much had happened for me to stay awake any longer.

My sister hugged me with her fingertips, and then Vijay gave me another suffocating squeeze, even the baby made appreciative noises. This time I couldn't help but shed a few tears because, despite their absurdity, these two people whom I hardly knew were full of warmth and sincerity. I had started to believe that happy, simple lives were confined to movies, and even then only after the movie had ended.

The bed was comfortable. I realised, with a funny feeling, that it was the first time I had ever slept alone. I lay in bed for a while, listening to the sounds of the night. They were different here, louder, and with more insects, though the air was cooler. Despite having an appointment with my father and his belt in the morning, I felt safe.

I thought of the grandfather. What would he expect me to do? Would he tell me to go back to The City? Would he scold me for undoing all his hard work, for upsetting his plans? I didn't think so, but I wished I could talk to him. I wanted to hear him tell me I was doing the right thing. And if he didn't, I wanted to tell him he was wrong.

I remembered the letter in my pocket and took it out to read.

To my dear young friend,
I am dying. I wish I could live to see you turn your dreams into reality, but my heart is weak and I am not so strong as to tell my heart when to stop beating. I will try not to give you reassurances. You are a woman and old enough to react to death in an appropriate way, if there is such a way.

Be careful in The City. Nothing is as it seems. Things are dangerous. When two rivers meet the rocks rise to the top. Such is the age that I am leaving, and in so many ways I am thankful for it. Many of us are too old to brave such a terrible time as the one you have been born into. You are the ones who must suffer, and this is unavoidable. Only a girl of heart and mind can survive. You will find many in The City who are living in a grave. It is their tragedy and you must not allow it to afflict you.

Things will draw you home. I know you are coming, but alas I do not know when, and there is no strength left in me to wait for you. Every day the ground I have walked all these years grows hard and cracked. I fear that if I wait too long it will split altogether and leave me with all kinds of troubles. You will find things changed. Ravi, your sister, Vijay, all changed. I do not know about your mother and father. You understand them better than me.

For an old man, young people are much more real. People of my age are so often jumbles of faded thoughts and images, and they slip through my fingers like dust. I want you to be young, but then you have little choice. You have chosen not to perish, and it is a brave choice, but your suffering will be real and painful. Others will suffer in other ways, perhaps long after they have left this world. But for you this world will be a world of screams. This is neither a good thing nor a bad thing.

I have little advice to give you. Trust yourself. If the world disintegrates before you then look inside your heart and you will find solid ground. Nothing is as it seems unless you trust your heart, and then everything is true. Who knows, we may meet again. I shall miss you, wherever I am going. You are lucky. For you I shall always be real. I do not know for myself. Even so close to death I feel that things are strange. All I have learned is that anything is possible, and that everything we perceive, no matter how ridiculous, is real nonetheless. This is the most unusual life I have ever lived and sometimes I regret my imminent departure from the playing fields of the insane. Things are to become more interesting yet. But in all fairness I scarcely believe that I could weather any more surprises. How unfair that after all these years, things still shock me every day. When life ceases to astonish or terrify, something is very wrong. Remember that if nothing else.

Your friend,

Needless to say, the letter left me with many questions. But I felt bad for having thought ill of him. He was my friend. I missed him, but I was too tired to cry.

As I felt myself falling asleep I could hear a thumping followed by a moan from outside. I wondered if the baby had fallen and hurt itself. But the thumping repeated itself again and again and the moaning continued, louder this time. And then I realised the window must have been open. I got up and closed it. Those weren't the noises I would have *chosen* to hear at that moment

211

in time, but it made me smile in spite of myself. I was glad my sister was happy.

Mr Laraby, how *are* you? No, I'm going to marry your brother, Mr, er, Bogart. Sorry. Coffee? Thank you . . . er, Vijay. Vijay Kumar, trans-Atlantic . . . husband, father . . . good, hot sweet strained frothing coffee, not black, not white, but brown, as a wise man once said. Wise man. Where is? . . . oh, dead. Permanently, I think. What am I doing? Oh God, today is the day I face the belt.

I tried desperately to reverse my thoughts, but it was too late, the present had caught up and reality had struck and light came streaming in through the window. Was this all the happiness I was allowed? A few hazy moments in between dreams and morning? Why had I tried so hard to remember?

I sipped the coffee. Today would be an ordeal. Tomorrow, in all probability, would be worse. And this wretched coffee was steeling my nerves, drawing me away from the only world where disguises were beautiful. Was I cursed? But no, this was no time for idle self-pity, today was the day when all I had learned would be tested.

Vijay was watching me with an interested expression. He looked very smart in gleaming black brogues, grey flannel trousers, and a white, starched shirt with silver cuff links. His hair was shining and his moustache looked as crisp as his shirt. He was not a handsome man, but he had that glow beside which classically handsome men seem cruel and inhuman (Armand, for example). He seemed in two minds, not sure whether I appreciated his presence or not.

I smiled and thanked him for the coffee, a little formally. I had spent so much time hardening this image in my mind, of a vile demon who had thrown my sister in a dungeon, that this man who stood in front of me seemed insubstantial, *translucent*. I wasn't suspicious of him any more, but this very welcome and even delightful transformation really did scrape at the boundaries of reality. I needed a little time to see whether

I could include Vijay Kumar in my list of Feasible Human Beings.

I didn't want to get out of bed with Vijay grinning at me. I needed to be on my own. But he refused to budge and my patience was wearing thin.

– Vijay, my sister is calling you.

He scurried off like a monkey after a banana. I smiled, remembering the intriguing noises I had heard before I slept. Who would have thought that Vijay would turn out to be such a successful husband? Had I been the elder sister, it was conceivable that it would have been I who had married Vijay Kumar. An interesting thought.

I bathed, trying to compose my thoughts, to concentrate on what I had to do. I couldn't expel the image of my father's face, screwed up in anger, locked in a *Some Things Have to be Done* expression. As I tried to get the soap out of my ear I realised that this could be my last moment of freedom.

I had successfully escaped an eligible rapist, a drunken gardener, and two generations of snail-eating, Indian-eating expatriates. But all were side-effects of the original sin of evading my father. But I was still free. If I wanted, I could hide out here with Vijay and my sister, or I could run away to the Himalayas and live as a goat-herder. But I couldn't run away from my mother. She was only minutes away from me now.

After my exile I had returned stronger and wiser, ready for battle, scarred, hardened, experienced. And here I was, too afraid to look in the mirror in case I noticed I was still a child.

I knew, without having to think about it, that my return was senseless and foolish. I could not succeed. In the end, it was all about guilt. Responsibility. Choosing pain. It was meaningless, but I had made my choice.

I gave up trying to free the soap suds from my ear and rubbed myself with a towel, harder and harder, long after the heat had banished any meaningful traces of water from my body. I could feel my skin screaming, in preparation for what was to come.

*   *   *

213

My sister patted my arm. Vijay grinned at me, as though that would make any difference. I curbed my perpetual desire to throw his good-natured bumblings back in his face and smiled, with obvious terror in my eyes. He kept on grinning. I wished I could be like him, or even like my sister, but all such possibilities had dried up a long time ago.

We went inside. There was nobody in the living room. It hadn't changed, except there was more dust. And it wasn't mine any more. The light bulb still dangled with annoying unsteadiness. My sister switched on the light, even though the room was flooded with sunlight. She smiled, as if to say, *It is All Right to Switch on the Light. This is Our House Too.* This considerate gesture missed the point altogether. I was certain that if I so much as looked at the light switch then that treacherous bulb would come splintering down, bringing half the ceiling with it and belt-swinging fathers from every direction.

I heard a pot clang in the kitchen. I couldn't move. She would go on cooking until the earth swallowed her whole. She didn't know I was standing there, only a few feet away. More pots clanging. I wondered, again, if I were making things worse for her by returning. I would interrupt her cooking. I should never have come. But I couldn't leave now. He could be outside the door, waiting for me. He might catch me as I tried to escape, and that would be even worse.

And then I heard a grunt. An unmistakable phelgmwhiskysweat grunt. Had I woken him? Or had it been my mother, clanging the pots. Either way, he would be angry.

I never went into their bedroom and this wasn't the time to break with tradition. I would wait. I couldn't sit down. The chairs were looking away, pretending not to notice me. So I would stand. Not moving. Not Breathing. Like a good daughter, silent and still. And when he came I would let him do what he had to do.

Another grunt, and footsteps, dusty feet flapping beneath old pyjamas. And he stood in the doorway, watching me. He looked small, and old. His stubble was white and stubborn. His eyes were very red and his oily hair sprouted from his head like weeds. His nails were long and dirty. He had been sleeping. I could smell the bed, and his whisky headache, from where he stood in the doorway. He squinted until I couldn't see his eyes any more, and then padded off into the kitchen, scratching his head with a noise like a saw aching through old rope.

I looked at my sister and she looked back at me, equally helpless. Vijay looked a little frightened, but when he saw that I had noticed he walked like a starving kitten into the kitchen. I heard him say, *Appa, Come and Greet your Daughter, she has Returned.*

My mother came rushing into the living room. She stopped when she saw me. She looked tired, but her eyes were wide with excitement. My father's voice came rasping from the kitchen, *What are you Doing? The Food is Burning.* She looked at me with a shy smile, and then hurried back into the kitchen.

What are you Standing There for, You Fool? I don't Want You Watching me While I Eat. Vijay, looking dejected, came ambling out of the kitchen, trying to conceal his powerlessness. He smiled at me and looked to my sister for help. She took my hand and led me into the kitchen while Vijay dawdled behind, not wanting to risk another undignified ejection.

My father was eating with his head almost in the plate. Rasam dribbled from his chin, but he didn't wipe it off. A grain of rice hung in his moustache. My mother was busy ladling this and that on to his plate, hefting pots and pans about. He glanced up at me between grunts, but kept eating with clockwork efficiency. I stood a little way behind my sister, but it didn't matter, he didn't look up.

– Appa, look, you have a visitor.

I didn't much like my sister's way of phrasing it, but her voice, as always, was soft and musical. I couldn't believe that it hadn't somehow found a way through those tattered pyjamas and into his heart. He paused for a moment, with dripping fingers halfway to his mouth, and then resumed eating. It was my turn.

I came from behind my sister and walked over to him. His hand shuffled more slowly between his mouth and his plate. I had told myself many times that I wouldn't fall at his feet. I would just stand there, in dignified surrender.

Eventually he sucked his fingers, belched, and looked up.

– So, you have come back.

– Yes, Appa.

– Better you had stayed away.

His hands were shaking as he slowly and deliberately dropped his plate on to the floor where the steel whirred against the tiles. He shuffled past me, wiping his chin with his sleeve. My sister called after him, *Appa, Where are you Going?* but his footsteps continued until I heard the door brush shut behind him.

My mother looked troubled and motioned to me to go after him. I went to the bedroom and opened the door. He was sitting on the bed, smoking a cigarette, and his unsteady hand was pouring whisky into a steel tumbler from a jug. The room was full of sweat and bad smells. The bed was not made, and the sheet had a shapeless urine stain that looked quite fresh. I stood just inside the door, waiting for him to speak. Without looking up, he threw the whisky tumbler against the wall behind me. I don't think he had intended for it to hit me. I wiped drops of whisky from my cheek.

– What did you come back for?

He hadn't looked up.

– Because this is my home, Appa.

– You have come back to laugh at me? The stupid old man who cannot control his own daughter.

– No, Appa.

– They all laugh at me now. They think I don't see them. But I know.

– I'll do whatever you want now, Appa.

– Do whatever you want. You don't interest me.

This was a strange way of putting it. It was as though he were trying to hurt my pride, as though he were talking to another man.

I drew closer until the smell stopped me in my tracks. I didn't know what to say any more. When I had come as close as I dared, he raised his head. His eyes were unfocused and lazy.

– Whore.

He said it so dispassionately, as though he were labelling a pickle jar. Without a word, he stood up and shuffled to where the tumbler lay on the floor, picking it up and returning to the bed to pour more whisky. I waited, but he didn't look up or speak.

How tall was my mother? Standing there like that, ashamed of her own breasts, she looked only two feet tall. She had to be taller than that. These dreams were getting stranger and stranger. There was no shock at awakening this time. I was almost pleased. It was better this way. Mrs Marceau and my father would never meet. Not out here. Be thankful for small mercies.

Now, what was my mother doing here so early in the morning?

– Amma, where is Appa?

– He has gone to the club.

– So early?

– It is two o'clock.

– Oh.

– He will be back in three hours. I can stay until four o'clock. I have to cook.

– Why, Amma?

– Because he is coming back at five o'clock.

– No, why do you have to *cook*?

I could see the words, rushing away in terror from my lips. I flapped my arms at them but it was no use.

– Because he is my husband.

She smiled. It was, I suppose, the correct answer, but her words carried a faint irony I had never detected before.

– You should talk to him again.

– I can't. He doesn't want to see me.

She lowered her head. I waited, but she said nothing.

– Did he say anything after I left?

She looked up again.

217

– After your sister was born your father had to work very hard. He wanted another son. Then you were born and he was very angry with me. He said all kinds of things. He said it was because I ate sweets while I was carrying you. He wanted me to give you up . . .

She played with her fingers.

– I would not do as he asked, and he did not have the courage to do it himself. When you were little he would act as though you did not exist. Then you left and he blamed me. He said you were God's curse to him.

– Did he hurt you?

She nodded.

– He wants you to marry, but he refuses to pay anything.

– Do *you* want me to marry?

– You should go away again.

It was too late. I had grasped the meaning of her words. My father would go on beating her until I did as he wished.

– What would happen to you if I went?

– Nothing.

– What would he do?

– He won't be angry for ever.

Unfortunately, we didn't know that for certain. My father had been angry for all of my life, and probably for many years before that.

– I want to be here with you, Amma. I'll marry whoever he wants me to marry.

– How? Who will pay for it . . . ?

I couldn't think of a reply.

I wasn't certain that the donkey was aware of my presence. His eyes were blackened with sorrowful shadows and his dusky skin looked faded, as though it had been left out in the sun too long.

The tonga driver was coarse but cheerful. He bellowed ghazals in between puffs on a smelly bidi. The words were not entirely correct. With genuine poetic ability he managed to transform lyrical sensuality into good-natured filth. He would turn around occasionally to see if he had shocked me, and when I returned his gaze without flinching he would whip the donkey with a stiff cane and resume his performance. He had a nasty habit of stubbing out his bidis on the poor donkey's backside. This precipitated a faint suggestion of activity from the beast, who was clearly unaware that death is the only remaining option when life can no longer be sustained.

The lilting motion of the tonga, combined with the bidi smell and the lustful musicality of the driver, pushed me into uncomfortable snatches of deep, sweltering sleep. Inevitably I was awoken when the donkey plunged into knee-deep potholes or stumbled over rubble. Greenish foam lathered around his bloody lips and dripped on to his knees. He didn't seem to notice. I wondered if he had any opinion of this man who sat behind him, singing profanely and using his backside as a trotting ashtray. Did he despise him? Or did he consider him a natural extension of his own tortured body?

The tonga was travelling slower than the sun. We had been travelling for a long time, always upwards, into the hills. I had seen few people. One or two men appeared from huts, but they didn't seem to be doing anything in particular. The driver had pointed to a number of huts along the way and had declared each of them to be his home. He had also claimed a number of women of all shapes and ages as *My Wife*. He had the sort of face that lacks any distinct features, a hardened mass of lines and stubble. His eyes were mere slits and I fancied I could see hard, scratchy hair growing from his eyelids.

As though wanting to display his entire range of on-the-job distractions, the driver retrieved a bottle of cloudy toddy from the straw at his feet and took a long swig until it dribbled down his bare chest. He offered it to me with a grin. I reached for the bottle and he became alarmed and pulled it away, laughing and cursing. Obviously he was unaware of my familiarity with all manner of European liquors.

The man's back was black and shiny. Sweat trickled down over the extended ridge of his spine. I wanted to wipe it off, but he seemed to care as little for it as the donkey did for the foam around his mouth. His back was very uneven. Bones protruded from all sorts of unlikely places, like the heads of baby birds clamouring for food. He wore dusty brown trousers that billowed around his waist. The uppermost crevice of his buttocks lurked under the edges of the cloth. I burned with curiosity to push my fingers inside that sweaty cave.

It was odd. A year ago I would never have considered sitting alone in a tonga behind such a man.

The road became steeper and more treacherous. The tonga began to slip backwards. The driver told me we would soon be there and whipped the donkey on. In response, the donkey came to a complete standstill and hung his head low, in acceptance of whatever fate lay in store. The driver became furious and jumped down from his seat to stare the donkey in the eye. He described in great detail the particular sexual deviance of every member of the donkey's extended family. The donkey was unperturbed by such slander and refused to acknowledge this fuming bully.

The driver punched him in the face, as he might punch a man. As donkey foam flew everywhere, I jumped down and pressed some money into the driver's hand, insisting that I would walk the rest of the way. He became even angrier and gave the donkey a few more quick slaps.

There was nothing else I could do. I said a silent prayer to whichever god watches over donkeys (though the existence of such a deity looks doubtful) and hurried up the slope, without looking back until the driver's cursing was just a faint echo.

I felt bad for abandoning the donkey, but there was little else I could have done. Anyway, the man's livelihood depended on the donkey, so I doubted he would do him any serious injury.

My walk led me to the top of the hill and to a wide plain surrounded by trees. There were eight huts in the clearing made from brick with roofs of straw. There were colourful flowerbeds outside each hut, and some distance away was a large vegetable patch. A few fluffy white goats ran away from me as I approached. In front of the second hut from my right, a man in orange robes was watering the flowers. His head was shaved and his skin was very pale. He looked up at me and smiled, and then continued watering. I walked over to him and he left his work to greet me.

– May I help you? You have come to join us?

– No. I am looking for my brother.

– I see. Your brother is one of us?

– Yes, I think so.

– What is his name?

– Ravi.

– Ravi . . . Ravi, there is no Ravi here.

– Oh. No Ravi?

– Unless you mean Ashwatthama.

– Ashwatthama?

– Yes. You see guruji wants us to forget our lives of sin and to find our true selves, to throw off the masks that, in our ignorance, we used to wear.

– I see.

– My name was Simon, but now I am Angulimala.

– Angulimala?

– Yes. Your brother used to be Ravi, and now he is Ashwatthama . . .

I wondered which Ashwatthama they had named him after.

– but I must tell you, he is also my brother now.

– Really?

– He is brother to all of us. Guruji teaches us not to root our hopes in the fickle ties of family, which, as the petals of a rose are held together by fear alone, bind us together. Instead, like the breeze that throws those petals into the wind, truth will set us free to find the brothers and sisters of our soul.

– I see. Well, could I see him now?

– Of course you may. Ashwatthama is resting, there.

He pointed to the hut furthest to my right and I smiled, a tight smile, and walked towards it. I hoped Ravi hadn't given them any money.

The door of the hut was ajar. I could smell incense, which

reminded me of Ambika and Maneka. Shaking the memory from my head, I pushed the door open and went inside. The hut was larger than it looked from the outside. The floor was well swept and the room was quite bare. There was a rug in the centre and lying on it, swathed in pillows, Ravi was snoring like a beached whale. His oily chest was bare and his waist and thighs were covered by a cloth. His stomach was partially obscured by a bundle of yellow hair which belonged to the woman sleeping on top of him. Her lower half was also covered by the cloth, but her upper body was naked and looked golden in the dusty sunlight.

I felt something brush my leg. It was a goat. He was trying to poke his head around me to look into the room. I pushed him behind me with my fingers and went outside, closing the door. Angulimala had gone. I wandered away from the huts towards the vegetable patch. I felt sick. The goat was trotting after me, a few yards behind. I hoped he would leave me alone.

I didn't like this. While some woman with golden hair and golden skin was snoring with her nose buried in my brother's stomach, I had to wait in a vegetable patch with this irritating goat. I wondered how long it would be before Ravi, or Ashwatthama, would wake up. Perhaps he would sleep all day. I thought about going back to the hut and waking them, but it wasn't a serious thought. I sat down and played with the grass between my fingers.

The goat tried to nuzzle his nose into my hair. I pushed him away but he did it again, as though trying to wake me up. I scratched him behind his ears and he wandered a few feet away from me and lay down on the grass. He looked like a fallen cloud, a shapeless bundle of white fluff lying unnoticed on the ground. His eyes were open, colourless and limp, staring at me.

I must have fallen asleep because when I looked up the goat had gone, leaving a few wisps of fur behind. The grass had left its imprint in my cheek and my hair was hot from the sun. I pulled myself up and looked back at the hut. The door was open now and I walked over to it. The edges of my vision were filled with grey dots and everything had a white haze about it. My head ached.

Ravi was gone but the girl was still sleeping. I shut the door, wanting to block her from my mind, and saw Ravi, his chest covered now, blinking at the sun. He was standing under a tree at the edge of the clearing. I watched him for a while and then he saw me and stared. He passed his hand in front of his eyes, as though to clear any false images, and then stared again before jogging towards me. I had never seen Ravi jog before. When he reached me, panting with exhaustion, he fell at my feet and remained there, his head in the dirt.

I didn't know how to react. I looked towards the hut, hoping the woman wouldn't come out. Ravi didn't seem to have any intention of getting up, so I told him to, perhaps a little sharply, and he did and clasped me by the shoulders. He was grinning all over. His eyes looked clearer, sharper, and it was the first time I had seen his face without a layer of stubble.

– I dreamed you would come back. I dreamed it. I knew you would. You had to –

I smiled, but I had no idea what to say to him.

– You look very well, Ravi.

– I am feeling very good – strong, healthy. You too look very good.

– What is this place?

– This is my home, you know. My spiritual abode . . .

Oh God.

– I have come here to set my spirit free.

– When did you come here?

– Not long ago. It was you who showed me the way.

– Me?

– Yes, of course, you, through your courage, and your vision. You taught me everything.

– I don't know that –

– So what have you been doing? You must be a film star now, or a model.

– No, nothing like that.

– Then what have you been doing? What new truths have you discovered, what wisdom have you learned?

– I saw Appa yesterday.

– Oh.

– He told me to go away. He says I don't interest him.

– Him! *He* doesn't interest *me!* For so many years he has ruled me, for so many years he has hurt me and held me down. Why should you care what he says?

– He will make Amma's life very miserable if I do not do as he asks.

– Is that all? Amma has her own path. Guruji teaches us to value the ashram, not the family.

– I have to do what he asks, Ravi.

– Perhaps. I will meditate on it. But now, what stories do you have to tell your brother?

The blonde woman came out of the hut. Without looking at us she crossed to the other side of the plain and disappeared from sight.

– Ravi, who is she?

– Her? She is Amrapali.

– Amrapali?

– In her previous life she was an Italian, and a drug-smoker. Now she is a spirit, nothing more.

– I see.

– Yes, guruji teaches us that the body is inessential, to be used or not to be used, as we wish. But the soul, the soul is –

– I see.

– Would you like to meet her?

– Not now. Can we go inside? It is very hot.

– Of course, of course. Come.

We went into the hut. Ravi asked me to sit on the rug, which had so recently heaved with the weight of his naked body, and *Amrapali's.* I declined and sat on the floor.

Ravi told me about his life in his *Spiritual Abode.* It turned out that *Guruji* had died some years ago. Only Angulimala, the man I had met watering the flowers, had ever seen him alive, or so he claimed. Ravi said this wasn't important, he said, *Guruji's Teachings Live. He was Never Born and Never Died. He only Visited this Planet.* I ignored this and interrogated Ravi about his new philosophy and what it meant to him. Ravi said that whenever anyone joined the ashram they had to surrender their material possessions to Angulimala, and to take an oath to refrain from any alcohol or drugs. He said that there were twenty of them, with others living on the other side of the hill. All of them had been unhappy, living lives that did not fulfil them, and had come to the ashram to be reborn. Ravi was the only Indian. The rest were Westerners, though Ravi said such trivial details were only of importance in the world they had left behind. He said that *Guruji* taught them that the body was only transient, but the soul was permanent. So there was no sin in *Gratifying the Senses*.

Ravi talked on, about life and death, maya and transcendence, and then left to fetch me some water. In a corner of the room, resting on three cushions piled on top of one another, was a photograph of me. The photograph was garlanded with small pink and white flowers, and an unlit stick of incense was placed beside it in a wooden holder.

I got up to take a closer look at the photograph. It was an old one. I must have been about sixteen. My hair hung loosely over my shoulders and my lips curved into a smile that didn't reach my eyes, which were large and vacant-looking. I think I used to always look like that, so distant and detached.

The door opened. It wasn't Ravi but the blonde woman, *Amrapali*. Her skin didn't look golden now, but pasty and mottled. She was wrapped in a purple cloth that revealed most of her large breasts.

– Where is Ashwatthama?

– You mean Ravi, my brother?

– I mean the one who used to be Ravi, but is now Ashwatthama. I felt like slapping her.

– He's busy. He has gone to fetch water.

The one who used to be Ravi came in at that moment, and looked from me, to Amrapali, to Amrapali's chest. He tried to introduce us, but I just glared at her. She whispered something in his ear and then stroked his chest with her fingertips, transfixing him with her eyes. She moved her hand down to touch his thigh and I coughed and Ravi started, and then she left. Ravi gave me my water and then sat down on the rug. I sat on the floor again, refusing to look him anywhere but in the eyes.

After Ravi's excitement and my anger had subsided, I told him in some detail of what I had been doing. I told him about Mr Aziz and Mrs Marceau, and about Raju and Ashok, but I didn't say anything about Armand. Ravi didn't interrupt me but listened with great concentration. I finished by telling him why I had come back, and about what my mother had told me about my father, and about why I had no choice but to do as he wished.

– And that man will pay no dowry.
– Nothing.
– That man is not worth the shit he was made from. For so many years he has spat on me, beaten me, told me I was less than a dog. And now I know it is not true. I should go back and take my belt and teach *him* a lesson or two.
– But Ravi, listen to me. I am in serious trouble.
– Not at all.

I looked at the ground.
– A problem is only a problem until you set it free.

I was glad Ravi wasn't unhappy any more, but I didn't know how much of the new Ravi I would be able to stand.
– If you will permit me, I have the solution. It is all very simple. Leave it to me.

He looked at me very confidently. Whatever idea Ravi had, I hoped for his sake that it was vaguely sensible. As far as I was concerned he was still my foolish, ridiculous brother, trying to prove his manhood and then losing critical slivers of it to robbers.

Of course I knew where his new confidence came from. That was obvious, and although I didn't like that woman, I didn't want to deny Ravi the only thing he had ever really wanted. If he was less unhappy now, then it was surely a good thing. But I had hoped that Ravi would have given up trying to give me advice. I didn't want to leave so soon, but if Ravi was going to revert to his wise, elder brother façade, then I would have to.

I recalled that Ravi's last piece of advice had been something about the virtues of matrimony.

6

My husband was a handsome man. He was charming too. He said I had a beautiful name, though very unusual. His name was nice too, Arjuna, my favourite Pandava. I'm not sure how to describe his eyes, *solitary* seems the right word.

We were married very soon, a three-day wedding with few guests who ate ferociously and spoke only to their husbands, wives, or children.

Arjuna had a taut, chiselled chest that cast neat flickering shadows beyond the glare of the fire. As I followed him around the flame for the first time, I thought of my mother. The second time I thought of my sister. The third time I thought of Ravi. The fourth time I thought of Raju. The fifth time I thought of the grandfather. The sixth belonged to my father, and most of the seventh as well. Only as I was coming to a halt did I look up at my husband's finely bevelled shoulder blades. His back was slender, like a girl's, and his longish, shiny hair was plastered firmly over the back of his neck, which looked very uncomfortable. He was tall, taller than Ravi, and he was thin as a giraffe, with the billiard balls of his spine forcing the skin into painful gymnastics.

His father and mother looked on with faces of approval. They looked like nice people. His father was a little severe perhaps, but he was a military man, quite high-ranking. She was a very soft woman. I was sure she used to be pretty, but her hips had ballooned prematurely, as is characteristic of endlessly reproductive women. She smiled a watery smile at everyone and everything. It was difficult to tell what she was thinking, but she seemed happy, in a shy, distant kind of way.

My parents looked similar to Arjuna's, only my mother was a little more assertive, and her hips were significantly less robust. My father and Arjuna's liked each other. One smirked a *Look, No Dowry* smirk, and the other grinned an *I am Richer than You* grin. It was the basis for a firm friendship. My mother talked a little to Arjuna's. They both seemed simultaneously relieved and anxious.

Vijay Kumar was happy and ebullient. He chatted to everyone about chow mein and how happy the bride looked while my sister popped up occasionally from behind his shoulder to correct him on a trivial point, or to praise him for some half-witted insight. Vijay accepted both praise and admonishment with good-natured enthusiasm, delighted that his wife should be so attentive. When my sister was particularly excited she would stand on tiptoe to reach Vijay's ear with her lips until they looked like a narcissistic two-headed monster.

Vijay and my sister liked Arjuna immensely. Vijay slapped him on his bare back, repeatedly stunning the room with open-handed thunder claps. I wasn't sure that my husband appreciated this rather strenuous male bonding, but he bore it all stoically.

Ravi watched the scene with delight. His involvement in all of this had been enormous. He stood quietly by himself like the author of a play waiting for the curtain call. Ravi had met Arjuna's sister at the ashram, where she had come to visit a friend. She had mentioned that her brother was in trouble. He was virulently opposed to marriage, wanting to pursue his career (he was training to be a dancer). His father, in turn, was virulently opposed to Arjuna's career. He wanted Arjuna to administer the family's lands, and was of the school of thought that accepts the divine power of marriage to free man of all rebellious urges. Interestingly, Arjuna's need for a speedy resolution to this deadlock was very similar to mine – his father also took it out on the mother.

Ravi had acted as go-between, negotiating an agreement. Arjuna and I would live together, ostensibly as husband and wife, but exempt from all marital obligations. Once again, it seemed, I had missed my chance to do *It*.

After the wedding, Arjuna and I adjourned to our new home. His father had consented, albeit reluctantly, to our living alone. Arjuna had promised him that after a year of freedom he would be willing to take over his filial duties. His father agreed, with the ready generosity of all mean-spirited people. Arjuna and I shared a bottle of beer to celebrate our success.

– I didn't expect you to drink alcohol.

– I didn't, before I went to The City.

– Yes, Ravi told me you ran away. I understand you had an eventful time.

It may seem surprising that we didn't know each other better. Certainly it would have surprised our parents, who were delighted that, under Ravi's watchful eye, we had spent so much time together. None of them knew we had been mere business acquaintances.

– Yes, a lot of things happened.

– I hope you were not unhappy.

– Everything will be all right when I'm free from my father.

– Sometimes I wish my father was dead. It would be better for everyone. I have thought many times of killing him.

– Why didn't you?

– Because some things are beyond our control. Because life wouldn't be life without the bad things.

– Perhaps life is hard enough without bad people making it worse.

– Perhaps.

He didn't seem interested in my arguments in favour of patricide. He looked sad, as though he had done something terribly wrong. I knew little about him, but I wanted to forgive him for whatever he had done to earn this look of helpless compassion.

– Have you ever eaten croissants?

– What?

– Croissants. French things, made from dough, very good.

– No, no I haven't.

– You should try them sometime.

– Yes, I must.

He looked happier now. We talked for some time. I told him about Maneka and her infatuation for Raju, and about the orang-utans. He found all this very amusing, but looked serious when I told him of my acting ambitions.

When I had finished he told me that he had lived in Cairo for a month with his uncle, who was a big diplomat. But his uncle had him sent home in disgrace after he caught him reading the Qur'ān. Arjuna's father had been a member of the RSS and was convinced that Hitler was a closet Hindu, with a secret agenda to spread the Vedas across Europe. His mother had trained to be a singer, and had continued this training in secret after his father officially banned her. But he found out after seeing her picture in the newspaper, so he forced her to smoke cigars to ruin her voice. Arjuna said his father had also tried to sew her lips together in a fit of rage, but Arjuna had run at him with a cricket bat, and it was then that he was exiled to Cairo.

Arjuna's father was opposed to his dancing. He considered it an effeminate profession and had once forced him to swallow a whole bottle of mascara after he caught him blackening his eyes in preparation for a performance. I laughed at this, but then I saw Arjuna's face and changed the subject. As compensation, I told him about my sister and Vijay, and the intriguing noises I had heard at night.

While Arjuna roared with laugher, it occurred to me that, legally at least, this man was my husband. It was an extraordinary idea. I wondered if I could be attracted to him and decided yes.

There were no uncertain pauses when we talked. Silences were focused and absorbed. Perhaps we could have lived quite happily together for the rest of our lives, but neither of us wanted anything so obvious as happiness.

– Do you feel married, Arjuna?

– No.

– Neither do I.

I regretted the question. My promiscuous mind was causing trouble again. I hoped he didn't think I was in love with him. I wasn't. But I didn't want him to think of me as a nuisance, to be disposed of as soon as possible. Either we were becoming friends, or we were passing time as two strangers might who happened to fall into the same well. I had no way of knowing, and Arjuna didn't seem to care.

I awoke the next morning to find the house empty. Arjuna hadn't told me where he was going, but if I were to have any life as an unmarried, married woman, then I would have to amuse myself. My sister hadn't learned to do this until she discovered the joys of waiting for Vijay. I decided to visit her. She might find it strange so soon after my wedding day, but she rarely found anything I did normal. I was a misfit, an outsider, and would always be so, married or not.

My sister loved me. But she loved me as she might love her own shadow, even as it terrified her in the lamplight, spinning wildly like a demon. I knew what she was thinking – who had given me my soul? Surely not the same God who supplied the rest of the family? Why had I so much hatred for small things? I couldn't tell her. The banality of her life didn't disgust me, it simply didn't *interest* me. I was happy she was happy. I was happy Vijay was happy. But as soon as they tried to *touch* me then I would leap like one possessed.

My explanation was the same as always. It all came down to imagination, the ability to turn what is into what isn't, with a simple shake of the mind.

The town hadn't changed. The air was cool and clean, and the sun was his old self again. Rumour had it that *Majick Movie House* was closing down, but I didn't care. A new bakery had opened. I made enquiries, but no one seemed to know if they stocked croissants. I would investigate. I wanted to buy some for Arjuna. The bakery was on my way, so I could buy the croissants and still be at my sister's in time for lunch. I was sure Arjuna would appreciate the gesture. I hadn't yet decided whether I actually *liked* croissants, but their symbolic value was unquestionable.

A few days ago I had seen *Breakfast at Tiffany's* again, with the drooling Ravi for company, and had noticed something truly extraordinary. Right at the beginning, before the credits, Holly Golightly strolls down the street drinking coffee, and eating a croissant! This ought to have been a minor epiphany, but it wasn't, because, for some time, I had felt my connection with Holly Golightly waning. It had all started with a dream . . .

I came into my apartment, fumbled for my keys, dropped them, and instead of picking them up I buzzed that funny little man upstairs. But who should appear on the staircase but a somewhat haggard-looking Ravi! He was wearing only a dhoti and his capacious stomach and deflated breasts were on display for all to see. But when he spoke his voice was ugly and alien to me.

It wasn't my Ravi any more, it was *her* Ravi, Holly's Ravi – pathetic, repellent, to be used and despised. I knew my line, *Don't be Cross, you Dear Little man. I might Let you Take those Pictures we Talked About,* but the entreaty in Ravi's frightened little eyes was too powerful to resist and I couldn't say a word.

Holly Golightly dissolved inside of me and I returned, no diamonds, no furs, only the same bemused, patient love for my unhappy brother. My isolation was complete. No grandfather, no Raju, no Ashok, and no Audrey . . .

A small child was pulling at my clothes. She was crying. I asked her what was the matter and she said she couldn't find her parents. I lifted her into my arms and wiped away her tears, and then I recognised her as Savitri, the little sister of the now deceased horrible man. I don't know whether she recognised me or not. She had that childish rationality that accepts all ridiculous coincidences as perfectly normal, so perhaps she did.

I asked her where she lost her parents and she grinned and said that while they were buying vegetables she had thrown tomatoes at some boys. The boys had chased her and she hadn't been able to find her way back.

As I was looking around for squashed projectiles, I saw Savitri's father. He was turning around and around, as though trying to maintain a three-hundred-and-sixty-degree view of the world. After his fourth or fifth revolution he saw us and Savitri waved to him. He didn't come running over as I had expected, but dragged his heels with a sullen face. As he approached he removed his glasses and squinted at me, as though I were a particle of ash lodged inside his eyeball. He snatched Savitri from my arms and dumped her next to him, holding her with his left hand while he slapped me across the cheek with his right. As he turned away, with Savitri contorting her neck to wave goodbye, I decided to forget the croissants and go straight to my sister's house.

When I arrived she was crawling on her hands and knees and the baby was chasing her with grim determination. When they saw me they stopped crawling and looked serious. After I had been given coffee and heard how wonderful Vijay looked in his new red tie, my sister gave me a sly, girlish look and asked me how things were with my husband. I said everything was fine.

– It's nice being married, isn't it?
– I don't know. I've only been married for twenty-four hours.
She giggled.
– But it's a nice twenty-four hours, isn't it?
I accepted the terrible reality that she was indeed talking about what I thought she was talking about.
– Well, I don't know.
She looked distraught.
– You don't know?
– Well, yes, it's nice.
She seemed happier.
– Good. So you really had a nice time with Arjuna?
– Well, yes.
– He is very handsome.
– Yes, I suppose so.
When the baby also made appreciative noises, I decided it was time to change the subject.

– I need to ask you a question.

– Is it about marriage?

– No.

– I know it isn't always nice at first, but –

– It's not about marriage.

She looked shocked at my sharp tone. I could still intimidate her very easily.

– It's about Amma.

– Why about Amma?

– Did you know that Appa beats her?

– Yes, of course.

– Why of course?

– He used to beat me too.

Incredible. He had never laid a finger on me.

– I see.

– Doesn't he beat you also?

I shook my head. She looked resentful, which I suppose was understandable.

– Why not?

– I don't know.

She thought for a while. It usually amused me to see my sister wearing her thinking face, but I was worried this time.

– I think he is afraid of you.

– Why?

– I don't know.

Vijay entered with a big smile. He and my sister had their usual moment of delirious passion and then he came to sit beside me and smiled, as though in a Who Has The Widest Mouth competition. I think he wanted to kiss me or hug me, but didn't quite dare. In the end he patted me on the back saying, *How Are You? How Are You?* over and over again. I smiled as sweetly as I could, relieved that he had restrained his affectionate impulses.

– Do you know who I just saw?

My sister gave a doting smile as though he were about to reveal all the secrets of the universe.

– I saw that terrible man's father.

– What man?

– The one who wanted to marry your sister.

My sister shuddered and began to repeat, *Horrible Man, Horrible Man*, over and over, until I silenced her with a glare.

– Did he say anything to you?

– Yes.

– What?

– I don't want to tell you.

My patience was beginning to fray.

– Why not?

– It isn't nice.

– Tell me anyway.

Vijay sighed.

– He asked me how my sister was.

– What is so terrible about that?

– Well, he said . . . oh, I don't know why I have to tell you –

– *Vijay!* What did he say?

He turned pale and my sister stroked his hand to help him through his ordeal. She gave me a look that said, *How Could You be so Horrible to Poor Vijay?*

– He said, *How is That Whore that you Call your Sister?*

– And what did you say?

– I said you were fine.

I almost exploded with laughter. Vijay, my sister, and the baby looked at me as though I were a strange and toxic fungus in a test tube. I continued laughing anyway.

– And then I told him that if I ever saw him again I'd kill him.

I stopped laughing and looked at Vijay with new respect.

– Thank you.

He didn't say anything. He didn't look like a good-natured fool any more. He looked calm inside, and strong. I was impressed.

– Well, shall we eat?

My sister was desperately trying to restore some emptiness to her life. All this substance terrified her. Substance in the man she loved was an intolerable quality. I needed to leave.

– I will eat with Amma. She must be alone now.

– I think Ravi is there.

– I'll go anyway. I need to talk to Ravi.

Before they could protest I kissed the baby, smiled sweetly at my sister, and, much to his surprise, slapped Vijay hard on the back. I needed to be walking, alone on the street. Things were moving too quickly.

The sun was reaching his highest point. He seemed to be in a hurry, and this made me walk even faster. I had this idea that if I didn't rush to the house then it would be dark before I got there, and my mother would have gone to sleep, and maybe, just maybe, I would never see her again. It was only a little time after noon, but this idea persisted and I found myself panting from the exertion of my forced march.

I needed to rest, and I sat by the side of the road.

It was as though events were moving faster than I was, as though time had a separate pace for me. I was a stranger in the eyes of my father, and my husband, and this made me invisible to everyone else. I did not exist, and though this was hardly a new feeling, it seemed ill-befitting for a girl who had returned home to rescue the ones who needed her.

Nobody needed my help except for my mother, but my mother, ironically, was convinced that she herself did not exist. One non-entity rescuing another – it was almost funny.

There was nothing for me to do any more, nowhere to go. People and cars and bicycles rushed by me, but I was only sitting, and nobody asked me my name and nobody stopped, not even to beat me or rob me. I wondered what would happen if I closed my eyes. I might awake to find everyone I knew dead and gone, and all the other people transformed into snakes who, on seeing that I was the only human left, reared up on to their tails and sank their teeth into my neck.

The sun was climbing higher and higher, faster and faster, hotter and hotter. I thought of my sister and Vijay. It was cool in their house. They would hardly notice the sun. Time moved slowly for them, peacefully, in tune with their own desires, and this world of chaos and madness that rocketed past me on the road was nothing more than a vague irritation, like the buzzing of a fly.

I stood up and considered returning to my sister. But then the thought struck me that perhaps she would not want me to return. Perhaps she wanted to live her uncomplicated life with Vijay alone, free from trouble. I had done nothing but condemn her all my life for her stupidity and her shallowness, and this had come back to haunt me. Perhaps if I had concentrated on my own life . . .

I walked on, towards my mother, through the heat and the noise. My steps were slower than before. There no longer seemed anything to hurry for. Something would happen. Nothing would happen. It was all the same in the end. After all that I had endured I had arrived back exactly where I had started. The only change was that my dreams had soured. I was trapped now in this ridiculous life in this infernal world. And that, was that.

The house looked smaller than I had ever known it to be. It was my father's creation, that house, it was his attempt at keeping howling winds and waves of sand firmly away from his own, carefully internalised madness. But it looked small and smiled sheepishly, as though embarrassed to be there, and I realised that anyone who looked at that house would know my father was a frightened man. I had never considered this before.

The door was open but I stayed outside. I felt I needed an invitation. I used to be a captive within those walls. Now I was a captive outside them. I wondered if prisoners felt that way when they were freed. That sort of freedom wasn't an act of kindness. Freedom was only meaningful if you had somewhere to go.

I shook my hair and walked into the living room.

Ravi was upstairs. I could smell him. Ravi was like a snail. He left a trail wherever he went, and that trail was considered unpleasant by most people. I liked it. But I liked Ravi, and that was also unusual.

My father was there too. I couldn't see him, and I couldn't smell him, but I knew he was there. The house was cold, or dark, or none of the two, I couldn't tell, but even so I was sure he was there. This tiny house lived in terror of him, and I knew the house well enough to sense that terror as soon as I walked in through the door. That would have pleased my father. He saw this terror as an extension of himself, which it was.

I stood in the centre of the room, listening, waiting for something to happen, and then I saw my mother sitting a few feet away from me, shelling peas. She had a small table in front of her with a bowl on it into which she threw the shelled peas, and she was watching me, curiously. I think she was also wondering about my new life as a married woman. At least she wouldn't ask me any questions about doing *It*. That much was certain.

There was a tacit (of course) understanding in her look. She might have asked me about my husband, had she been playing the game, but she didn't. She just smiled.

Another gaggle of peas popped into the bowl. My mother's fingers seemed to work independently, independent of the resignation in her eyes. They were light and deft and it seemed they were the only part of her body that was real. The rest of her was transparent, and her voice, when it finally left her throat, seemed to come from another, more distant corner of the room.

– You are here.

It could have been a question or a statement. It didn't matter. I wanted to say *Am I?* or *No, I am Not*, but that would have been unfair.

I sat down beside her and helped her with the shelling. I wasn't very good at it, but I enjoyed working with her, drawing as close as I could to the part of her that didn't shudder with denial of its own being.

Ravi came bounding down the stairs. He seemed to take a long time about it, and someone who did not know Ravi might have thought that he was doing it deliberately, jumping up and down on each step like a small boy, as though hoping to fall right through the wood. But we did know Ravi. He was doing his best.

– Ah, you are here?

– Yes, Ravi.

– How is your husband?

He said it gleefully. I wanted to be annoyed, but instead I smiled. My hand collided with my mother's on its way to the bowl. Her hand was cold, but light and nimble. I tried to touch it again but she was too fast for me. The peas came first, though this was not a deliberate choice.

– He is fine.

– Good, good. So, married now?

– Yes, Ravi.

– Good, good.

My mother's lips twitched.

– Ravi, bring me some water.

He bounded off again. At once the dutiful son, delighted to be of assistance, to show his worth in front of the only ones who would pretend to appreciate him without making that pretence so obvious as to hurt his feelings.

My mother stopped shelling for a moment and glanced at me, as though to elicit some response. I had nothing to say and didn't return her glance. She continued shelling. Ravi returned with the water.

– Here is the water, Amma.

That affirmation was unnecessary as Ravi had already spilt most of it into the bowl. My mother smiled her thanks through pursed lips, her cat's smile.

Ravi stood in front of us both, his hands on his hips.

– So, Arjuna is well?

– Yes, Ravi. He is fine.

– Good, good. Well, all's well that ends well, isn't it?

He beamed at us both, but neither my mother nor I could manage any more smiles. Ravi didn't seem to mind. He whispered, *Appa is Here*, and then addressed the room in his usual bellow.

– Well, well, married now, married. Isn't that the best thing in the world? Everyone is happy now. *Every*one.

It felt as though my mother's silence was louder than Ravi's shouting. It seemed to drown out his words, which only made him shout louder.

– Yes yes, everyone is happy!

Ravi's rather wishful assertion was immediately contradicted by the appearance of a man who, as far as I knew, had never been happy. He glanced first at my mother, and then at Ravi, and then at me. He had been sleeping, that was obvious from his hair and from the creases the sheet had left in his pockmarked skin. I think, had I not been present, that he would have given Ravi, and *perhaps* my mother, a few slaps with his tobacco-stained hand. But instead he snorted, and jerked his chin in my direction. This, I felt, was a gesture to the effect that I had now re-entered reality, as defined by his own drunken parameters. I acknowledged this approbation with a few moments of silence.

My silences, unlike my mother's, were carefully stylised to convey different meanings. My father had the capacity to understand them, though he did not always use this.

My mother went on shelling peas. I did not know if she understood my silences. Sometimes I felt that she understood them too well. She shared them. Her silences and my silences met in the middle and formed one great silence, though only she was capable of perceiving the whole. This, of course, left me in a decidedly uneasy position, but perhaps that was common to all daughters.

I watched her. A handful of peas slipped from her hand and fell to the floor, scurrying away like shiny, round insects. She bit her lip, and continued to shell, while Ravi vainly pursued the disappearing peas.

My father tried to kick Ravi's backside and missed, and it was only then that I realised how drunk he was. He had fallen asleep, apparently for some time, but still his movements were so slow and disconnected that even Ravi was able to evade him. Ravi looked quite pleased with himself, though I could see he was trying his best not to show it.

I worked hard on a different type of silence, a silence of pacification. It didn't seem to work.

– How is your husband?

This was the same question that Ravi had asked, but from my father's throat it was cruel and mocking.

I did not reply. This was not calculated. I was, against my will, very frightened. Ravi answered on my behalf.

– He is very well, Appa. Arjuna is very well.

My father aimed another kick at Ravi, and missed by several feet. This time Ravi was unable to prevent a grin from invading his face.

– I did not want to marry him, Appa. He did not want to marry me. I did it because you wanted it.

I had truly not intended to say that. As far as I was concerned, I *hadn't* said it. But there were the words, fluttering away from me like little winged demons. My silences had a nasty habit of disintegrating.

I wanted to look at my mother, but my head wouldn't turn. I couldn't hear the peas popping into the bowl any more.

Ravi had veered dangerously close to my father. There was a look of astonished alarm on his face. He was trying to attract my attention, waving his arms when he thought my father couldn't see him. My father turned on him, his open hand raised.

– What are you doing, fool!

– Sorry, Appa. She says funny things sometimes. She goes mad, quite mad.

My father stared at Ravi so hard that I feared he would break into a million pieces. That look was far worse than any damage he could have inflicted with his fist. Ravi turned pale and seemed to wither away, becoming one with the wall. I didn't look at him.

– Is this true?

– Yes, Appa, it is true.

– Why are you telling me?

I didn't know. I said nothing.

– You are trying to make a fool of me again? Isn't once enough? Already I am the laughing stock.

– No, Appa.

– Then why are you telling me?

– I don't know, Appa.

He stared at me. There was real understanding in his eyes, and real hatred. I was causing him too much trouble. I was a fool. Only a fool would marry to placate their father and then, the day after, confess that the whole thing had been a farce.

– You . . .

He pointed at Ravi.

– go buy cigarettes.

Ravi went. I knew my father didn't need cigarettes. Perhaps Ravi knew, but didn't want to admit it to himself. I watched him go.

My mother stood up, leaving the peas to their own devices. I didn't want her to involve herself in any of this, it didn't seem fair. Supposedly, I had done all of this for her. And now I was undoing it.

She walked over to my father and took him by the arm. She said something like, *It Doesn't Matter*, *Let her Go*. I couldn't decipher the exact words.

I watched my father hit my mother. His hand moved very slowly. She could have jumped out of the way. *I* would have jumped out of the way.

He walked over to me and grabbed my arm. I struggled, but his grip was too tight. I tried to force my fingers into his face, to hurt him, but his flesh felt so ugly that I withdrew my hand. It was like rancid, unwashed dough.

He dragged me through the doorway, into the sunlight. My mother was back there, in the house of fear. The light was hot and blinding. My father's fingers were embedded in the flesh of my arm, pushing deeper and deeper into blood and bone. I said something like, *Appa*, *Let me go Now*, but I don't think he heard me.

We walked like some misshapen, multilated beast, tripping, stumbling, rushing on towards a collision that lay outside of any rational history. The pavement glared up at us, ringing out its condemnations in a dirty, mindless voice. I could see people all around us but their startled silhouettes were pathetic like insects beside our relentless madness. He pushed me on, faster and faster, and I looked up for the sun and found him looking away. For a sickly second I was an unsteady two-year-old, hobbling after my father on sad, wistful legs, and then I was fifteen, drowning in a grave of dreams, and then all of that receded and I was as old as he was, as hard as he was, as driven as he was, and I walked with him, in front of him, faster than him, adrenalin exploding in my furious chest, determined to show him the resolution that his demented life demanded.

My head struck his shoulder sending sparks of insanity flashing into my skull. My eyes felt as though they would leap from my face, joining his world. I rested my head against his shoulder, trying to still the aching of my mind, and I saw a shape behind us. Craning my neck, I saw a familiar form shuffling against the horizon, following us. She walked absurdly slowly, encumbered by the heat and by the masses of cloth that strangled her legs – no urgency, no protest, no mad rush to the rescue, just a dogged, ambling shuffle. She so rarely left the house on her own.

I used to live in my dreams. I thought they were more real than reality. But when I looked back at my mother, when I looked sideways at my father, I thought *Reality is a Dream*, and I was scared. I would never be fifteen again, not unless I could forget that sight, but some sights lay eggs.

We were nearly there, at my house, Arjuna's house, where no children had been or ever would be conceived.

As we turned a corner I looked back again. She was still there, still moving, still steady and strangely assured. Our eyes met, or they might have met, it was difficult to say, the light was too bright. The heat had left her form swathed in a grey haze. Dust rose, incandescent in the sunstorm, to fight the air around her head. But still she walked, never slackening or quickening her pace.

The door was open. Arjuna's shoes were inside the doorway, but I could see no sign of him. My father pulled me inside and let go of my arm. I followed him. There was no reason to run. I was as much a part of the madness as he was now.

Coffee was boiling on the stove. I walked over and turned it off. This was a calculated gesture. My father snorted. I took this as a kind of acknowledgement. He was in my home now.

I could hear music. It sounded muffled. My father headed towards it, fists clenched. I had no idea what he planned to do. He tried two doors without success, and then opened a third that led to Arjuna's bedroom. The music came rushing out, loud and triumphant. I watched as my father took two steps inside, faltered, and clapped his hand to his head as though in pain. His fingers clenched and then wrapped themselves around the doorframe.

I walked up to him and looked inside the room.

Arjuna was sleeping. Lying on his chest, also sleeping, was a man. They were both naked.

I turned to look at my father. He was staring. His mouth was wide open and a purple vein pulsed like a snake in his forehead.

I heard footsteps behind me and turned to see my mother enter the house. She placed her sandals by the door and went into the kitchen. My father had not moved. His grip had tightened around the doorframe, and it seemed that it was only luck that kept him standing.

My mother crept up to us and pressed a glass of water into my father's hand. He looked at it, as though he didn't know what to do with it. Gently, she helped him lift it to his mouth and he drank a few drops. My mother was supporting him now with one hand under his elbow, while the other ensured that the glass didn't tumble to the ground.

I looked at him again, and then at my mother. She returned my look, her eyes wide with concealed thought. She tightened her grip around his elbow and led him away from the door and into the kitchen. I followed.

My mother left my father leaning against a wall. He looked like a man made from straw and mud alone. I could see no flesh or blood in him any more. She took me by both hands and moved her face close to mine. I was shaking slightly.

– You should go now. There is nothing for you to do here.

245

– But what about you, Amma?

– I have to go home. There are things to do.

I must have looked astonished, because she smiled again, but it was not a happy smile. There were tears in her eyes, but those tears were ever present, it only required certain shades of light to see them.

She kissed me on my forehead and left me standing in the hallway. I watched as she fetched my father from the kitchen and, still supporting him by the elbow, led him out of the house and into the sunlight.

ACKNOWLEDGEMENTS

Deep affection and gratitude to Ato, Victoria, Tim, Alexandra, Kadija, Salima and my parents, of course.

A NOTE ON THE AUTHOR

RAJEEV BALASUBRAMANYAM was born in 1974 in Lancashire, England, and is a graduate of both Oxford and Cambridge Universities. *In Beautiful Disguises* is his first novel, and was a winner of the 1999 Betty Trask Award and an Ian St James Short Story Award, 1999.

A NOTE ON THE TYPE

The text of this book is set in Berling roman. A modern face designed by K. E. Forsberg between 1951–58. In spite of its youth it does carry the characteristics of an old face. The serifs are inclined and blunt, and the g has a straight ear.